RESTED WATERS

BOOKS BY DEBORAH FLETCHER MELLO

Harlequin Kimani Romance

Promises To A Stallion
Lost In A Stallion's Arms
Tame A Wild Stallion
To Love A Stallion
Always Means Forever
In The Light of Love

Harlequin Kimani Arabesque

Forever And A Day
The Right Side of Love
A Love For All Time
Take Me To Heart

RESTED WATERS

A NOVEL

BY

Deborah Fletcher Mello

MaGREGOR PRESS

This is a work of fiction. All names, characters, places, incidents and dialogue, are either the product of the author's imagination or are used fictitiously, and any resemblance to actual persons, living or dead, business establishments, events or locales is entirely coincidental.

Published by MaGregor Press

ISBN-13: 978-0615456638
ISBN-10: 0615456634

RESTED WATERS

Printed in the United States of America
First printing, May 2011
Designed by Richard Wayne Williams, Jr.
Photograph by Camille Kauer

To my son-shine,
Matthew Mello

WITH NOTHING MORE LEFT TO LOSE...

****

No matter how you slice and butter it, my mama had been a straight-up, stone-cold whore. She was happiest when a stranger's lips were meeting hers for the very first time, alien hands exploring the lush curves of her body. When the lips became too familiar and the hands well known, there was no more pleasure for Lavinia Tucker. Lavinia had tolerated Manroot Tucker the longest and only because their coupling had produced me, Janay Tucker.

And now Manroot was dead. My father died yesterday. He died in his sleep, a resident of the Louisiana State Penitentiary. I was six years old the last time I saw Manroot. Back then I used to call him Daddy. I'd not called him anything since March 11, 1964, when he had wrapped his thick arms around me, tucked a pale yellow blanket against my small body and passed me to my grandfather, James Tucker. He'd kissed me for the last time as he apologized, dark tears running in streams down his coal-black face. Diana Ross and her Supremes had been singing *Baby Love* on the old radio in the kitchen.

My hands shook as I read the neatly typed telegram. Its bold, black print suddenly revived the many memories that still haunted me. I inhaled sharply, the bitter remembrances of my father, and my mother, and a road we'd traveled together only briefly, pulling me back toward a numbness I'd struggled for so long to overcome and forget.

Outside, the bearer of bad news pulled his dark panel truck out of the driveway and onto the main road, the bright white printing on the vehicle's side fading in the distance. I looked anxiously toward the fields for my husband Everett, knowing that he'd not be so easily found but hopeful nonetheless.

On the mantel above the fireplace, a photo of my parents seemed to loom to the forefront, grappling for my attention. Their smiles were genuine, joy shining in his eyes, satisfaction in hers. Mommy and Daddy. Manroot and Lavinia. Her and him. Them. Now Manroot was dead, and I had no choice but to remember.

My mother, Lavinia Pappas Tucker, had been the type of woman men only loved between the hours of midnight and dawn. Once the sun rose and daylight blessed the green grass, no man truly loved

Lavinia, and Lavinia surely hadn't ever loved any one man. Manroot had been the only fool to think that he could sugarcoat Lavinia's heart with any honest emotion. It would have been enough for most women to have a man like Manroot loving them, but it had never been enough for my mama. Not even I had been enough for Lavinia.

Lavinia had been miserable with her everyday existence. Most words out of her mouth had always been bitter ramblings spattered with stinging curses. Lavinia's spirit had been scarred, the wound deeper than the deep, pink cut that ran down the right side of her face.

Lavinia had died laughing. She'd looked at me with those deep, sapphire-blue eyes, one tear rolling down her cheek, and she'd been laughing. Laughing at my daddy. I could remember vividly how she sat on the edge of that big brass bed, stretching a pair of ebony nylons up her thin, porcelain legs. She grinned this sugary smile at me, tossed her sable hair from side to side, and had whispered secret girl things in my direction. Laughter tugged at her thin, cotton-candy colored lips.

Tears sprang to the edges of my eyes, dampness clouding my view, but I blinked them back. I did not care to cry, not yet. The tears would flow soon enough. There would be no stopping them. Once the hurt of my past became too much to bear, the tears would erupt in a volcanic explosion, and then I would have to fight to stop them.

As though sniffing roses in the flower garden, I inhaled the dark reflections that could wake me from my sleep and walk in silence beside me when I least expected them. They came storming into the room on the sheet of paper that carried the news of my father's death. They would not be ignored. Not this day. This day was theirs, and they'd come demanding my full attention, seeping deep into every crevice and crack on my body.

The day I was born, Lavinia nicknamed me Black Beauty. She called me her half-and-half china doll, an intricate blend of her European ancestry and Manroot's blue-black pedigree. Mostly, I was just a half-white, mocha-colored black girl with straight hair, turquoise eyes, a crazy black father, and an even crazier white mother. My saving grace was a grandfather who at least had an ounce of sanity.

Now, I loved Manroot like every six-year-old loves a daddy who calls her Beauty in the mornings when he lifts her to his broad shoulders to reach for the new day's sun. He always smelled of mild tobacco and foamy aftershave, his shiny, bald head shimmering in the sunlight. His pockets were always filled with sweet surprises, and his arms were never unwilling to wrap my small body in warm hugs or stroke the hurt out of my heart. I had surely loved my daddy.

I placed the telegram back into its envelope, heaving a heavy sigh. Tucking the ivory mailer into the back pocket of my too tight, bright white, cut-off shorts, I headed out the door toward the gardens where my grandfather, Daddy James, worked diligently, fussing over a new crop of tomato plants. Kneeling on the ground beside him, I placed my hand over his own soil-stained paw, rubbing my other palm against his back.

"What's the matter with you?" he asked, kissing my cheek gently.

"Telegram came from Angola."

The old man nodded. "What Manroot want now?"

I squeezed his hand, pausing briefly.

"Don't waste my time, Black," he said firmly, calling me by my nickname. "I've got too much work to get done. What does that daddy of yours want from us now?"

I took a deep breath before responding. "A decent burial. He died yesterday."

Daddy James inhaled sharply, nodding his gray head slowly. "Long time coming. Manroot done been to them crossroads more times than I can count and he kept on coming back."

He sighed heavily, sitting his large body down onto the mound of rich, red soil behind him. "Did he suffer?"

"Message says he passed in his sleep."

He sighed again, continuing to bob his curly head up and down.

"Bring my boy home," he said finally, smearing dirt from his hand to his cheek. "We'll bury him here. Bury him right here next to Titus, Chauncey, and Eloise."

"Yes, sir," I said, rising to my feet. "I'll take care of everything."

"You take care of it," he repeated, shooing me away with a quick flip of his wrist. "You take care of it."

Heading toward the large farmhouse, I looked back over my shoulder and watched as Daddy James fought to still the tepid waters that threatened to fall from his large brown eyes. His struggle was for naught as the warm saline pushed past his thick lashes. The Hershey's Special Dark chocolate complexion contrasted sharply beneath his silvery-gray crown of kinky curls. Blue-black skin enveloped the flawless curvatures of his chiseled jawline like expensive silk draped against granite and the tears rolled easily over the round of his cheeks. Dropping down into his lap, the light wave of water came to rest upon the front of his faded blue overalls.

It is unnatural for a parent to bury a child. None should feel that weight. Children should be made to see their parents grow old and weary. They should have to sit beside them and hold their wrinkled hands as they pass from this world. Passing only on cool, fall nights when dark skies are clear and bright stars are calling their names loudly.

Daddy James has had to bury all of his children. Chauncey Tyler Tucker had been the first, found dead in the back swamps behind his home. There had been no sane reason for it, years of fear and hatred dictating his time before he was ready to go.

His only daughter Eloise had been next, passing one year later from pregnancy complications. Daddy James had thought her condition could have been avoided had she just kept her legs shut tight.

Not long after Eloise, Daddy James' first-born son, Titus Manfred Tucker, was called home to meet his maker. Titus dropped dead from a heart attack while working in a Carolina steel mill. Now Manroot, his youngest son, was gone. His life had been snatched away from him as quickly and as quietly as his freedom had been taken some thirty-odd years earlier.

Daddy James had been made to mourn one more time, a child he'd carried close to his heart. God should find some shame in that. If anyone was less deserving of such heartache, it was Daddy James. He was deserving of so much more, and if I could see it, then I had no understanding how the Almighty Father could be so blind.

Back inside the house, I curled up in the window seat that looked out over the front porch. Staring off into the distance, I marveled at the nonsensical attitudes that attributed so much to God's miraculous ways. I had given up on God long ago, figuring that to have lost so much before I'd reached the age of seven meant God had long since given up on me. Daddy James' faith in the good Lord, however, had always been unwavering, fortified by a weekly fix of glory, glory, hallelujahs during Sunday morning church service.

I heaved a sigh. Making funeral arrangements had almost become as common place as planning a child's birthday party I thought suddenly. As I contemplated the choral selections and scriptures for the program, I wondered why I had been made to plan what I thought was more than my fair share of funerals.

My mama's had been the first as I'd sat stoically next to Daddy James nodding my head up and down when he'd leaned to ask my opinion. Now I had to do my daddy's. When you totaled the number of days that had passed between the two, one would have thought it would have gotten easier by now.

Staring out the window, I saw that Daddy James had gone back to his vegetables. Though I could not hear him, I knew that he was singing, and I could almost feel the swell of his deep baritone voice gliding across a hymn. Daddy James always sang spirituals when his heart was heavy. Daddy James' singing was as close to God as I could ever imagine being.

Out of the corner of my eye, I caught sight of Everett as he sauntered toward Daddy James, his arms laden with an assortment of farm tools. They engaged in brief conversation before Everett dropped the utensils to his feet and wrapped his arms around my grandfather's shoulders. Instinctively I knew he wanted to make it all better for the both of us. The man was a rock of gold, as precious to me as any treasure could ever be, and I marveled at how abundantly his love for me and grandfather flowed.

Everett worked daily to bandage my hurts. His understanding of my pain though was limited to the screams that woke us from my nightmares, the saturated bedclothes that disturbed our sleep with humiliating discomfort, and the rank depressions that spun silence between us, and washed anger and frustration over my soul.

I'd not noticed as Everett came to stand in the doorway, crossing over to be by my side. His sudden presence was almost startling and I jumped, my heart beating harshly in my chest. I reached out to take his hand, entwining my fingers between his. As his warm flesh brushed lightly against mine I was suddenly aware of just how cold my body had become. A shiver ran up the length of my spine, spreading through my torso and out into my limbs.

"Manroot's dead," I said, my voice void of any emotion. "Manroot's dead."

Everett leaned to kiss my forehead, wrapping his thick arms about my narrow shoulders. He whispered words of comfort into my ear, his large hands stroking the length of my back. I would need his hands later I thought to myself, once the sun had settled down for the evening. I would need his hands to push away the moments of recall that would envelope my rest and leave me sweating profusely by his side. I would welcome the comfort of his hands then, the warmth of his appendages tenderly kneading and caressing my flesh. At that moment though, his hands were irritating, unwanted intrusions upon my emotions.

Pushing him away, I reached for the telephone. Picking up the receiver, I dialed the prison first, then Mr. Goodwin Boyd of Boyd Funeral Home, and Reverend Winston Taylor of White Rock Baptist Church. Only then, when the wheels were turning to bring my father back to where it all began, did I take one quick moment to hang my head against my husband's chest and cry.

Time walked slowly as the house began to fill with people coming to pay their respects. Elderly women pulled rank inside my small kitchen, over-filling paper plates with an assortment of food that seemed to appear out of nowhere. The house smelled of fried chicken and collard greens, thick cooking aromas that spilled from room to room. Daddy James' voice boomed in the distance as he greeted well-wishers who either had known Manroot when, or just wanted to pretend that they did. Hands passed over my back and shoulders, kisses pressed against my forehead, but I sat oblivious to most of it.

From across the room, Daddy James beckoned me to join him, holding tight to my hand as he had when all the others in our family had passed on. He pulled me out the kitchen door and across the fields toward the pond. Everett followed close behind us. At the edge of the reservoir, we three stood side by side, inhaling the dampness, watching the rays from the setting sun dance off the surface of the water.

"It's time to let it go, Black," Daddy James said, the boom of his voice intruding upon the silence.

I looked up at him. He was still as wondrous in my eyes as he had been when I was three years old and barely reached his knee.

Everett reached out to take my other hand. His dark eyes searched the lines of my profile. My husband smiled, an easy bend of his full lips that brushed comfort across my spirit. "Daddy James is right," he said softly. "If you don't talk about it now, you are never going to get over it. Never, and we can't live like that. Not anymore."

The two men pulled me to the ground to sit between them. I leaned my head against Everett's shoulder. "I don't know what to say—" I started, dropping my chin against my chest. "I don't remember anything."

"Yes, you do," Daddy James said. "You just don't want to."

I shook my head. "Tell me about them first," I said softly. "Tell me about them...before..." My words trailed off into the soft breeze gliding through the evening air.

Daddy James nodded his head slowly, cleared his voice, and then spoke, painting the picture of my history before me.

AND SO IT WAS IN THE BEGINNING...

****

Manroot Tucker looked up and down the road through scotch-hazed eyes, swaying awkwardly back and forth. The young white girl giggled excitedly as she wrapped her arms around his thick waist, guiding him toward the back of an old brick building. He giggled with her, having no clue as to what she found so funny. Together they staggered up the back fire escape, kicking an old, gray cat out of the way as they searched for her rear door. On the third floor, lights flicked off inside one apartment and Manroot could see the window shade being lifted ever so slightly as someone peered out curiously.

"Mind your business, you nosy bitch," the girl giggled with a thick accent, flipping her hand in the window's direction. "My man will kick your old ass if you mess with us. Won't you, baby?" she said to him, goosing his broad backside. The window shade dropped quickly.

Manroot snickered. "I'll take care of you, baby."

As the young woman struggled to get a key into the door lock, Manroot leaned back against the porch railing. Although his mind was glazed, painted over by a thick coat of cheap alcohol, he could not help but appreciate the statuesque figure before him. He'd had his eye on her for some time, ever since that brief moment when she'd brushed against him brazenly, her bright red lips turned up in a seductive smile. Tonight, she had sashayed into the after-hours club, a pale peach dress clinging like wet paint to her firm body. She was a pretty girl, with long, russet-toned hair that hung in smooth spirals down her back, and deep, ocean-blue eyes that danced in the dim light. Her pale complexion was smeared with far too much pancake makeup, but Manroot was too drunk to truly care.

Now, a white girl in an after-hours club that catered to colored folks stood out like a sore thumb, and this girl had wanted to stand out. The way she'd pranced in, swaying her lean hips at each drunken fool who catcalled or whistled in her direction clearly announced her intentions. The women had eyed her maliciously, knowing that she was up to no good, but keeping their distance because she could easily bring the kind of trouble none of them needed. White girl start crying and complaining and someone's ass was going to jail. Those with any sense crossed to the other side of the room to avoid the blue eyes whispering for attention. Those either too drunk, or too stupid, fell over themselves to get to her.

Although she appeared to be in her mid-twenties, Manroot guessed that she was probably much younger than she looked. Even though they had two-stepped and shimmied across the dance floor while polishing off a bottle of scotch, he still had no idea what her name was. He laughed loudly.

"What's so funny?" she questioned, glancing back over her shoulder to stare at him.

"Dead man told me a joke once 'bout this voodoo woman from N'Orleans. She'd wrapped this spell round him and he won't no more good after that."

"So?"

Manroot laughed again. "That's right. So."

The girl shrugged, then laughed along with him as she reached for his hand, pulling him inside behind her.

Banging his knee against a table, Manroot swore loudly, rubbing the bruised shin with a callused palm. "Turn on some light, woman!"

"Don't need no light," she whispered, pulling him close to her. "Just lean your body next to mine and I'll lead you where you need to go," she said coyly.

Manroot chuckled as he wrapped his arms around her, lifting her off the floor. She folded her legs around his waist as he pressed his full lips against the inner curve of her breast.

"What your name?" he asked, inhaling the sweet scent of jasmine upon her skin.

"Lavinia," she answered, just before she kissed him, allowing her tongue to dance inside his mouth.

"Mmmmm," Manroot purred, coming up for a breath of air. "Lead on, Miss 'Luv-in-ya'."

His hands were hot and as Lavinia kissed him hungrily she pushed and pulled at the large appendages, allowing them to fall in strategic places along her body. The heat from his hands burned like melting wax dripping from a scented candle.

As Manroot dropped his hulking body against Lavinia's petite frame, the girl gasped loudly, her small hands clasped about his broad back. They fell back against an unmade bed, the sheets tossed to the floor. Manroot laughed as she struggled beneath the weight of him, refusing to let him go. He maintained control, his body gliding against hers, flesh savoring flesh as if it were a last meal. The young woman panted heavily, struggling for air as the heat bristled between them, rapture choking all of her senses. Their loving was intense, the crest of it coming in a sudden burst that left them both breathless against the surface of the mattress.

The next morning Manroot stirred reluctantly, Lavinia's small body twisted awkwardly against his back. Turning around to face her, he leaned up easily on his thick arms. Her breathing was mellow, a slow exchange of morning air and nocturnal breath. Lavinia's makeup lay smeared against the dingy white pillowcase, her face flush from the heat in the room. The dress she'd worn was wrapped haphazardly around her waist, her breasts standing at full attention. The sight of her caused a rush of energy to surge through his body, a hard shudder shaking him where he lay. As he leaned down to kiss her bare shoulder, Manroot thought her much prettier without all the makeup.

Lavinia jumped, startled out of a sound sleep. The large black man leaning over her smiled sweetly, an even row of ivory teeth gleaming down at her.

Pulling her hands to her face, she pushed the length of hair out of her eyes, sending the auburn strands down her back. Manroot laughed, then kissed her forehead lightly, brushing his thick lips down the length of her face. A crimson blush rose to Lavinia's ivory cheeks.

"I am surprised you are still here", she said, her accent more pronounced than Manroot had remembered. She leaned over the edge of the bedside, reaching for a pack of cigarettes on the night table.

Manroot rolled back against the pillows, pulling his arms above his head, his nude body sprawled in full glory, as he wrapped a warm palm around his manhood. "Why?"

Lavinia shrugged, pulling a cigarette to her lips. "Thought you would have to go back home to your woman." She fumbled unsuccessfully with a damp pack of matches, then threw it and the cigarette to the floor. She swore, the manure-filled expletive tainting the early morning air as she kicked angrily at the tangled covers around her feet.

Manroot laughed again. Reaching out he pulled her against him, kissing her boldly. Lavinia pushed against him, struggling to free herself from his hold. When he let go, still laughing, she slapped his face hard, the palm of her hand stinging against his cheek. The glimmer in Manroot's eyes dimmed ever so slightly. His nostrils flared as he inhaled, drawing in breath as if preparing to go under water. Manroot pushed her away, drawing himself up from the bed. His naked body stood majestically, a six-foot, eight-inch tower of taut muscle locked beneath black marble. He shook his head slowly as he reached for his clothes.

Immediately regretting what she had done, Lavinia reached out for him, clasping him around the waist. She pressed her lips to his abdomen, kissing the taut muscle in apology. With a firm hand, Manroot pushed her back against the bed, a wave of anger saturating his face.

"You want me to leave you be, you just say so. Next time you hit me, I'm gone kill you."

Tears rose to Lavinia's eyes as she pulled her knees to her chest, wrapping her arms around her body. She struggled to look indifferent. "Go to hell."

Manroot tucked his wrinkled dress shirt into a pair of tailored pants and laughed. "Next time, and only if I'm in the mood."

"You bastard! You think you can come in here and..."

Before the woman could blink Manroot reached a heavy hand in her direction and gripped her around the throat, leaning his face up close to hers. He could almost smell the sudden fear that filled her, its faint scent blending with the last essence of her perfume and the remnants of his sex that still clung to her skin.

"I come in here 'cause you invited me. You wanted it and I gave it to you good. Real good. Now, I'm leaving. But just remember what I said, put your hands on me again and I'll kill you. You understand?"

Lavinia nodded ever so slightly, the pressure of Manroot's hands unnerving. Releasing his grip, Manroot let her fall back against the mattress. Her fingers rose to her throat, rubbing at the bruised skin. Manroot studied her momentarily, then reached into his pants pocket, and pulled out a roll of bills. Counting off the currency, he placed twenty dollars in her hand.

"You knows where to find me," he said, leaning down to kiss her cheek, his thick lips lingering a second longer than expected. He cupped a palm beneath her chin and lifted her gaze to meet his. "I'll be there by eleven. Don't keep me waiting."

The woman smiled sweetly, her head bobbing up and down as she assented, still clutching tightly to the green bills that lined her palm.

Outside, Manroot inhaled deeply, taking in the cool air. The rise of sunlight was just beginning to filter over the horizon. Morning sounds hummed lightly in the distance and Manroot could feel a rush of new day activity rolling in his direction. Needing a bath and a fresh change of clothes, he lowered his head slightly and headed toward home.

He could hear his woman's curses even before he placed his key in the door. Her anger rushed to greet him, kissing him in the entranceway.

"How you stay out all night and don't come home?" Ruth Ann Baisden asked angrily. "How you go off with some other woman and leave me here alone like you done?"

Manroot eyed her irritatingly, not bothering to respond. Dropping his keys onto the kitchen table, he plopped down onto a thinly padded chair, kicking his shoes off beneath the seat. He yawned widely, stretching his body upwards.

Standing with her hands on her hips, Ruth Ann continued to berate him, tears rolling down her cinnamon-colored cheeks. "How you do me wrong like that, Manroot? You answer me. I want to know how you gone do me wrong like that?" The woman's body shook beneath a pale peach nightgown edged in white eyelet. Manroot eyed her curiously.

"Who say I been with some other woman? How you know I ain't been working?"

Ruth Ann sucked her teeth. "Tch. Don't play me stupid, Manroot Tucker. I done heard how you went off with that piece a white trash last night. Everybody talking 'bout it. Here you got a decent woman sitting here home waiting for you and you go chasing after some trashy whore, and a cracker whore at that."

Manroot laughed, leaning his large body back in the chair. "Since when you become a decent woman? If I remember correctly it won't too long ago that you was selling it for two dollars and fifty cents, if you could."

Ruth Ann stood angrily before him, the tension swelling in her orange shaped face. "And what you pay her for it?"

"She give it to me for free just like you done," he answered, reaching out to grab her around the waist.

Ruth Ann pushed angrily against him. "Don't you put your hands on me you son of a—"

Manroot laughed again as the words stuck in her throat. He had reached a hand down the front of her nightgown to pull gently at her right breast, the sensation of his touch cutting off her words. Fingering the large, round nipple, he brushed it against his cheek, the wealth of it blossoming candy-hard beneath his touch. Only the thin nylon fabric separated her bare flesh from his lips. Pushing the gauzy cloth aside, he suckled her slowly, his tongue dancing along the round of her bosom. Sneaking his other hand around the curve of her waist, he clasped the cheeks of her buttocks beneath his large palm.

Ruth Ann could feel her anger subsiding as the pleasure of his touch swept through her. "You ain't shit, Manroot Tucker," she whispered as she leaned down to kiss his forehead, caressing the sides of his face with her own. "You less than shit, you lying, cheating, no-good bastard."

Manroot grunted, continuing to lick and kiss the fleshy tissue. Inhaling swiftly, Ruth Ann shuddered as Manroot suddenly thrust a large hand between her thighs, her breath catching tight in her throat. He moved as if invited, pushing and pulling at her private playground. He massaged her gently as she stood awkwardly above him, her legs splayed open like two lean vises around his arm. She could feel herself rocking against his fingers, need rising swiftly as all evidence of objection dissipated with the beat he was tapping against her flesh. "Damn you," she sputtered before plunging her tongue deep into his eardrum.

In one swift movement Manroot released himself from his pants and pulled Ruth Ann down into his lap. She collapsed easily against the swollen tissue as Manroot stretched the length of himself deep inside her. His fingers just shy of bruising, he clutched at the round of her behind, lifting and dropping her against himself. The chair beneath them rocked precariously against the linoleum floor, threatening to spill them both to the ground. As the tingling in his crotch increased, and his breathing came in shorter gasps, Manroot lifted his hips anxiously, plunging deeper within her. Ruth Ann cried out loudly, a mixture of pain and pleasure teasing her inner thighs. Rising warmth crept quickly up into her abdomen. Just as she thought she could take no more of his strapping body, the fullness of him seeming to grow thicker and thicker with each thrust, her pleasure grew exponentially. She could feel the delicate lining of her insides unfolding around him, crying out for more, and more is what he gave her.

A row of orgasms, one after the other, rocked her. When her legs were more rubber than flesh, and she could feel the room spinning around her, she fell heavily against him in a limp faint, his lips still locked around her nipple. Beneath her, Manroot shuddered, his swollen member slipping down between his own legs. Pausing only to catch his breath, he lifted her from his lap and dropped her across the kitchen table.

Standing above her, perspiration seeped from Manroot's pores, falling in large drops against his shirt, the table, and Ruth Ann's brow. He swiped at the salty moisture with his index finger, flicking it down to the floor. Pulling at the shirt that still covered his torso, he popped the line of buttons, sending them flying around the room. The sweat-stained fabric fell to the floor beneath his feet.

Manroot's broad chest heaved up and down in rhythmic palpitations. Dark chocolate muscles shimmered in the morning sunlight that flowed past the red gingham curtains that covered the windows. His upper body faded into a tight line at his waist. A soft fuzz of baby hair curled between his breastbone. There was no fat beneath the dark tissue. Manroot's body was a solid mass of perfectly sculpted flesh. Ruth Ann gasped at the beauty of him, her eyes falling from his chest, past the slightly protruding navel, down toward the wicked length of his maleness.

Ruth Ann shuddered as she envisioned the pale white woman who threatened to disrupt the complacent existence she'd established with Manroot. Images of the woman's white hands and thin pink lips touching Manroot made her stomach suddenly quiver with nausea. Ruth Ann swallowed back the bile film threatening to spew from her midsection. *No*, she thought. She would not allow it. *No other woman was ever going to come between her and Manroot.*

She had endured his philandering more times than she cared to count, but Manroot had always come home to her. Last night was the first time he'd stayed gone and she knew that this was not good. This was not good at all.

Reaching for him, Ruth Ann pulled at the dark flesh, wanting more of him. But Manroot stopped her, disengaged himself from her grasp, and zipped himself back into his pants. She leaned up weakly onto her elbows, her body still spent from their loving. "What's the matter?"

Manroot shook his head and shrugged, his shoulders reaching up toward the tin ceiling. "Got business to take care of. I need to get me a bath and get dressed."

Ruth Ann stared at him, a stunned expression painted across her face. Manroot had never before turned down her advances. "What that white girl do to you?" she shouted, rising from the table as she struggled to pull her clothes into place. "How you gone do me like this, Manroot?"

Manroot laughed as he headed up the single flight of stairs. Shaking his head, he never once looked back behind him. Locked behind the bathroom door Manroot studied his reflection in the mirror. A dark shadow lay cross his scalp and chin. He brushed his hands atop his skull relishing the sensation of freshly sprouted stubble against his palm. He sighed. On the other side of the door he could still hear Ruth Ann, her crying reminiscent of a yapping dog you wanted to kick.

After dropping his slacks and briefs to the floor, Manroot relieved himself. In the back of his mind he could not help but think how peaceful it could be were he to flush Ruth Ann and her incessant noise away as easily. She had begun to grate on his already worn nerves.

Lathering his chin and head, Manroot shaved the dark fuzz away until his hand ran smoothly across the black flesh. Satisfied, he stepped into a tub of warm water, the porcelain vessel stained heavily from age. Soaping himself thoroughly, he could not wait to rinse the feel of Ruth Ann from his skin. Her touch had suddenly become as undesirable as the rest of her. He soaped himself again, rinsing the suds down the drain. When he felt cleansed, he lifted his body up and out of the tub, wrapping a thin towel around his midsection. The worn cloth barely covered his nudity.

"It's time to move on," he thought out loud as he swiped at the moisture along his flesh. "Time Manroot Tucker made his way someplace else," he mumbled, his voice barely audible. He nodded his head slowly, his decision, once made, ever so final.

Exiting the small room, he paused when he heard Ruth Ann sniffling in the bedroom. She knew that he would only take so much before her tears would set him off. He felt the irritation rising as he wondered just how far she intended to push him this morning.

Ruth Ann lay across the freshly made bed as Manroot pulled clothes from the closet. Draping a charcoal gray suit against his body, he ignored her efforts to get his attention. Her griping began to take its toll.

"Manroot? Manroot?" she whined, clutching at her breasts. "Why you doing me wrong, Manroot?"

He sighed heavily, clenching a heavy fist against his side.

"When you coming home, Manroot? When you gone be back?"

Manroot turned to stare at Ruth Ann's tear-streaked face. The woman's hair was curled tightly, the delicate style flattering to her round face. Her nightgown, though old, the eyelet torn around the hem, contrasted nicely against her brown complexion. Moisture spilled past her deep black eyes, sadness spilling out into the room. Manroot had had enough. He had never meant for their relationship to be permanent. In fact, Ruth Ann had only been a pleasant diversion to pass some time. He had fully intended to leave months ago, but one thing or another had held him hostage, allowing Ruth Ann to hold onto hope that wasn't there. Weeks earlier would have been better, but now was as good a time as any for him to leave.

"Ain't coming back," he pronounced, pulling his clothes from the closet and dresser drawers. "Done told you too many times, a man wants some peace when he comes home, not this shit."

"I can do better, Manroot. I can," she wept, dropping to her hands and knees. "Please, Manroot," she begged, wrapping herself around his legs.

Manroot stared down at her, his expression reflecting his annoyance. "Don't," he said, pushing her away from him. "This for the best. I got to go."

Turning his back on her, Manroot headed down the stairs, a cardboard suitcase in hand. As he headed for the front door, he could hear Ruth Ann screaming behind him.

"She gone pay for this, Manroot Tucker! That cracker bitch gone pay for what she done. You gone come back. You wait and see. You gone come back!"

Manroot laughed, dropped fifty dollars on the table in the hall, then closed the door behind him. Hell would have to freeze before he'd ever consider coming back to Ruth Ann Baisden.

****

Manroot sat off in the corner, a bottle of Jack Daniels at his elbow, a half-empty glass in his hand. Music played in the background, a jukebox spinning hits by The Platters, Frankie Lymon, and Fats Domino. The small club smelled heavy, a rank mixture of body odor hidden beneath pungent perfumes and cheap colognes, clouding the air. Manroot inhaled deeply, the acrid fumes rising in his nostrils. As he studied the couples grinding against each other on the dance floor, his annoyance quickly turned to a low rage. He glanced at the gold watch on his wrist. The clock's hands read half past eleven. Manroot bit hard against his bottom lip. He had told her not to keep him waiting.

He jumped ever so slightly as long hands reached across his shoulders, wrapping him about the chest. He looked up into a honey-colored canvas, cheeks and lips painted brightly in conflicting shades of red. The woman smiled widely, a mouth full of teeth gleaming yellow under the dim lights.

"Hey there, Manroot. Heard 'bout you and Ruth Ann. Feel like some company?"

Manroot lifted the woman's arms from around his chest, pulling himself free from her grasp. "You ain't waste no time, huh, Beverly?"

The skinny woman named Beverly continued grinning, shaking her head. "Why should a woman waste time going after something she wants?" She stood boldly, her hands clutched against her thin hips. "So, what you say about me and you spending some time together? You interested in that, Manroot?"

Manroot leaned in closely, eyeing her from head to foot. A soft chuckle passed his lips. Easing back in his seat he lifted his glass and drained it empty, dropping the glass to the table. "No, I ain't interested, Beverly. I sho' enough ain't interested in you," he responded, refilling his glass from the liquor bottle on the table.

The skinny woman huffed, sputtering like a fish out of water. Pouting as she gasped for air, she turned and thrashed back to the bar, cursing Manroot all the way. Cutting her eyes at him, she whispered to a short, obese woman with mocha skin, who sat at the bar beside her, both of them shaking their heads with disdain. Before word of Manroot rejecting Beverly could be spread about the room, Lavinia walked through the door.

Manroot watched as she eased herself into the smoke-filled club, a floral-print, silk dress falling in neat lines around her curves. Her long hair fell in soft waves over her shoulders, a white carnation tucked behind her left ear. Once again her face was heavily made up, crimson lipstick coating her thin lips, a palate of color brushed heavily across her cheeks. Her hips tripped boldly across the floor as she made her way to the bar, leaning to whisper to the bartender. Wiping a smoky glass dry with a dirty rag, the man nodded his head toward the table where Manroot sat. Lavinia smiled coyly as she headed in Manroot's direction.

Coming to stand beside him at the table, she grinned boldly, her brazen movements entertaining all the eyes upon her. Leaning toward him, her breasts brushing against his cheek, she kissed him hard, pushing her tongue into his mouth. Manroot allowed her to work her lips over his, never lifting his hands from where they lay folded against his lap. Satisfied that she had indeed made an entrance, Lavinia broke the kiss. She tossed her purse onto the table, and took a seat in the chair beside Manroot. She grinned at him again.

Manroot leaned forward. Wrapping his arms around her, he locked his fingers together behind her chair. The grin across her face faded as she read the anger in his eyes. The fury etched in the lines of his brow burned like a brush fire.

"You kept me waiting. It's almost midnight," he whispered between clenched teeth.

"I...I am sorry," she stammered quietly, lowering her gaze to her lap. "I did not mean to be late. It could not be helped."

Manroot nodded, lifting her chin. "When I say don't keep me waiting, I mean don't keep me waiting. You understand?"

Lavinia nodded.

Manroot rose from his seat, tossing a shower of dollar bills onto the table. "Let's go," he ordered, pulling her to her feet.

"But, I just got here," Lavinia sputtered, incredulous. "I thought we would spend some time—"

Manroot's look was cutting, sapping her words from her breath. Lavinia nodded her head, following behind him as he pushed his way through the crowd to the door. As they exited, the two women at the bar whispered bitterly, racing to spread gossip about Manroot and the white woman.

Side by side the couple made their way down the dark streets, cutting through even darker alleys toward Lavinia's home. Just before they rounded the bend toward her building, Manroot pushed her into a blackened doorway, their bodies hidden from the streetlights and any peering eyes. Lavinia shook intensely as Manroot held her against the doorframe of the local insurance office, her face and body pushed against the glass. His touch was bruising as he pushed her dress up around her waist, ripping her nylon panties from her buttocks. His body was hard as he pressed himself against her, leaning his weight heavily upon her small person. With probing fingers, he parted her legs roughly. She could feel herself nodding as he whispered into her ear, her head banging into the glass.

"Now, when I tell you to do something you best do it and do it right. This..," he said pulling harshly at the silky fluff of her crotch, "...this belong to me now. You do right and I'll take real good care of it. You do wrong...," he pulled again at the strands of female hair, the gesture painful. "You don't ever want to do me wrong. You understand?"

Lavinia's head bobbed up and down as a faint "yes" fell like a whisper out of her lipstick-smeared mouth. Manroot continued. "Now, next time you come strutting in some club like a fifty cent whore, I'm gone beat you like one and I don't never want to see you with you face painted up like that no more. You gone be my woman you best act like it. Do I make myself clear?"

Lavinia nodded again, tears falling from her eyes. "Yes," she whispered one last time. "Yes."

Manroot's head waved up and down against his shoulders as he turned her body around to face him. The white carnation from her hair lay battered at her feet, the delicate petals bruised around the edges. Wrapping his arms around her, he kissed her lightly, brushing her tears away with the back of his fingers. "Let's go home, Miss 'Luv-in-ya'."

Lavinia took his hand, stepped out of her torn panties, and led him home, stopping only to kick the old, gray cat off the stairs. Inside, she turned on the lights, placed her purse and keys on the kitchen counter, and watched as Manroot looked over the small, three-room apartment. Her eyes dropped to the floor when he turned to stare at her.

"You scared of me?" he asked, his voice coming in a deep whisper.

She looked up at him, not sure if she should answer, then she nodded her head yes. Manroot sat down onto a dusty, brown floral sofa in the makeshift living room.

"Come here," he commanded.

Lavinia made her way to his side and sat down.

"Don't you ever be afraid of me if you doing right. You act right and I won't never do nothing to hurt you." Manroot traced a finger along the curve of her profile, the tip of his finger resting lightly against her bottom lip.

Lavinia nodded again.

Brushing his large hand across her knee, Manroot smiled wickedly, his thick lips parting into a wide grin. "You do right, baby, and Manroot gone love you real good."

Lavinia shuddered as his hands stroked her thin legs. Easing her back against the cushions Manroot continued smiling as he brushed up and down her legs, tossing her red high heels off into the corner. Lavinia's body reacted on its own accord, giving into the seduction of the man's touch.

With one hand, Manroot reached for her breasts, unbuttoning the top of her dress and pulling the firm, orange-sized tissue from the black silk bra. Lavinia shuddered as he skillfully kneaded the rose-colored nipples between his dark fingers. They blossomed to full attention and he smiled his satisfaction. His other hand still danced up and down the length of her inner thighs. Manroot's grin was permanent as he watched her close her eyes, unable to resist the intensity of the pleasure sweeping over her.

"You like this don't you, baby? You like Manroot loving you, huh?"

Lavinia could barely nod, her teeth bruising her lower lip. His dark laughter crept up her stomach, pausing momentarily at her breasts until his thick lips reached hers. He tasted sweet against her tongue and she kissed him voraciously, pulling at him anxiously with her tiny hands. The kisses were passionate, his mouth covering hers. Lavinia could feel him swelling against her thigh as his manhood grew between them. She heard herself gasp as she reached down to take hold of him, kneading the dark flesh within her palm.

An orgasm suddenly ripped through her body and she shook uncontrollably.

Manroot nodded his head with satisfaction, his expression boasting just how much he intended to explore before their loving would be finished for the night. He purred into her ear. "Manroot gone love you real good, baby."

Manroot took her from behind, his wide hips pushing and pulling against her until they both cried out with pleasure, clutching at each other against the sweat-stained sofa.

Their breathing was heavy, deep gasps seeking to fill their lungs. The rush of adrenaline eased slowly as they lay stretched against the couch. Lifting himself off her, Manroot dropped back against the other end of the sofa. Lavinia could not help but laugh as she watched him sprawled across the seat, one leg tossed over the back of the couch and the other hanging over hers toward the floor. Manroot smiled back, his lust-filled expression painted in sweat.

"Is that what you wanted?" he asked her, scratching at his inner thigh. "Did Manroot love you good, baby?"

Lavinia nodded her head yes. She still could not find the energy to answer him properly. Manroot laughed. Rubbing a palm against his bald head, he stretched his limbs upward, arching his back off the sofa. A wide yawn tiptoed past his lips.

"Are you tired?" Lavinia finally asked, her tone low, her words nothing but a whisper.

Manroot shook his head. "Nah. My body just feeling relaxed is all."

Lavinia shifted her torso up and around to lie back against Manroot's long legs. Her hair fell down over his crotch, tickling the dark muscle. It made Manroot laugh again.

"So, what happened to your woman?" Lavinia questioned, hesitancy edging her words. "She did not seem to be the type who would let you go so easily."

Shrugging his shoulders, Manroot thought about Ruth Ann, then pushed the memories from his mind. "Like I said before. Do right, and Manroot will take good care of you. Do wrong and you gone have to pay a hard price. I'm with you now. You got a problem with that?"

Lavinia shook her head from side to side, her hair brushing against him once more. "I am glad to hear that. I worked very hard to be with you. I don't want to think it won't last but for only a short time."

Manroot shrugged his shoulders. "I ain't promising nothing. I'm here now. Don't know what tomorrow gone bring."

Lavinia did not respond, her gaze flowing off into the distance. His words were not the words she wanted to hear. *In time though*, she thought. *In time.*

Nuzzling against him, she ran her hands along the length of his leg, slowly kneading the tight flesh. His skin felt warm, the firm tissue hard against her palm. Peering up at his face, she smiled coyly, pushing out her lips as though to blow him a kiss. The grin returned to Manroot's face.

Having resting long enough for Manroot to catch his breath and incite his organ back into operation, the sexual acrobatics continued across the living room floor, down the length of the small hallway, and into her bedroom. When Manroot finally laid his head against a pillow to sleep, the sun sat perched within a thick, blue blanket of sky. Lavinia watched him as he slumbered beside her, his dark body a striking contrast next to her own pale complexion. The sweet spot between her legs throbbed, a painful remembrance of what the previous night had done for her. She leaned to kiss his brow, brushing her hands against his bald head. "Yes," she thought aloud. "You have loved me good, my man. You have loved me good and soon you will truly love me."

****

They arrived before the sun. Chauncey and Titus Tucker arrived first, Manroot pulling into the yard right behind them. A faint light peeked from a kitchen window and they knew their father was up and ready, patiently waiting for the three of them to find their way home. As they exited their vehicles, James stepped onto the back porch, his thumbs hooked behind the straps of his denim overalls. The patriarch nodded his head agreeably, a gnawed toothpick spinning from one side of his mouth to the other.

His sons greeted him warmly, chattering in low whispers as though the depth of their voices might pull the morning up and out before anyone was ready to greet her. They were each eager to get started and their anxiousness spilled out across their faces.

"So," Titus whispered into the damp air. "What are we doing?"

Chauncey wrung his hands together, nodding his head. "Yeah, Pops. What you want us to do first?"

James nodded his head toward the back fields. "Got us a lot of land to get ready. Field's just about ready for planting."

The three younger men looked off toward where their father was gazing. The land stretched into the darkness, faint shadows quivering beneath the faint rays of a quarter moon.

"Thought you were going to let them Baxter boys sharecrop them back fields?" Titus questioned.

James shook his head. "Changed my mind. I let them have the fifty acres down on the south end. We gone plant the back fields this year."

"Why's that, Daddy?" Manroot asked, going to stand by his father's side.

James shrugged. "I want your mama to be able to see how well the land is doing. These here fields are your mama's fields and ain't nobody planting here but us."

Manroot nodded his head, then headed for the barn. "What you two waiting for?" he asked, looking back over his shoulder toward his two older brothers. "We got work to do."

Falling in step with their younger sibling, Titus and Chauncey joined him as their father looked on behind them. "I'm blessed to have them three boys", James whispered into the darkness. "Got me three fine boys." Humming softly, he eased himself back into the house. There was much to be done inside before he could even think about joining his sons out on the land, and the sooner he got started, the better.

An hour later daybreak was beginning to peer over the horizon. The slow rise of light unfolded lazily, stretching color up and over the dark earth. In no time, the dusky shadows were consumed by varying shades of green and brown, the freshly painted farm house and barn coloring the backdrop with red brick and white washed siding. By mid-day, the heat had followed the sunrise, tagging along behind like a bothersome sibling. The three men worked diligently, their solid bodies brimming with sweat. As they toiled in the rich soil, the inky ground tattooed the soles of their work boots and stained the legs of their jeans and overalls. Beads of moisture rolled down their black coffee-colored complexions. Dirt dusted the white fabric of their tee shirts, leaving an ashy film against the cotton. Every so often one of them would reach to swipe his hand along his brow, sweeping sweat up and out of his eyes. It was just past one o'clock when their father called for them to come eat lunch.

As Manroot approached the back porch, he pulled his shirt off, dropping the sweaty fabric against the back banister. His brothers followed suit. Turning on the faucet behind the house, he leaned down to let the cold water run over his head and shoulders, rinsing the dust and grime from his face, hands and arms. Titus and Chauncey joined him, wanting to carry as little of the dirt to the table as possible. James stood on the bottom step, clutching three towels for them to dry the water from their skin.

Sitting down at the kitchen table the three siblings waited for their father to join them. They could hear him upstairs fussing over Miss Lucy. It was not too long before the man sat down at the head of the table, his hands clasped together in front of him.

"Mama okay?" Titus asked, inching his chair closer to the table.

James nodded his head yes. "She's just fine. She done finished her lunch and is taking a nap. Your mama needs her rest. Later on you boys need to go on up and spend some time with her before you leaves here."

The boys nodded their understanding, knowing that their father's comment was more of a command than a suggestion.

"Let's bless this food," James commanded, lifting his hands in prayer. "Heavenly Father, thank you for this food we are about to receive. Bless it, dear Lord, that it may nourish our bodies and strengthen our souls. Continue, dear Lord, to shower your blessings down upon us and know that we remain your faithful servants. Amen."

"Amen," Titus, Chauncey, and Manroot chimed in before reaching for the bowls of hot food. The aroma of stewed beef with carrots and potatoes was tantalizing, teasing the hunger in their stomachs.

As the four men ate, their laughter boomeranged around the room. Titus regaled them with tales of Chauncey's latest escapade and James roared with laughter at his son's antics. It had been some time since he'd last laughed so with his boys. It felt good to have them together, happy, after a hard day's work.

.

As James wiped a faint tear from his eye, he turned his attention to Manroot, smiling warmly at his youngest son. "So, boy, what you been up to lately?"

Manroot shrugged. "Keeping my behind out a trouble mostly."

James nodded his approval.

"Uh huh," Chauncey murmured, cutting his eye over to his other brother. "Ain't what me and Titus been hearing."

Titus grinned, reaching over to tap Manroot against his shoulder. "Yeah, we hear you done found yourself a heap a trouble."

Manroot lowered his head slightly, raising his eyes questioningly. "What you done hear?"

"Heard you keeping time with someone other than Ruth Ann. Seems Manroot done moved on to another woman, Daddy," Titus said, turning to grin at their father.

Manroot pushed his lips out, running his thick tongue over the outer line of his mouth. "I don't keep time with any one woman. I'm enjoying as many as I can."

James shook his head. "Boy, you gone learn your lesson the hard way. I can see it coming."

Manroot shrugged. "What? Like them two ain't doing the same thing."

"Not like we hear you doing it, little brother," Chauncey smirked. "Hear you done lost your taste for blackberry. Hear vanilla cream more your flavor these days."

Titus laughed, slapping palms with Chauncey.

Manroot glanced nervously toward his father, then cut his eyes back at his brothers. His gaze was beseeching, begging them to drop the subject before it went any further.

"Blackberry, cherry, chocolate, or almond. Like I said, I'm keeping time with as many women as I can. You two jealous?"

Titus shoved a fork full of rice and gravy into his mouth. Shaking his head no, he grunted, savoring the food against his tongue. "Not me," he finally muttered. "Just hopes you know what you doing."

James stared from one son to the other, then leaned back against his chair, its front legs rising slightly off the ground.

"Something I need to know, boy?" he asked, raising his thick eyebrows questioningly.

Manroot shook his head, lifting his eyes to glare at his brothers. "No, sir. Like I say, I'm just trying to stay out a trouble."

James studied his sons, knowing there was more to what had been said between them than he had been privy to. *Soon enough,* he thought to himself. *I'll find out soon enough.* He let the chair fall back against the floor, nodding his head slowly.

Titus and Chauncey stole glances between themselves, fighting to keep from laughing. They were amused by their little brother's sudden discomfort. Manroot found no humor in their teasing. He'd deal with them later, he thought, when they were away from their father's judging gaze. Turning his attention back to his plate, Manroot ate the china dish clean. The other three did the same.

With the dishes washed and put away, the siblings made their way back to the fields. The sun continued to thrash its harsh rays against their tarry complexions as they raced to finish a good day's labor. Out of his father's earshot, Manroot cursed his brothers.

"You two think you're funny!"

Titus and Chauncey laughed. "You the one that's funny. How long you think it gone take for Daddy to find out about that white woman?"

"Mind your business. What I do ain't none of your business."

"Uump," Titus grunted, cutting his eye at Manroot. "Our business when we know we gone have to watch your back. You done gone and got these folks all upset. What you think you doing anyway? Ain't we done taught you to hit it and get out? Shoot, you got to be a fool to keep dipping in that rice pudding like you doing."

Manroot shrugged, leaning against the wooden hoe in his hand. "Ain't like I'm planning on staying. Things is just feeling good right now." He clutched his hand tight against his crotch.

Chauncey shook his head. "Just don't do nothing stupid. You just lucky these folks don't take to no foreigners. White man don't take too kindly to you being sweet on his woman."

"White man can go to hell."

"White man gone send you to hell you don't watch out," Titus retorted. "Just be careful. I ain't in no mood to be getting my ass kicked looking after you."

"Keep messing in my business and I'm the one gone be kicking some ass."

Titus grinned. "Still think you can take me don't you, little bit?"

Manroot grinned back. "Who you calling little?"

Titus dropped his own garden tool to the ground. "Bring it on, little bit. Show me what you got."

Titus lowered his body ever so slightly, the mass of black muscle tensing in preparation. Manroot positioned himself carefully, then lunged at his oldest brother. Chauncey whooped a loud cry into the air and egged them both on with his hoots and howls. On the porch James watched with amusement, leaning his thick body against the porch rail. His sons still carried on as though they were eight years old. Despite their frequent antics, he was proud of each of them. They were fine men and he was pleased they were still so close. Heaving a slow sigh, he stepped off the porch and headed toward the fields where his children lay wrestling. It would be dark soon and there was still a good amount of work to be done. No point in letting them waste but so much of that energy.

****

As hours spun into days and the days into nights, Manroot looked forward to the time he spent with the white woman. He enjoyed the stories she told of vast river ways and land unlike the rich red soil that stretched beneath their feet. Lavinia could make him laugh even when he fought hard not to. There was a gleam in her eyes that easily lifted his full lips over his teeth into a warm bending of joyous laughter. He had never loved before and thought this to be as close to it as he could possibly get. This felt right, calming the beast that hulked beneath his soul.

Lavinia was enamored with this man she had yearned to possess. She'd found a gentleness within him that others would never see, and Manroot made her feel special. She was considered an outsider here in the Southern U. S. of A., away from the European continent she'd once called home. Her mannerisms were not like those of her Southern counterpart. Other white women thought her to be common and trashy because of her passion for Negro men. The colored women didn't care much for her either and she struggled daily to be accepted by someone.

Manroot had opened doors for her that otherwise would have remained closed. People respected Manroot and if they didn't, they feared him, and that was more than enough for her.

Out on the back porch, Manroot stood leaning down over the old wooden balcony, watching the neighborhood children playing below. Lavinia pressed her palm against the small of his back as she came to stand beside him, the warm air brushing color against her skin.

"What are you doing, Manroot?"

The man grunted, shrugging his shoulders. "Just watching them kids playing. I can remember when I use to play like that." A faint smile pressed against his lips.

"Those were happy times for me also. The country side was so beautiful and there were fields of flowers for me and my sisters to trample in."

Manroot clasped his hands in front of him, resting his elbows on the railing. "Me and my brothers were lucky 'cause our daddy had land for us to play on. Daddy says children need land to run on."

"I would like one day to meet this father of yours. He sounds like he is very special to you."

Manroot nodded, his bald dome shining in the sunlight. "Him and my mama both real special. Cain't nobody touch them two." His thick chest swelled with pride, the wealth of it shimmering past his thick lashes.

The woman smiled, tracing the line of his face against her fingers. "Their son is very special also," she whispered, dropping her eyes.

Manroot pulled her hand to his mouth and kissed her palm. Meeting her eyes, he smiled, then leaned to plant a kiss against her mouth. His tongue lightly traced the outline of her lips before he lifted his head to stare back down to the pavement below. A curtain of silence enveloped them, and with the exception of the giggles and cries rising from below, they could almost hear each other breathe.

A little girl with an eggnog complexion and rows of sienna plaits jumped awkwardly through a tattered clothesline, the makeshift rope fraying around her thin ankles. Two copper-colored boys bounced a rubber ball between themselves, sometimes stopping to make fun of the girl or each other. A small infant could be heard crying out a window and kiddy cries skipped in the wind.

"Do you ever think about having children?" Lavinia asked, smiling down at the youngsters below.

Manroot shrugged his shoulders. "Sometimes. Wants me some kids someday. Man needs children to carry on his name. Man got a settle down first though. Can't take care no kids if you too busy running."

Lavinia nodded her head slowly. "You ever think about having children with me?"

Manroot laughed, amused by her boldness. "Man don't think about having children with no one woman less he married to her. If it happen before that then that's one thing, but can't waste no energy thinking 'bout it. Who in the hell goes round thinking 'bout disaster? It happen you deal with it but until it hit no point in playing with your luck." He laughed again. "Why you want to know that anyway?"

Lavinia breathed in a heavy sigh, then laughed a low laugh with him. She shifted her gaze out into the distance. "No reason. Just curious. Sometimes I daydream about what it would be like to be your wife and give you sons."

"Well, don't. I done told you before, whatever happens with us happens. Right now, what we got feels real good. Don't mess that up daydreaming 'bout stuff that might not ever happen."

"Do not get upset. I was just asking."

Manroot shook his head. He would never understand why most women were always worrying about things they didn't need to. If it wasn't having a man that had them tied up in knots, it was whether the man they did have would marry them and give them babies. Didn't make much sense to him. Lavinia knew better than to push him for any type of commitment. He'd told her before to just enjoy what they had while they had it. He wasn't making any promises about tomorrow.

Standing up straight, he pulled her close, wrapping his arms over her shoulders. "I'm gone be away for a while. I have to go take care of some business for my daddy. I won't be gone but so long."

Lavinia bit her bottom lip as she nodded her head. "What kind of business?"

Manroot shrugged. "Nothing you'd be interested in knowing 'bout. Just got to go buy and sell some land for my daddy."

"But I am interested in what you do."

Manroot sighed. It was not his way to share his business with any woman. Women who knew too much about what the Tuckers did and did not have, or how profitable their land holdings were for them, quickly wanted to become part of the family. It made it harder to get rid of them when a man thought about leaving.

"Like I said," Manroot finally responded. "It's nothing you need to be knowing 'bout." He studied her expression, sensing that there was more she wanted to ask, but she didn't. She smiled sweetly instead, turning to stare out into the distance.

From some place close, the sound of music rose in the air, the volume steadily increasing out an open window. Tab Hunter was crooning, the lyrics of *Young Love* billowing through the warm air. Manroot smiled as he pulled her close, draping his arms around her body.

"Dance with me," he whispered into her ear, his body gliding comfortably against hers.

They shuffled easily from one end of the porch to the other, never once releasing the hold they had on each other. When the song stopped, the laughter of children once again filled the open space.

Lavinia hung her head slightly, nodding slowly. "Will you come back to me?" she asked, her voice barely audible as she whispered back.

Manroot pulled her closer, bending her body tightly against his. "Won't nothin' keep me from it," he answered, and down below, the childish laughter of joy and happy skipped into the wind.

****

Lavinia stirred a pot of thick red gravy, taking quick glances out the rear window down to the street below. The summer heat had disappeared since Manroot had moved his few possessions into her home and his large body into her heart. The heavy wool sweater wrapped around her shoulders was doing very little to ward off the chilling autumn air seeping under the back door. She hummed a soft tune to herself.

Manroot had been gone for two months now, on business he'd told her when he'd kissed her good-bye. Since they had no telephone, there had been no way to call him, nor for him to call her. He had written once though, sweet words telling her that all was well, that he missed her, and would soon be home.

Every day she'd gone to her job at the local chicken and grits restaurant hoping that he'd be waiting outside to collect her when her shift was through. But each time she'd walked out the door, searching anxiously for his presence, she'd been disappointed. The nights had grown lonely since she did not dare dress herself up and go dance at any of her favorite night spots. Heaven help her were Manroot to hear she'd been out dancing with other men while he'd been away.

Lavinia loved to dance. She always had, even before she'd come to the United States. It exhilarated her to flaunt her body across a dance floor, the center of attention beneath a flood of lights. Men paid homage to her vanity when they sought to wrap their hands around her thin waist to guide her hips from side to side. She enjoyed the attention from men who appreciated her beauty with sweet, lingering words, and hard, stone-carved bodies.

It had been a Negro man who'd brought her here and now it was a Negro man who kept her. Her first husband had paid for the ticket that had taken her away from her family and home. He'd moved her into the very apartment she still lived in and every weekend he had taken her dancing, showing her off like a prized possession he'd won at the state fair. They'd met in Edinburgh. He'd been a striking black soldier who'd dazzled her with his maple syrup skin, dark brown eyes and thick, blue-black hair. One day he'd gone away, on business, and the only thing that had returned was a box filled with his personal possessions and an official government letter saying that he was dead.

Many a man had passed through his bed since that day. Not one of them had been lighter than brown bread. Lavinia had only wanted strong, Negro men since her husband had stolen his first kiss from her in her daddy's barn. It was only by accident that she had happened upon Manroot. He'd come to collect a rent payment from the manager of the restaurant where she worked. He'd strolled in through the front door, as bold as you please, oblivious to the scornful stares of the few white patrons who sat dining. In the kitchen, he'd leaned over the counters, laughing with the cook. When she'd walked in, he'd given her this wide, full grin that had warmed his face and her spirit. He'd tipped his hat with a courteous hello, finished his business, and walked out the same way he'd come in. No other colored man she knew would have been so brazen.

After that, she'd gone looking for him. Her search had taken her into the Negro nightclubs that stretched down West Main Street and there she'd sat every night she could until she'd found him. It hadn't taken long. That fateful night he'd been seated at the bar, a thin, cinnamon-toast girl named Ruth Ann on his arm. The girl had wrapped herself possessively around him, warning off all the other women with a bitter smile and a hateful stare. The one and only time Manroot had risen from his seat without Ruth Ann by his side, and sauntered toward the rear of the bar, Lavinia followed, brushing up against him as he headed into the men's room. Her smile had been all inviting as she'd allowed her hand to brush lightly against his groin.

It had gone like that for many a night until the one night he'd come without Ruth Ann. That night she'd purchased a bottle of scotch and had carried it and two glasses over to the table where he sat. They'd laughed and he had danced with her, grinding his thick body against hers, and when they were through, she'd brought him home. It had been her intentions to control the relationship much as she'd controlled all the others, but Manroot had never been controlled by anyone, and it soon became crystal clear that Lavinia was not going to be the first.

Nausea rose from her belly to the back of her throat as the smell of heavily spiced tomato sauce floated to her nose. Suppressing the urge to vomit she wiped her hands on her apron and sat herself down on a chair. Rubbing her hands across her abdomen, she smiled faintly. Her monthly flow had stopped coming shortly after Manroot had arrived and she knew she carried his seed inside. She had been too afraid to share the news with him before he'd gone off, but she knew there would be no choice once he returned. The bulge through her waistline would not soon disappear, and her dresses no longer hid the fullness growing within her.

Lavinia hoped it would be a boy, a miniature, cocoa-brown version of Manroot. If she bore him a son, she thought, he would not be so angry about her becoming pregnant. Sometimes Manroot's ire frightened her. His temper was quick and his rage could be tormenting. He had never hit her, but she believed that he was capable. It was the promised threats of pain that she had come to fear most.

She tapped her foot anxiously, smiling at the thought of holding her own little black baby doll in her arms. A little boy would always love her, she thought to herself, her smile growing wider. Sons clung to their mothers long after adulthood consumed them. Manroot would teach their son to watch over her like he did for his own mama.

As she sat with her eyes closed, her body perched precariously against a wooden stool, she imagined she heard him calling her name from somewhere below. As the calls grew louder, Manroot's footsteps fell heavily against the back steps. Lavinia was suddenly consumed with surprise and excitement. Manroot stomped his feet against the tattered rug that lay on the rear porch outside and Lavinia jumped to greet him when she heard him turning the knob on the door. She wrung her hands with excitement. The grin on his face was wide and warming as he pulled himself inside, dropping his bags to the floor. Lavinia rushed into his arms, throwing her own around his neck and her lips against his. The kiss was warm and searching, their tongues meeting like two old friends.

Closing the door, Manroot sat down in a chair, pulling Lavinia onto his lap. His kisses were tender as he washed his lips over her cheeks and chin, brushing along her eyes and forehead. His hands flowed across her shoulders and back, pausing at the crest of her full breasts. As they fell to her stomach, Lavinia stiffened ever so slightly, knowing the moment of truth had arrived. Manroot pulled his mouth from hers as his eyes darted from her stomach to her face and back again. Lavinia placed her own hand over his. He pushed her gently off his lap, lifting her blouse high above her waist. Her stomach protruded knowingly, the snow-white tissue stretching across a map of blue-green veins. He nodded his head slowly, leaning forward to brush his cheek against her belly.

"I think it's gone be a boy," she whispered. "I hope to give you a son. Want me a beautiful colored baby like his daddy."

Manroot laughed, pulling her back down to his lap. "Don't much matter, Miss 'Luv-in-ya'. Don't matter much what this baby is. It's my baby and that's all that matters with me."

Lavinia kissed him excitedly as they laughed and giggled together on that kitchen chair. Time was theirs, ticking slowly, until the pot on the stove gurgled, spewing its contents across the stove. Jumping to her feet, Lavinia rushed to turn the flame off under the large, cast iron utensil. Cursing, she wiped up the mess across the porcelain stovetop.

"Are you hungry?" she asked, turning around to face him.

Manroot shook his head no. "Not been too long since I had me some food. Stopped by to see my mama before I come back up here."

Lavinia nodded, disappointed that he'd not come home to her first. Manroot could see the hurt in her eyes, but knew there would be no complaining from Lavinia. Rising to his feet, he extended his arm, taking her hand in his own. Pulling her behind him, he led her into the bedroom, dropping his body onto the bed. Standing above him, Lavinia smiled warmly, elated to have him back with her. That he had not been angry about the child that would soon be coming filled her with complete euphoria.

Lavinia stepped slowly out of her clothes. As Manroot sat watching her, she loosened the tight bun at the back of her scalp, her thick hair falling down upon her shoulders. The cascading waves rested over her breasts. Manroot smiled at the protrusion of baby that reached out toward him begging to be loved. Reaching out with a large hand, he stroked it tenderly, imagining the day his child would lie in his arms. It was pure love that swirled past his thick eyelashes to dance along the round of the woman's face and down the length of her body.

Needing to feel her close to him, he loved her ever so gently, fearful that he might hurt her, or the child she carried inside. Lavinia clung to him, not wanting to let go. The faint brush of hair along his torso tickled her cheeks as she rested her head against his chest. Straddling her body over his she rode him gently, savoring the sweet sensations. The explosion through her pelvis came quickly as Manroot's own orgasm painted the walls of her femininity. It had been a long time and he was pleased to finally be back at home.

Hours later, they still lay side by side, Manroot's body curved protectively around hers. His hand stroked the pregnant bulge. As he shifted his body, Lavinia lifted hers from the bed, rising to turn on a light. Flooding the darkness with cool white light, she reached for her tortoise-shell hairbrush, pulling it through her long strands. Manroot leaned up on one arm to watch her as she braided her hair into a large plait down her back.

"Where are my pants?" he asked softly, his deep voice breaking through the silence.

Lavinia reached down to the floor to hand him the gray wool slacks he'd arrived home in. She sat down beside him as he reached into the pocket to pull an overly large roll of green paper from the pouch. Her mouth fell open, her chin dropping to her chest as he counted off a number of bills, pressing them into her hands.

"Business was better than I anticipated. You go buy yourself something pretty and get some stuff for my baby, too."

Lavinia nodded her head, kissing him on the mouth as she clutched the three hundred dollars in her palm. She did not dare ask him how he came about so much money knowing that to do so would send him out the door. If he wanted her to know he would tell her when he was ready.

"Come back to bed," he commanded, pulling gently at her arm. Lavinia smiled, turned off the light, and lay back down beside him.

"Show me how you love me," she whispered, wrapping her arms around him. "Show me good."

Nodding his head, Manroot grinned into the darkness, and complied.

****

James Tucker looked out his screen door into the front yard. He thought he'd heard a car pull up and he'd been right. He watched his youngest son ease himself out of the passenger side of an old Ford pickup truck. Ollie Madison waved a lazy hand in his direction, tilting his head hello.

"Hey there, Ollie. How you been?" James called out, returning the wave.

"Been just fine, Mr. James. How's the missus coming along?"

James nodded his head. "Miss Lucy's doing real well, thank you."

Ollie nodded, then waved one last time before pulling his old vehicle, which was more rust than steel, out of the yard and up the dirt road. Father and son stared, each eyeing the other with some reservation before James turned, slamming the screen door behind him. Manroot followed, gliding up the porch steps.

"Hey, Pop," Manroot nodded, standing tall in a linen suit the color of corn silk. James turned to stare at the child who bore more resemblance to him than all his other children. He noted the gleam across Manroot's bald crown, the dark skin atop his head and freshly shaven face. The suit was new, complimented by a white silk shirt, matching tie, and two-toned shoes in cream and caramel, soft as a baby's bottom, leather. Manroot was polished nicely and James could not help but smile in spite of wanting to slap the grin off his son's handsome face.

"Boy, you done lost your mind?" he asked heading into the kitchen to fix his wife some supper. Manroot followed closely on his heels.

"What you mean?"

"Everybody talking 'bout you carrying on with that white woman. How long you think it gone take before they put a rope around that thick neck a yours and send you swinging from one them trees downtown for the rest a them ignorant boys to learn a lesson from? What happen with you and Ruth Ann?"

Manroot shrugged, knowing his father really did not want an answer. The older man continued. "Your brothers come by this afternoon and said that there's been a lot a talk 'bout how you done moved in with her and now she telling everybody you gone marry her. Now, I know I ain't raise you to do something as fool as that."

Manroot clasped his hands together as he watched his father pile food upon a plate. Creamed corn, fried okra, rice, and smothered chicken cut into small pieces steamed lightly beneath brown gravy.

"Me and Lavinia having us a baby. Ain't having no child a mine born a bastard. This baby gone carry my name proper."

James looked up from what he was doing, a large wooden spoon frozen mid-air in his hands. "Damn, boy. If you had to be getting someone pregnant why couldn't it have been Ruth or any one a them other girls you was chasing? I swear I ain't raise you to be so stupid. We still live in the *deep* South, Manroot. These folks don't care until you upset they balance. Do you know what this could do to you? This shit could sure enough get your black ass hung 'cause you gone upset the balance if you marry that white girl." The older man sighed.

Manroot laughed. "Don't you fret none, Daddy. Ain't nobody gone mess with me. People 'round here don't mess with none of us Tucker boys if they want to live to tell about it."

James grunted. "Who is this girl?"

"Her name's Luv-in-ya", Manroot said, pronouncing her name as though his tongue was wrapped in thick syrup. "She's from Europe." He smiled proudly, tucking his thumbs beneath the lapels of his jacket.

"Well, she obviously ain't got no good sense either going and getting herself pregnant for your black ass."

Manroot shrugged again, still grinning.

James passed him the plate of food. "Go feed your mama. You tell her she gone be a grandma."

Manroot nodded as James headed out the back door. Pulling at his overalls, he called back over his shoulder. "Manroot."

"Yes, sir?"

"If that your baby you make sure you does right by it or you gone have to answer to me. I can't do nothing 'bout how you be treating these women out here, but you don't do right by any grandchild a mine and you won't have to worry none 'bout these white folks, 'cause I'm gone whoop your ass. You hear me?"

As James headed toward the back fields Manroot paused, then started up the stairs toward his parent's bedroom. There was no need to respond. His father knew his message had been clear.

Slipping quietly into the room, Manroot smiled warmly at the frail figure whose limp body lay supported by a mountain of pillows. The afternoon sunlight poured into the room, falling in bright striations against the hand-sewn quilt. He placed the tray of food against the night table, dropping his large body onto the edge of the bed.

"Hey, mama," he said, leaning to kiss her wrinkled cheek. Unable to speak, Lucille Tucker blinked her eyes closed, then open. The gleam in them smiled back at him. Manroot adjusted the pillows beneath her small body so that she could sit up and eat comfortably. Last Christmas Eve Miss Lucy's petite frame had been besieged by a stroke, leaving her paralyzed from the neck down and unable to speak. It had been her husband's loving care and her children's constant attention that had brought a semblance of life back into her eyes.

The doctors had advised them to place her in a home for the disabled, but James refused. His love for his wife was boundless and he trusted they'd get through whatever befell them. He knew that not being able to take care of Lucy would be far more difficult for him to deal with than taking care of her every need would ever be.

After tucking the covers around his mother's body, Manroot began to feed her as carefully, and as lovingly, as he could remember her doing for him when he'd been a small child cuddled against her lap. He grinned broadly as he eased small spoonful's of food into her mouth, waited patiently while she chewed, then wiped at the edges of her lips with a cloth napkin.

"It sure smells good, Mama. I hope it taste good too."

Her eyes blinked rapidly.

"Daddy done found out 'bout 'Luv-in ya', Mama. He won't happy 'bouts it neither."

His mother's eyes whispered that she'd told him so.

"Don't know how to tell him how much I love her, Mama." Manroot shrugged. "Can't hardly tell 'Luv-in-ya' how I feels bout her. I just hope she knows 'cause there ain't never been no woman who makes me feel like she do. Never." Manroot sighed heavily before continuing.

Placing the spoon onto the plate, Manroot covered his mother's tiny fingers with his hand. "We gone have us a baby, Mama. I'm gone be a daddy. You gone be a grandma again."

Lucy stared at him, then blinked her eyes closed, shutting them tightly. A moment passed before she opened them. The gleam had faded ever so slightly and Manroot could feel her disappointment at his news.

"Didn't plan it, Mama," he said softly, his head hanging low. "It just happened, but I'm gone do right. I'm gone marry her and give my baby my name proper."

Lucy's eyes smiled ever so faintly, the dark orbs shaking her head for her.

"I want you to meet her, Mama. I think you'd like her. I really do."

Lucy's eyes dropped to the bed covers. Manroot lifted the spoon, placing one last morsel past the woman's lips. He watched as she chewed slowly, her eyes brushing along his face, caressing him gently. He missed his mother's small voice, the gentle tones with the not so gentle words that had made him do right more times than he could ever count.

Her eyes had scolded him repeatedly since he'd first told her about Lavinia. He had only shared news of the ivory beauty with the one person who could no longer voice judgment with her too-frank words. It had become too easy for him to ignore the opinions behind her silent eyes.

Manroot sighed, resting the plate on the night table by the bed. Lifting his mother slightly he readjusted the pillows, wanting to bring her as much comfort as he could. Stretching his body alongside hers, he rested his head against her shoulder, wrapping her fingers between his own.

Lucy's eyes searched past her son's head toward the sunlight streaming through the large front window. How she missed standing in front of that window to stare out over the land that she and James had worked so hard to hold onto. God had been good to them despite the many barriers that had stood in their way and they'd been blessed with good children who'd grown to be decent adults. The older ones went to church on a regular basis, their faith firmly grounded. This made her happy. Manroot though was always going in a different direction, treading down a path contrary to the road she and her husband wanted for him.

Thinking of her children, Lucy's eyes shone brightly, the sparkle brighter than the sunshine outside. Manroot was the child that she worried most about. Being the baby, he'd been spoiled by all the others and in some ways, it had made him selfish. No less loving than any of his siblings, but definitely selfish. When she'd been able, she'd had to constantly remind him to do right by people no matter who they were. But Manroot had a hardness in him. He could be mean spirited, and many times, he'd act rashly with no thought to the consequences. Now she feared the worst for him and had no way to tell him.

Rising from the bed, Manroot kissed his mother, taking the dirty dishes with him as he said goodbye. Father and son passed each other on the staircase. Their eyes met, lingering briefly. James stopped short, placing his hand against the younger man's shoulder.

"Baby coming means someone's dying. A spirit got to pass for that child to be having life."

Manroot nodded. "That's what the old folks say."

"That's what your mama would say."

Manroot nodded again.

James paused, searching his son's face for a semblance of understanding. "Your mama's getting tired, Manroot. That stroke done took lots out of her. It's gone be her time before any of us knows it."

Manroot studied his father's face, a pained expression across his own.

"Come see your mama again real soon, son. She likes it when you children come spend time with her. You bring this woman when you come too. Don't be having no woman carrying the Tucker name who ain't been in this house to pay your mama her respects."

Manroot nodded. "Yes, sir."

James squeezed his son's shoulder gently, then lifted his tired body up the rest of the stairs. He stood at the entrance to his wife's bedroom, his hand on the doorknob as he waited for the front door to close behind his youngest child. When the door clicked shut and the footsteps faded off the front porch, he turned the handle and went inside.

Lucy lay peacefully, her dark eyes staring off into the distance. James leaned to switch on the eight-track tape player the boys had bought him for his birthday. Nat King Cole slid into the room, maple syrup dripping down the walls. James smiled at the beautiful woman whose eyes cradled him in her heart. How they loved some Nat King Cole.

As her husband eased his oversized body onto the bed beside her, Miss Lucy closed her eyes, wanting to feel his arms wrapped tightly around her. She longed to feel his gentle caresses brushing along the length of her arms, falling against her thin waist, and over her small hips and thighs. She fought back the tears that burned at the edges of the eyes, knowing the hands were there, but that she could no longer feel the heat from their touch.

James cuddled her closer, rocking her gently in his arms. His tears fell against her cheek as he leaned to kiss her brow. The salted water blended with her own tears, rolling off the curve of her chin.

A low hum rose from James' throat. Miss Lucy found great comfort in his presence. They needed no words to share the emotions that flowed like a river between them. After forty-one years of marriage, they fed off each other's energy, their thoughts in complete sync, one with the other.

Silently they prayed for their son. Lucy's prayers asked that her child be as loving toward this woman as his father was toward her. Asking that Manroot find some control over his jealousy and anger, knowing that no matter how much he might love this Lavinia, the mean streak within him could easily cause them both a great deal of pain.

James prayed that his son would see the error of his ways. This white woman could do nothing but rain disaster down upon him. This was neither the time nor the place for such a union, and history should have shown Manroot what lay in wait for him.

Whispering a silent amen in the back of their minds, both knew they could do no more for the children they loved so dearly. It was past time for them to learn from their own mistakes, but as Lucy drifted slowly off to sleep, her instincts told her Manroot had now made his own bed, and James knew his son would have to pay for his hubris.

****

The four men stood side by side, their hands pushed deep into their pants pockets. Dark blue suits adorned their immense bodies, a wealth of navy fabric fitting perfectly around their frames. The chatter between them was casual, easy conversation between family members. On the other side of the room, Lavinia stood nervously with Manroot's sister, Eloise, who fretted over their mother, trying to ease any discomfort she presumed the elder woman to be feeling. Eloise's daughter sat in a large, wingback chair, kicking her small, brown legs back and forth against the fabric.

Miss Lucy's eyes scanned the white woman's face and she wished she could tell her daughter to stop fussing about and sit down out of her way. Every so often, the woman would smile down at her or over to the child, but mostly her eyes were on Manroot, inhaling his every motion. The woman's nervousness was genuine, but it was the glow in her eyes when she and Manroot stared toward each other as if they were alone that made Miss Lucy happy. It was love and Miss Lucy was grateful for that. It would not be easy for them and their love might be the only thing to pull them through.

The knock on the front door brought the excitement in the room to another level. What little color blessed Lavinia's face drained away slowly, blending her pale complexion into the ivory maternity dress she wore. She quickly crossed the room to go stand by Manroot's side. Titus and Chauncey opened a narrow path to allow her in. Daddy James pulled his suit jacket closed, buttoning it neatly, and headed for the foyer. His boisterous greeting and deep laughter welcomed the visitor at the door.

Daddy James and Reverend Robert T. Prescott entered the room arm in arm. The newly ordained Reverend Prescott extended his arm to shake hands with the other Tucker men and then knelt down to whisper his greetings to Miss Lucy. He winked an eye toward Eloise.

"So, this is the lovely bride," he said, turning his attention to Lavinia. A toothy grin greeted her.

"Hello, Reverend Prescott," Lavinia smiled. "Thank you for coming to marry us."

"Oh, it's my pleasure," Reverend Prescott beamed. "This family been part a my church for as long as we all remember, as way back as when my grand-daddy was pastor. We're all family here and it's an honor to welcome such a pretty sight into the family."

Behind him, Eloise grunted, then rolled her eyes, and twisted up her mouth as though she'd bitten into something sour. From where she lay on the red, velvet-covered sofa, Miss Lucy glared up at her daughter, appalled that the young woman would behave so uncivilized in front of their young pastor. Daddy James' stern look echoed his wife's sentiments. Rolling her eyes, Eloise knelt down to button her child's shoe.

"Well, let's get this ceremony moving," Manroot said, reaching for Lavinia's hand. His father nodded his head, then strolled over to stand by Miss Lucy's side. He brushed his hand gently against her hair.

As the Tucker children gathered in front of the pastor, Eloise on Lavinia's left, and Titus and Chauncey to the right of their brother, Daddy James leaned down to pick up the little girl who'd fallen asleep against the chair back. As he nuzzled the child close, he smiled down at his wife. Tears misted in both of their eyes as Reverend Prescott blessed the union. As the pastor pronounced them man and wife, Miss Lucy sighed heavily, blinking back the tears as Manroot scooped Lavinia up into his arms and kissed her warmly.

When all was done, Daddy James passed his grandchild back to her mother, then extended his large hand out to shake Manroot's. He gripped his son's fingers tightly as he pulled the man into a close hug.

"Congratulations," Daddy James said into Lavinia's ear as he reached out to wrap his arms around her, "and welcome into this here family."

"Thank you," the woman smiled back, beaming up at the two broad men who held her closely. "Thank you so much, Mr. Tucker."

"You family now. You best call me James."

Lavinia smiled again, nodding her head up and down.

"Well," Eloise said, clearing her voice loudly. "Why don't we all go get some food. There's plenty to eat."

"Sounds good," Titus muttered.

"Yep, food smells ready to me," Chauncey chimed. Both men headed toward the kitchen.

The women laughed as Eloise led Reverend Prescott toward the dining room.

"I need to take Miss Lucy back upstairs so she can rest," Daddy James said, leaning to pull the brightly colored quilt from around his wife's body.

"I'll do it, Daddy," Manroot said, reaching past his father to lift his mother up into his arms. "I'll take care of her."

Daddy James nodded, kissing his wife tenderly. Miss Lucy smiled, stroking both of their cheeks with a gentle look. As Manroot headed up the stairs, Daddy James extended his elbow and guided Lavinia toward the dining room for the wedding celebration.

In his mother's bedroom, Manroot laid her gently down onto the bed, propping her against the pillows as he drew the covers up to tuck her in. Miss Lucy smiled up at him. Manroot watched his mother's eyes as they spoke to him, and he believed her to be as happy for him as he was for himself. He nodded his head slowly, leaning to kiss his mother's cheek.

"I love her, Mama. I truly do and I'm gone be a real good husband. I promise I will."

Miss Lucy continued to smile, then closed her eyes and drifted off to sleep.

****

Travis Teeter ran the gas and convenience store on Hillandale Road, a mile down from the new Piggly Wiggly Supermarket. He'd taken it over from his daddy just a year earlier. There was little going on in town that Travis did not think he had some knowledge about, or so he thought the Saturday morning he stood in front of the large coolers in deep conversation with the Bates brothers. He'd been whispering loudly about Lavinia Tucker, peppering his comments with idioms like 'white trash' and 'whore'. His ranting about her giving decent white women a bad name had reached many an ear since he'd seen her pregnant frame walk past his doorway earlier in the day.

Off in the back, searching through the baskets of sewing notions, Eloise Tucker's ears perked up, the tight curls at the back of her skull pulling against her tightened jaw. Everyone knew that Travis Teeter's problem with Lavinia came from the very public rejection she'd given him months earlier when Manroot had been gone, and Travis's interest had been keen. In fact, Lavinia's rejection had not only involved a harsh slap to the man's right cheek, but had also included a large wad of spit hurled in his ruddy face. This had come only after he'd cornered her against the dry goods, offering to show her what a real man was all about. Lavinia had been all too clear, pronouncing what his lily-white, red-freckled, two-inch dick would never do for her, and her declaration had not been pretty to witness.

Eloise dropped her purchases on the counter just as her brothers entered the store. Titus leaned against the door frame, a toothpick clutched between his teeth. His dark eyes fell into narrowed slits as he pushed his hands deep into his pockets. Manroot and Chauncey came to stand on either side of their sister, peeking at the items she'd placed on the wooden counter top to be rung up. The Bates brothers, Griffin and Duncan, both took this as a cue to make their exit, nodding a quick greeting as they made their way out of the store. Travis smiled weakly, rushing behind the counter to complete the transaction.

Manroot nodded in Travis's direction, turning his attention to his sister. "You seen 'Luv-in-ya'?"

Eloise nodded, raising her eyes to stare into Travis's. "She went next door to bring Miss Hattie the cake she made for her."

Manroot nodded. Travis counted the change Manroot handed him, then packed the canvas sack, his hands shaking. Manroot watched him closely.

"How you been, Travis?"

"Fine, thank you, Tucker. How's everything been with you?"

Manroot nodded. "Ain't got no complaints really except word going round 'bout people having lots to say 'bout my new wife."

Travis dropped his eyes. "You don't say?"

"Yes, sir. Man can do something right crazy he think another man disrespecting his woman. You know? Wouldn't be right for a man to allow no talk to go on and he not do anything about it."

The head of red curls nodded feverishly. "A man should protect what's his."

Manroot grinned, a wide toothy grin shining over Travis. As he reached quickly for his sister's parcels, Travis flinched, taking a step back from the counter. "You have a nice day now," Manroot said with a smile.

Travis nodded his head, still shaking in his gray, snake-skin boots, as the Tucker siblings made their way out of his store. He brushed his hands over his brow, cursing under his breath. "Goddamn niggers. Them three think they own this goddamn town." Travis raced to the window to peer out toward the street just as Lavinia met Manroot on the sidewalk. His nostrils flared with disgust as he bit his bottom lip.

Crossing his arms over his chest, he stared as the Tucker men made their way down the road toward Manroot's brand new, shiny, black Buick. Each brother stood as tall as the other. Chauncey was bulkier than the other two, though all of them were mammoth in size. For as long as Travis could remember the Tucker boys had done just as they pleased and no man in Creekton, white or black, had been fearless enough to question them.

It had begun with their great granddaddy, Silas Tucker. Silas had been the wealthiest, most influential landowner in the small community of Creekton. A generous and good-natured man, Silas had been the epitome of Euro-southern gentry. He had governed his vast acreage with a firm but fair hand.

Silas had not fathered any children. His first wife, Priscilla, had been barren and had died childless only three years after their marriage. Since Silas had never been the sort of master who pestered after his slaves, there were no cafe-au-lait, mulatto children running around that belonged to him.

Soon after Priscilla's death though, Silas purchased a beautiful slave named Naomi. Naomi was an exquisite beauty boasting a long, lithe frame draped with skin the shade of midnight and large, blue-black eyes that could make the strongest man drop to his knees. Silas Tucker had paid a small fortune for her and in no time, he'd taken her into his house, his bed, and his heart. Naomi soon became the second great love of Silas' life. He then did what no Southern white man in his right mind would have done. He took the woman to Europe and married her, moving Naomi back into his home as his wife.

The news was whispered about in small circles at first. Good white women who never had a negative word for anyone were suddenly speaking ill of Silas Tucker, mortified by his actions. The men in the barbershop made jokes, laughing at the absurdity of his transgression. Then the Baptist ministers preached from the pulpit about the horror of it all.

Before long the uproar in Creekton stampeded across the borders. The slave population took cover, not wanting to draw any undue attention upon themselves, fearful the fallout would cost them their lives.

They came first in small groups, well-dressed white men, pointing out the error of Silas' way. Then they came in droves, angry mobs threatening to destroy his property, land, and human life. But Silas stood firm, greeting them with his own pronouncements or buck shot from his rifle, whichever they preferred. Soon, those most bothered by it, sold Silas their land for hefty sums, two and three times the value. Those who stayed ignored him, proclaiming Silas an eccentric fool who'd soon grow weary of the colored girl.

Naomi bore Silas one child, Franklin Tucker. Franklin grew up amongst the cotton, corn, and tobacco, tending to the cattle, hogs, and chickens. His father schooled him at home, refusing to allow his son's dark complexion keep him from being educated. Eventually Franklin was sent overseas for schooling, bringing back to Creekton a fountain of worldly knowledge possessed by few others. Franklin grew into a tall, indigo prince who soon presided over the land of the Tucker estate.

When Naomi and Silas passed on, it was Franklin, a charcoal replica of his daddy, who owned most of Creekton. Now, there had come a point when no one would have dared go up against Silas Tucker, and even in death the man's spirit was both revered, and feared. It was not long before Franklin walked in his father's shoes, forging his own footsteps.

Tempered with compassion and intelligence, Franklin fought daily battles to maintain his father's legacy. On no less than six separate occasions, the tax man had claimed monies delinquent and restitution due. Payments were contingent on the time of day and the mood of the sheriff. And more than once, Franklin had found it necessary to pull himself out of a bind, relying on his instincts and the good grace of a benevolent God.

Franklin believed in sharing his wealth. Colored sharecroppers and field hands soon found their own sense of worth as Franklin sold them their own small acreage, sometimes only on the spit of a promise and the clasp of a handshake.

When Franklin married Elaine Cropper, a robust woman with a pecan complexion, and she bore James, father again passed on to son all the privileges afforded one who possessed so great an asset as a piece of land. The Tucker men had been born into worth inked on the faded yellow papers deeded to their ancestors and passed down the family tree.

Now, no man had ever given any serious thought to going up against any of the Tuckers. At least no man with any common sense. Over the years, the Tuckers had sold off some of their property, but James still laid claim to the original plantation and a hefty sum of acreage. Although the Tuckers may not have appeared to be outwardly wealthy, they had money and plenty of it and in Creekton, the color green had been bigger than white, or not white, could ever be. Their neighbors may not have shared their dinner table, but they did not pass up an opportunity to benefit from the Tucker's plentiful bounty.

Travis spewed spit to the ground, jealousy tiptoeing through the pit of his stomach. Biting at a hangnail on his thumb, he smiled weakly as a customer brushed through the door, sending him back to the food-lined shelves.

Manroot pulled his shiny new vehicle onto the dirt driveway leading toward the family home. The dry dust rose in low swirls as the tree-lined pathway welcomed their coming. Crape myrtle in shades of pink, white, and lavender bowed above them, the flowering blossoms waltzing in the cool breeze. Manroot looked into the rear view mirror to watch Lavinia. Her face had grown heavy with sadness when Eloise had related the conversation between Travis Teeter and the Baxters. No matter how often she heard it, she could not get used to the constant whisperings about her and Manroot.

He had told her on more than one occasion not to place any stock in what anyone else had to say about their lives. He'd told her that as long as they loved each other nothing else mattered. It was hurtful though, as she struggled to hold her head up high beneath the cloud of disparaging remarks that hovered about them. Even Manroot's family had been less than kind, his father pulling no punches about what he thought about the relationship. They'd been forced to embrace her though, once Manroot had made it clear that she would be a Tucker. One could never say the Tuckers did not take care of their own.

Manroot sighed, his gaze flickering between the rear view mirror and the stretch of road ahead of them.

Eloise's daughter, Candy, stood on the front porch of the Tucker home, tears streaming down her face. As her uncles brushed past her to go inside, her sobs grew louder.

"Girl, shut that noise up," Chauncey yelled over his shoulder. "Every time I see you, you crying."

Candy wiped her eyes, pushing her lips out to pout. As her mother eased her way up the steps, Candy ran to grab her leg.

"What's wrong now, Candy?" Eloise asked, kissing the six-year-old on her forehead.

"Don't want to stay with Grampy James. This house smells bad. He smells bad."

Eloise smacked the child's legs, stinging the tanned flesh with a heavy palm. "Girl, I know your rude self ain't been carrying on no such foolishness since I been gone."

Daddy James met the two at the door. "She been crying since you pulled out of the yard. I told her to stay out on the porch if it smelled so bad. She lucky I ain't take a switch to her behind."

Eloise kissed her father on the cheek, glaring at her daughter. "Candy Louise Alexander, girl, you better apologize to Daddy James right now."

Candy wrapped her arms around her torso, resolute. "No. Wanna go home."

In the other room, Chauncey and Titus laughed. Candy swung about on her heels to glare in their direction. Stomping her foot, she shot a hard glare past their heads, throwing her hands on her bony hips. "I wanna go home," she screamed, her small voice vibrating around the room.

As Candy took a deep breath in, filling her lungs with air to scream back out, Manroot came from across the room. Grasping the front of her pink sweater, he lifted her off the floor, raising her to his eye-level. Candy gasped loudly as she stared into her uncle's face, his dark eyes intensely angry. The cry caught in her throat as her black, patent-leather shoes over snow-white ankle socks swung beneath her, the tears frightened out of her gaping eyes. Manroot stared at her hard, his gaze all-telling.

"Shut it up now. Your grandma upstairs resting and you carrying on like a little fool. Shut it up before I shut it up for you."

"Manroot, if you don't put my child down, you better," Eloise said with little enthusiasm, emptying her bags onto the kitchen table. "Put that girl down."

"I'm gone tear her little butt up if she don't start acting right," Manroot said, glaring at his niece.

Eloise sucked her teeth. "Just put her down. You know she only act up when she tired."

"Tired my behind," James piped in. "That girl act like she ain't had no home training the way she carry on sometimes."

As Candy swung in the air she could feel her full bladder threatening to burst to the floor beneath her. "I gots to go pee, Uncle Manroot. I'se got to go bad," she whispered.

Manroot's nostrils flared as he kissed her chubby cheek, lowered her ever so slightly, and then dropped her to the floor. As Candy landed on the polished hard wood with a loud thump, Chauncey and Titus burst into laughter for the second time. Picking herself up, Candy wiped the tears from her eyes, brushed the dust off her dress, then raced up the steps toward the bathroom. Shaking her head, Eloise joined in the laughter with her brothers. Lavinia sat at the kitchen table, a bowl of freshly picked string beans in her lap. Snapping the ends from the green pods, she heaved a slow sigh through her heavy belly.

"What you think Manroot gone do when that baby of his gone be crying for something?" Chauncey asked.

Titus chuckled. "Probably have that baby swinging so much it gone think it's a monkey in a tree."

Manroot pushed at his brother teasingly. "Me and Lavinia gone have us a good baby. Ain't gone be no spoiled sight like Miss Candy-pants is."

Eloise cut her eyes at Manroot. "My baby ain't spoiled. She special and you need to treat her that way. You ain't got no call to be scaring my child like that."

Manroot wrapped his arms around his sister. "Scare you like that if I needs to."

Eloise kissed her brother's cheek. "Just leaves my child be."

James grunted, seating himself beside Lavinia. "Candy might not be such a handful she had a daddy to keep her in check."

Eloise's mouth fell into a tight line as she bit back her tongue. The silence that filled the room hung heavily. In the distance, they could hear Candy's faint voice telling her grandmother how Manroot had manhandled her. Choosing her words carefully, Eloise spoke slowly, her tone cutting.

"Daddy, I don't want to have this fight with you again but you ain't got no call to say something like that. Candy got a daddy. He just can't be with us right now. She also got you and her uncles to keep her in line, and for the time being that is going to have to do. Earl gone be back soon to help me with Candy but right now we just got to be patient."

James stared hard at his daughter, shaking his head. "One day you gone use the good sense God gave you, girl. Candy's daddy ain't coming back. Earl Alexander done left you. He probably up North somewhere lying to some other woman, making promises he ain't got no intentions of keeping. It's been how long now? Five years and you ain't heard nothing from him. Told you when he wouldn't marry you that he won't planning on being around for no length of time. Candy ain't got no daddy worth telling about and you a fool if you think he is."

Her brother's firm hand against her shoulder stalled the angry words ready to spill out of her mouth. Manroot squeezed his sister gently, dispelling the tirade threatening to pour from her wounded pride. Although they all knew James was right, Eloise hurt each time her father felt it necessary to paint the truth across her face.

"I need to go give Mama her bath," she said instead, wringing her wet hands against a towel. "Lavinia, can you come help me?"

Lavinia nodded her head, her eyes darting back and forth between James and his children. Rising slowly from her seat, she smiled a faint smile as she heaved herself past her in-laws and up the stairs behind Eloise.

In the bathroom, Eloise cursed under her breath as she ran a metal basin full with lukewarm water. "He ain't gone ever let it die. Never. Them boys of his can do whatever they want and he don't never say nothing. I always got to hear about my mistakes. Gone keep bringing them up in my face until the day I die."

Lavinia said nothing, knowing when it was best to keep her mouth shut. She noted the tears that fell from Eloise's eyes and reached a frail, pink hand out to comfort her. Eloise gave her a thin, weak smile, silently mouthing her thanks.

"How are you feeling?" she asked, turning her attention to the pregnant woman.

"Ready for this baby to come. It is getting very difficult to breathe."

"That's cause you carrying so high. Carrying high like that usually means you got yourself a girl. I carried high when I was pregnant with Candy."

Lavinia's eyes widened. "Don't say that. I want this baby to be a boy for Manroot. We wants us a son."

Eloise laughed. "Don't you worry none. Manroot gone loves it no matter what it is. He just wants to be a daddy."

Lavinia smiled again as Eloise led her into the matriarch's bedroom. At the foot of the bed, Candy sat with her legs crossed beneath her, her childish ramblings greeting them at the door. The child's chatter bounced against the walls as she stripped the clothes from a rag doll.

Against the pillows, Lucy Tucker lay awkwardly, her body spilling heavy over to one side. Both women knew instantly that Lucy had not heard a word of the child's chatter. Neither could say for certain if she'd even known Candy had ever been there. Darkness had replaced the twinkle in the older woman's eyes. An emptiness had entombed the bright sparkle they each knew so well, and it was Lavinia who eased her way back down the stairs to tell the Tucker men that their wife and mother was gone.

****

When the angel of death came swooping down to wrap his dark wings around Miss Lucy, he set off a chain of events that left them each spinning in a vicious cycle they would not find so easy to escape from.

Lucy Tucker was buried in an ivory dress of Battenberg lace, white gloves adorning her fragile hands, a faint smile posed upon her lips. The turnout was impressive as a congregation of friends and family packed the small Baptist church to pay their respects. All her children cried, leaning to kiss her cheek one last time before the heavy mahogany casket was sealed tight and lowered into the rich, red soil. James paved the way, a mournful expression frozen across his face, softness found only in his large, dark eyes.

It was those large, dark eyes wishing his wife well on her journey home that first noticed the look of panic that pulled at Lavinia. It was those dark eyes that saw the quick ripple of contraction stretching across her abdomen and followed the line of fluid which seeped from beneath her skirt, down her swollen legs, to puddle against the wood planked floor. It was those dark eyes that spoke silently to the scared woman seeping with embarrassment, not wanting to draw attention from the occasion at hand.

Theirs was a silent conversation mediated by something greater than either of them. Lavinia nodded and smiled faintly, reaching to grasp her father-in-law's large brown hand. His fingers held her tightly, flooding her with a strength she did not know she had, and it was he who kept her from crying out as the onset of labor took hold.

As mourners gathered in silent celebration over plates of fried chicken and home-spun foods, Janay Lucille Tucker was pulled from her mother's womb, a chocolate-milk mass of beautiful baby. Tears streamed down Manroot's face as he peered beneath the pastel blanket to see his mother's reflection in the ice-blue eyes staring back at him. Behind him, his father stared off into the distance, marveling at the passing of souls.

James lifted the small bundle from her mother's arms, walking her to the large bay window in the front of the room. Lifting the small child to stare out over the green pastures, he marveled at the newness of his second grandchild and the quiet white woman lying in his grandmother's bed. She'd brought life back into the home that a better part of him had wanted to bury with his beloved Lucy. He studied the baby who suckled her own tongue, the pale eyes already searching.

"She got old people's eyes," he announced out loud, not really caring if any one of them heard him.

"What does that mean?" Lavinia asked curiously, her voice barely audible.

James tossed her a quick glance, then let his gaze drop back on his grandchild. "Mean she got an old soul. Mean she know more at this very moment than any of us will ever know in a lifetime."

Manroot rolled his eyes, shrugging his shoulders lightly as Lavinia glanced up at him.

James continued. "Mean she done lived too many lives before she even took breath," he finished. He nodded his head knowingly, placing the tiny infant into her father's outstretched arms.

"Do right by this baby or it's you and me," he said, directing his comments at Manroot. "You and me. Don't you ever forget that," he repeated, his voice a shade away from a whisper.

Manroot nodded, then kissed the child's cheek as his father went back downstairs to call for the preacher to come bless the new baby.

Manroot and Lavinia sat huddled together over their newborn child. The little girl suckled lightly at her mother's breast, the pale eyes darting around and about. Lavinia could feel the hot flash of tears wanting to spill down along her cheeks. She cleared her throat, then leaned heavily against Manroot.

"I am sorry I did not give you a son," she whispered, her faint voice a nervous quiver.

Manroot chuckled. "What you sorry for woman? You done give me a fine baby. She healthy and she pretty as a picture. Man loves his daughters, too. You know this here girl already has me wrapped right round her little finger. You ain't got nothing to be sorry for."

Lavinia smiled a weak smile, though the feeling was not in her heart. The child should have been a boy, she thought silently, heaving a heavy sigh. Aloud, she said instead, "I love you, Manroot."

Leaning to kiss her, Manroot smiled back. "Me too, baby. And I sure 'nuff loves our baby girl here."

It was just one month later when Manroot and Lavinia walked into Travis Teeter's store, their infant girl pressed against her father's broad chest. Manroot was the picture of paternal pride as he showed off his daughter to everyone who would stop to look. The tiny child gushed and spewed contentment as her parents beamed with joy.

Travis nodded then grunted his greetings and congratulations as he rang up their purchases, silently wishing the young family out of his store. No one noticed the dark shadow who'd eased into the doorway behind them. It was only when they turned to leave, Lavinia leading the way, that Manroot caught sight of the bitter woman, her eyes blazing with malevolence.

It happened too quickly for words to capture. Afterwards, not even Travis could recall clearly all that had occurred in the swift moments before Lavinia lay screaming across the display of vegetables, blood spewing a crimson line down the summer-picked peaches and vine-ripened tomatoes.

Travis could not remember precisely when Manroot had pushed the tiny infant into his arms or how the man had grabbed Ruth Ann's hand, dripping with blood from the silvery length of a pearl handled carving knife. Nor could he recollect when Manroot had smashed his fist into the woman's face sending her backward through the front door, shattering the glass panes beneath her.

What he did remember though, with vivid clarity, was the large, black man's hurt as he sat cradling his wife's lacerated face in his lap. He remembered the blood splattered down the infant's cheek and her father's gentle touch as he wiped it from her eyes. He remembered the tender tears that spilled out of the man's heart when he whispered the white woman's name into her hair. He remembered the bloodied colored woman who lay sprawled in his doorway, laughing and crying an evil, hateful laugh and the glazed eyes filled with malice that stared at him with knowing recognition as he leaned to inspect her damage. It was these memories that haunted the man's racist heart until the day he died.

****

In the distance, she could hear her child crying. Though she knew she should rise from her bed to tend to the hungry baby, she could not find the energy or the will to lift her head from the pillow. Reaching up to touch her face, she lightly caressed the puckered length of flesh. The doctors had said nothing could be done to rid her of the protruding scar. Hot tears fell angrily from her eyes as the baby's wails grew louder and increasingly distressed.

Lavinia tossed the covers to the floor, rolling her body to the edge of the bed. Lifting herself up, she pulled herself to her feet, dragging her body across the room to the cradle. Janay lay cringing, her tiny face creased in red wrinkles, baby tears dripping against her cheeks. Lifting the infant from the crib, Lavinia cradled her awkwardly, rocking the child uneasily against her breast. She would have to make a bottle she thought suddenly. Her milk had dried weeks ago and her breasts were empty. She sighed heavily as she made her way toward the kitchen and the refrigerator, the child clutched awkwardly beneath her arm.

Lined neatly in a row, four bottles sat on the top shelf waiting for her. "Manroot has been busy," she said aloud jiggling the baby against her side. "What a good daddy you have, little girl."

Adjusting the infant against her lap, she looked down into the child's face as she pushed the rubber nipple into the infant's mouth, Lavinia could not feel the maternal yearnings that she had wanted so wholeheartedly the months before. There was no emotion for this female person, with her crystal complexion and innocent beauty, who'd become the light of her father's life. Lavinia regretted her child had not been a boy.

Back in her bedroom, she lay the baby back into her cradle. Once again, the child began to cry, despite the bottle of cold milk that Lavinia had laid by her side. The noise crept inside her head, whispering loudly about her being a bad mother. A son would have understood, Lavinia thought, pulling her hands through her hair. A son would have been sensitive to her pain. This daughter of hers was selfish, pointing out Lavinia's faults. This daughter looked at her with a critical gaze, pointing out her weaknesses. Lavinia's hand slapped the side of the small child's face, the imprint of her palm painted in red against the baby's cheek. The child cried harder until Lavinia could take no more and crawled back into the bed, pulling the covers over her head. Hours later, it was Manroot's screams that pulled her to her feet, his verbal tirade slapping against the corners of her mind.

"What the hell is wrong with you? Why this child crying like this? Miss Hannah say this baby been crying all day and when she knocked on the door you wouldn't answer. Woman, why ain't you taking care of my baby?"

Lavinia shook the cloud of sleep from her head, wiping at her eyes with the back of her hands. "I didn't hear..."

Disgust filled Manroot's eyes as he stared at the woman before him. She needed a bath, her hair twisted in oily, stringy knots atop her crown. Filth clung to the flannel night gown and the bare skin which peeked from beneath. Her face was still bruised around the scar where Ruth Ann had slashed her. He inhaled deeply.

"Clean yourself up. We're leaving," he commanded, turning an about face out the door. In the kitchen he filled the sink with warm water, stripped the baby naked, and cradled her gently in the water. Trails of baby shit floated against the water as he soaped the foul excrement from her skin. The tan of her bottom had started to welt in a purplish rash from having been left in the soiled diaper. Manroot could feel the rage rising.

Tears still fell from the child's eyes as she struggled against him, wanting nothing more than to be held tight against someone who cared. Wrapping a large blue towel around the small bundle, Manroot pulled her close, placing a warm bottle of milk into her mouth. Janay sucked hungrily on the nipple, filling her stomach. When she finished, Manroot dressed her, coating her blistered bottom with homemade salve, then tossed her gently over his shoulder to pat a burp from her mid-section. Only when she lay content in his arms, drifting off into a deep sleep, did Manroot think of laying his baby daughter back against the cushions of his own bed.

In the bathroom, Lavinia wrapped a towel around her own body, pulling a brush through her tangled hair. The bath had made her feel better. She inhaled swiftly as Manroot pushed the bathroom door open. Fear shot across her face, throughout her body, and she dropped to the floor, her knees giving way beneath her.

"I'm sorry...," she sputtered, clutching the towel in front of her.

Manroot shook his head from side to side, then reached a large hand out to pull her from her seat on the tiled surface.

Grinding his back teeth, he pulled her close, wrapping his arms around her. Hugging her tightly, he did not let go, fearing that if he did, he might hit her. What he did not want to do was hit her. The minutes that passed were cathartic. Sobs filled Lavinia as Manroot cradled her firmly, his arms strong and protective. He let her cry, the tears washing over his bare chest and when she was all cried out, still clasped within his arms, he leaned down to kiss her face, running his lips gently across the disfiguring scar.

"Get dressed," Manroot commanded, his tone ever so soft. "Pack a bag for you and one for the baby, too."

"Where are we going?"

"To Daddy James'. You ain't ready to be looking after Beauty yet. My daddy'll give you a hand until you starts to feel better. I have to go away on business for a while."

Tears filled her eyes once again. "Please, Manroot, don't leave..."

Manroot silenced her words with a quick kiss on her lips and pat on her backside. "I'm going. Daddy James will keep an eye on you both."

Nodding, Lavinia exited to the bedroom. As she caught sight of the sleeping infant she sighed deeply. She suddenly longed for the moments before the child had been born and the cinnamon-toast girl had taken her beauty away from her.

Lavinia's depression grew deeper with each day that Manroot was gone. Her father-in-law took over caring for the baby as there was no way that Lavinia could have done it herself. And it was becoming increasingly evident that she had no interest in trying.

That Saturday it rained all day, the icy moisture falling in flash showers out of the gray sky. The day seemed longer than any day she could recall and suddenly the four walls around her felt as though they were closing in. She felt an intense urge to get away and for the first time since her accident, Lavinia dressed herself, applied her makeup, and left.

James sighed heavily as he rocked the tiny infant in his lap. The warm bottle fit awkwardly in the baby's small hands as she struggled to hold the glass container. She gurgled contentedly as milk poured out the side of her mouth, dripping down against her pale pink shirt and cotton diaper. Her tiny feet kicked out eagerly, the bare toes curling up tightly against her grandfather's leg.

Staring out into the distance James was conscious of the time, noting the sun's slow climb upward in the sky. Cornfields swayed in the foreground. There had been no sign of Lavinia since the previous evening and he knew that this was not good. He sulked quietly, debating whether or not he would tell Manroot about his wife's coming and going. For his son to know might mean more trouble than any of them needed to be bothered with. He knew he might better be able to talk some sense into the foolish girl if only she were around long enough for him to speak with.

Lavinia had started going out the second month after Manroot had been gone. The first week he'd worried, waiting up for her until she returned. The second week he'd not cared. The child was in safe hands and that was all that was of any real importance to him. His son's woman could run the streets as she pleased as long as his grandchild did not suffer any from her indiscretions. But now he worried about Manroot's reaction.

James noted her arrival as she made her way slowly up the dirt path. The dress she wore was too tight, a slinky red number cut high on the thigh and low along her cleavage. Her face was caked heavily with makeup, the scar hidden under a thick coat of foundation and blush. Baby fat still clung to her broad hips and thick waist and she barely resembled the young woman Manroot had brought home for them to meet. James grunted in her direction as she made her way up the front steps.

Lavinia blushed ever so faintly as she greeted him good-morning, dropping into the rocking chair on the other end of the porch. Kicking her high pumps off her swollen feet, she extended the length of her legs and twisted her ankles in a circular pattern. Not once did she acknowledge her daughter napping comfortably in the elder man's lap.

"I think you best be leaving. You need to go back to your own home."

Lavinia sat up straight, leaning her shoulders toward him. "Why?"

"You do what you need to do but you ain't gone do it under my roof. My son'll be home soon and I won't have you acting so disrespectful under my roof."

Lavinia bristled, then slumped back down into her chair. "I've not done anything wrong. I just need to be out. I enjoy the dancing, that's all. Manroot should not be angry about dancing and you can tell him that."

James stared at her briefly then swung his attention back to the horizon. "Between you and my boy. You explain it however you likes, but you still getting out of my house with it."

"Fine. I will take my child and we shall go today."

"No. Baby stays until her daddy come for her."

"She is my child and if I leave, so does she."

James came to his feet, swinging the small bundle up against his shoulder. "She leaves when her daddy comes and only when he comes."

His voice was cutting, edged in blades of barbed wire. Lavinia cringed knowing that there would be no argument. Giving it one last thought she shrugged her shoulders, not really caring one way or the other. She really did not want to take the child with her if the truth were to be known. Let the old man be burdened. Lavinia rose to feet, gripping her high-heeled pumps in her hand.

As she studied the man before her, thoughts of Manroot struck her broadside. He would not take her leaving lightly. He would not understand her need to feel whole again. He would not want to hear why she needed to feel like a woman who was more than just his wife and the mother of the daughter he doted upon. She dropped back to her seat, allowing the leather shoes to fall back against the porch floor. Pulling her hands through her hair, she sobbed quietly, oblivious to the man's stares. What she needed most was for Manroot to be home to make everything well.

"If I must, I will go, but please let me stay. I will not go dancing any more. I do not want to do anything that will make Manroot angry with me."

James sighed heavily as his eyes followed the woman's words, his gaze falling down to the tears that dripped against her cheek. The child cuddled close to his chest, thrusting a small thumb into her mouth to suckle. He kissed the tanned forehead, brushing her silky hair against his lips. She smelled sweet, a moist blend of talcum powder and Ivory soap.

"Why you start acting like this? What done got into you? This here baby needs a mama and you ain't even trying to act like one. This ain't like the woman my boy brought home. You ain't the woman he done give the Tucker name to. What done happen to you?"

Lavinia stared out past him, not quite sure how she should answer. She was not even sure if she could, having no words to explain her heartache. She said nothing, her eyes dropping back to the floor.

"You act right you can stay. You want to go back out catting around in the streets, you gots to leave. Your choice," he proclaimed, closing the front door behind his exit. "You decide."

Lavinia breathed a sigh of relief. Though there was little for her to be relieved about. Her father-in-law was right. She was not the woman Manroot had brought home. She had stopped being the wife he'd married and there was no part of her that still wanted to be a mother. She'd not had the son she'd hoped for and she had no longing for a daughter. This time her sigh was one of discontent.

The air around her smelled earthy, a heavy fragrance topped with dampness. Every so often, the pungent fumes from the roses would waft past her nostrils, taunting the richness of the red clay. Inhaling deeply, the thick aroma coated her senses, laying a blanket of comfort across her shoulders.

How could she possibly make any of them understand her feelings? She had no understanding of it, except to know that she no longer felt herself worthy of Manroot's love. It was not so much that her face was scarred, but since the attack, so was her spirit. It was the lack of spirit that made her feel ugliest. What could she possible offer her man when she felt so low? What could she possible instill in a daughter when she herself felt so undeserving? Especially a daughter she did not want.

The makeup felt heavy on her skin, she thought, the waxy coating suddenly uncomfortable. Pressing her fingers against her face, she sighed again. When she could hide the scar behind a mask of paint, and dance with a man who knew nothing of her, in that moment she felt better. She could forget her own pain. Manroot would definitely never understand. Never.

****

Seated around a low table with one brother at his right elbow and the other at his left, Manroot leaned forward in the wooden chair, tipping the back legs up in the air. He tapped his foot anxiously as the three men whispered in low hums between themselves.

"...said she ain't do nothing but sit at a table by herself and drink all night."

"Joe Dempsy say she was dancing with some guy from Elliston come through here, but that she left by herself."

"Jessie Lee and Anna Mae say she was sneaking about but they ain't know who with. I don't trust nothing Anna Mae got to say though 'cause she'll lie through her teeth if she thinks she can get something from it."

Manroot chewed on his lower lip, then banged the table with his fist. An elderly man sitting alone at the bar turned to stare in their direction, then spun himself back around in his seat. Manroot took a deep breath, slowly pushing the dry air back out.

"I ain't putting up with this shit. She should have been home taking care of Beauty. I ain't marry no whore."

Titus shrugged. "She ain't been right since she come home from that hospital."

Chauncey nodded in agreement. "Something like that can change a person."

"I don't care," Manroot hissed. "Ain't no wife of mine got cause to be acting like some cheap tramp."

Chauncey filled his brother's empty glass, filling it to the brim with cheap gin. "What did Pop have to say 'bout it?"

Manroot shrugged, hunching his thick shoulders forward. "He ain't said nothing yet."

Titus shook his head. "See what the old man got to say before you do anything foolish."

"I ain't gone do nothing but beat her ass. She ain't gone be shaming me and she ain't gone be shaming the Tucker name."

Titus dropped a hand onto his brother's shoulder. "Don't put your hands on that woman. You know Daddy ain't gone put up with you putting your hands on no woman, for no reason."

Manroot came to his feet. "Daddy took care of Mama the way he saw fit and I'm gone take care of my woman the way I sees fit. She ain't gone be disrespecting me and thinking she getting away with it."

Chauncey and Titus cut their eyes at each other, then Manroot. Chauncey stood up to look his brother in the eye. "She ain't worth you going to jail for. You better think about what's best for that baby before you does anything, you hear me?"

Downing the last of his drink, Manroot met his brother's eye, staring at him intensely. With nothing else to say, he spun around on his heels, slammed out the door, and headed up the street. Outside the damp air seeped under his clothes, chilling his skin. No one had anticipated the wave of cold air that was sweeping through the country side. The damp mist and frosty temperatures were tainting miles and miles of crops. It would not be a good season for produce if this kept up.

As Manroot took the back steps two at a time, he could feel himself on the verge of exploding. How could Lavinia have shamed him so? How could this woman love him and do him wrong like this? He wanted answers more than anything else, and he wanted it to stop. He wanted Lavinia back the way she'd been when she'd danced into his heart, twirling herself around ever fiber in his soul.

As he slammed the door shut, Lavinia jumped from her seat. The baby sat contentedly on the floor at her feet chewing on the hem of her skirt. She knew instantly that Manroot was angry and that he was ready for a fight. Stooping down, she lifted the small child into her arms and pressed her close to her chest. He would not hurt her if she held onto Beauty.

The silence between them was thunderous. He did not need to say anything for Lavinia to know what he was thinking. She hung her head, biting against her tongue.

Manroot stood with his fists clenched. His jaw was frozen in a tight line, the veins popping against the length of his neck. When his daughter smiled at him, gurgling excitedly as she reached out her arms to be held, he felt the tension fading. It was an instantaneous relaxation of taut muscle, his anger assuaged by something sweeter. Walking to Lavinia's side, he pulled the child from her arms, hugging the infant warmly.

"Hey there," Lavinia mumbled. "Didn't expect you to come home so early today."

Manroot pursed his lips, nodding his head. "We need to talk."

"What is the matter?"

"Why you been sneaking around, going to the clubs when you should have been home here with this baby?"

Lavinia took a deep breath. "I have done nothing wrong, Manroot. I've not been with any other men."

"But you ain't been home. You been out drinking in the clubs like some whore. I ain't marry no whore."

"I am not a whore."

"So what you need to be going out for?"

Lavinia wrung her hands together, twisting a cloth diaper between her palms. "I just wanted to go dancing. You were not here to be with me and I needed to feel alive again."

"Being a wife and mama don't make you feel alive?"

"I need more than that, Manroot. It is so lonely when you are not here. How can I make you understand how lonely it gets?"

Manroot shifted the baby to his other shoulder. "I ain't putting up with this. You stay home when I go away. Men be out there talking 'bout you like you trash and I ain't gone have you acting like it. You understand me?"

Lavinia nodded.

"Here," he said, passing the baby back to her. "Beauty smell like she done messed her pants. Clean her up so I can take her over to see my Daddy."

Lavinia nodded one last time, then fled from the room and Manroot's sight.

James listened as his son rambled on incessantly, the man's emotions raining outrage, disappointment, disbelief, and apprehension. But his eyes never left the little girl who crawled along the floor beneath their feet, stopping occasionally to pull something into her mouth. He'd glance into his son's face every so often as he stooped down to pull the offensive matter from the child's grasp. He'd nod his head agreeably, whilst pushing out his mouth in a soft pucker, a toothpick sticking past his lips.

When Manroot finally settled down, relaxing his heavy limbs against the porch steps, James cleared his throat and rested down beside him. They sat quietly, filling the entrance way with their large bodies as the little girl would use their torso's to pull herself up on her wobbly legs before falling back onto a diapered behind.

"Lavinia the first woman you truly loved, ain't she?" James asked, chewing on a much gnawed toothpick.

Manroot shrugged.

"I know she is cause you would have packed and left by now if you didn't."

His son shrugged again, leaning to kiss his baby girl's cheek.

"Ruth Ann cutting her face like she done took a lot out of Lavinia. You expecting her to go back to being normal and she don't feel normal. She don't look normal and she be thinking that you don't care about her the same no more."

"Lavinia knows I care about her."

"Does she? Since it happened you been gone more than you been home. What that girl suppose to think when she don't even see you no more? When you is home you stay gone in the streets most times or you giving all your attention to the baby."

"And what about that, Daddy? She don't look after Beauty the way she should be. She ain't been no fit mother."

"Was she a fit mother before the accident?"

Manroot shrugged again. "Not like she should have been. Like something wrong. Sometimes I think she be hating Beauty for being born and she the one say she wanted this baby."

"Do you think you be treating her the same since it happen?"

Manroot sat pensively before responding. "It's hard, Daddy. Every time I look at her face I think about it being my fault. This wouldn't have happened if I had done something 'bout Ruth Ann."

"Boy, what could you have done? You ain't know Ruth Ann lost her mind like that. Ruth Ann was hell bent on hurting someone and you didn't put Lavinia in front of her knife to help her do it."

"No, sir, but I didn't do nothing to keep her safe from it either."

James sighed. "Can't change what done happen, but you can make it easier for her to deal with. Lavinia need to know you loves her. You show her and she won't be looking nowhere else for no other man to show her."

Manroot nodded his head slowly, tear-misted eyes staring deep into his father's face as his daughter squealed with delight beside him.

The child lay sleeping in her crib where Manroot had gently placed her, tucking the blankets from the foot of the small mattress around her body. She didn't appear to have a care in the world, Lavinia thought as she stared down at her child. She slumbered contentedly and all seemed as well for the baby as anything could ever be. Lavinia couldn't help but want the same for herself, regretting that every aspect of her life seemed so out of focus. She couldn't help but wonder what differences birthing a son could have made. She winced, bitterness and a rush of anger painting her expression.

She knew they all looked at her with a critical eye, wondering what it was about her that kept her from bonding with her own child. She had looked in the mirror and had asked the same questions. There were no answers as to why she felt nothing at all for the small person who was her spitting image in chocolate, Manroot's bloodline flowing in the warm coloration of her complexion. But she felt nothing at all for the baby, every waking moment spent wishing the little girl away.

The child stirred ever so slightly, and Lavinia inhaled a deep breath, holding it deep in her lungs. Manroot had gone, again, and were the little girl to wake, disturbing her few minutes of peace, she didn't know what she might do. Lavinia wished for a hole to fall in, dirt filling in the space around her. She wanted to cry, but had no more tears to shed. She wanted to scream, but knew that there was no one who would come to comfort her cries. She was lonely and she couldn't begin to fathom how the little girl could be any sort of companion for her. She exhaled, blowing the air out harshly.

Wishful thinking became disappointment when the child stretched the length of her small body against the bedding, her face twisting with discomfort. The cries were muffled gasps of air at first, rising to a full crescendo within a moment's time. Lavinia continued to stare down at her, her expression blank, the lines of her face frozen with indifference. She made no motion to comfort the crying child, wanting nothing more than to have the noise cease as quickly as it started, the child disappearing from her sight.

Lavinia reached a shaking hand down into the crib, pressing her palm and fingers over the baby's face. She marveled at how easy it was to cut off the child's airway, her own flesh obstructing the child's breathing. Her palm fit snugly over the baby's mouth and nose, the fingers pulled taut to prevent any air from seeping through. Lavinia watched as the child struggled beneath the weight of her arm, the tears ceasing almost as quickly as they'd come, the little girl's light eyes suddenly piercing her own.

The sound of Manroot opening and closing the front door startled Lavinia from the trance she'd fallen into. The baby gulped a large breath of air, then lay still, her gaze still focused up toward her mother. It was only when Manroot called the woman's name that the child shifted her attention elsewhere, rolling onto her stomach to seek out the sound of her father's voice.

Lavinia took a step back, clutching her hand against her chest, the appendage suddenly shaking uncontrollably. A sob caught in her throat as she dropped down to the bed and curled her body against the mattress. As she pulled the cotton sheet up and over her torso, she suddenly wanted nothing more than to put all of this behind her. She wanted to forget the little girl who should have been a boy, and to dance the hurt away against a man who had no knowledge of the depravity in her heart.

****

The months that passed were quiet. The small girl child grew steady on her feet, rambling words in semi-coherent sentences. Her father's love and adoration intensified with each passing day, as did her grandfather's. It was her mother's emotions that struggled in turmoil, discontent brewing to a bitter restlessness.

Janay sat in the center of her mother's bed, her back curled up against the large bed pillows. A bowl of raspberry Jell-O was tucked between her chubby legs and her small fingers were wrapped around a large, silver spoon. Using both hands, the little girl carefully guided the gelatinous sugar into her mouth, smiling brightly as the chilled sweetness melted against her tongue. Lavinia smiled back at her daughter as she pulled her clothes over her head, smoothing a newly purchased dress around her hips.

"Now, don't you go making a mess on that bed, little girl. Mama has no time to be cleaning up a mess."

Janay smiled. "Beauty good girl."

Lavinia nodded her head. "That's right. You be a good girl for your mama."

Seated in front of the mirror, Lavinia carefully decorated her face, giving meticulous attention to covering the scar on her cheek with the heavy foundation and blush that she wore when Manroot was not around.

Janay giggled. "Daddy want yello'?"

Lavinia waved a hand at her. "Daddy is away on business. Daddy doesn't want any Jell-O."

"Mama want yello?" the little girl asked, lifting her spoon up and out toward her mother.

"No. Now hush up and eat so you can go to bed."

"Mama go bye-bye?"

Lavinia nodded her head up and down, pressing her bright red lips together. "Yes, mama is going bye-bye."

"Beauty want to go wit' you."

"No, now finish your Jell-O. You are going to bed."

The child screwed her face up to cry, her bottom lip quivering slightly. "Want my daddy."

Lavinia cut her eyes at the little girl, taking a deep breath in. "Don't you dare start. You cry and I'm going to give you something to cry for."

Janay dropped her spoon into the empty bowl. "Beauty go see my Daddy James?"

"Beauty is going to bed. Now, shut that noise up!" Lavinia shouted, her voice rising unnecessarily.

Janay stared quietly at her mother, tears falling down her tiny cheeks. "Want my daddy."

Annoyed, Lavinia rose from her seat and smacked the child's leg, stinging the tender flesh with the palm of her hand. Crying out, Janay grabbed the painful limb, rubbing the rising red bruise with her tiny hand. Lavinia raised her arm threateningly, her hand waving like a weapon over her head.

"Cry and see if I don't give you some more. Now why you have to be such a bad girl for? Why do you have to make me hurt you?"

Choking back her sobs, Janay lay back against the bedspread, folding her small body around a large pillow. Her skin still burned. She wiped at her eyes with the back of one hand while the other rubbed the soreness out of the rising black and blue mark on her lower limb. Lavinia stared back at the child, then shook her head approvingly. "That's a good girl. You be good now."

Lifting the little girl from where she lay, Lavinia dropped her into the crib and laid a newly filled bottle of milk beside her. "Go to sleep now like a good baby". Lavinia leaned to kiss her again. "That's my Beauty. Beauty is a good girl."

The child smiled, cradling the bottle close to her chest. "Beauty good girl?"

"Good girl," her mother smiled, turning her attention back to her reflection in the mirror. When the makeup met with her approval and she felt ready, she cut off the lights. Leaning into the crib one last time, she kissed the child's forehead, and pulled a cotton blanket up around her shoulders.

"Now, you stay in this bed until Mama comes home, okay? You be a bad girl and Mama will spank you good, you understand?"

Janay blinked her eyes.

Leaving the door cracked, Lavinia switched on the hall light, casting a faint glow into the bedroom. Outside, a car horn sounded for her and as she rushed to jump into the waiting vehicle. She did not bother to soothe the sobs rising from the small bed inside.

The little girl was use to the darkness, but she did not like it. She was scared and though no one would respond to her cries, she still sobbed, sobbing only because she wished her daddy would come home and hold her. When her daddy was home, she was never left alone. When her daddy was home she fell asleep in his arms and that was far better than the emptiness of her crib and the loneliness of the apartment.

Hours later, her mother returned, a strange man in tow. Janay cowered in the corner of her crib knowing better than to call out or give any indication that she was still awake. She hated the giggling and loud whispers and couldn't understand why her mother seemingly enjoyed the men who appeared to be hurting her. Every so often one would lean to peer down at her, reaching a hand in to brush the hair against her brow. The first time it had happened, Beauty had mistaken the dark face for her father's and when she'd reached up to be held, her mother's anger had been fierce, the smacks stinging. Beauty no longer reached for the strange black men who sometimes stopped to stare down at her.

Squeezing her eyes shut, she'd lay quietly, pretending to be asleep. Only when the noises stopped and the door closed behind the strange men, would Beauty finally rest, waiting for it all to continue on the following day, and the one after that, and the one after that.

Lavinia's discontent grew like a fungus. Depression consumed her days as she froze her reflection hour after hour in front of her dressing table mirror. Staring at the unsightly scar only fueled the woman's anxiety and a dark hatred for the mundane chores of her life ran command over her soul. Those nights when Manroot was gone, she would dress the ugly line, shielding it away from prying eyes. Then she would dance herself into someone else's life, stepping out in the high heels of a world that did not include a child she didn't want or a man who didn't want her. The dancing made her feel better. The men she danced with gave her back her control.

"When you get bigger Mama will show you how to make your face pretty with the makeup," Lavinia said, winking an eye toward her daughter.

Janay sat curled up on the new, heavy brass bed, stroking her face with a sable makeup brush. "Beauty gone be pretty just like you, Mama?"

Lavinia laughed. "Yes, you will. You will be as pretty as your Mama."

"Mama, can I go see Daddy James, please? Do I have to stay home?"

Lavinia shrugged. "Not tonight. Maybe tomorrow. I won't be gone long."

Janay sighed, knowing better than to ask again. Crawling under the heavy covers, she snuggled her face into the full pillows, smelling her father's scent along the pillow case. She missed her father. He'd been gone a long time this last time. When he was gone her mother was different and it scared her, but there was no one she could tell and not have her mother hurt her.

Manroot had departed the day after her sixth birthday party. He'd dazzled her with cake and ice cream, balloons and gifts, then he'd kissed her cheek and said good-bye. He'd only whispered something spiteful at Lavinia, which had made the woman even angrier.

The first night had been the worst. The simple act of breathing had brought Lavinia's wrath upon her. The beatings had been brutal, leaving hideous bruises across her back and buttocks. Her hair had been pulled, her face shoved into her own excrement when the brutality had made her soil herself.

It had gotten better the second night, forced only to lay in ice cold water while her mother cursed her birth and called her names. There had been no sleep, the knife by her mother's bedside pressed against her throat when she thought to close her eyes. After a week there was only the name calling, and an occasional slap, and when the bruises were gone, a quick visit to her grandfather's house to kiss his cheek, spend a brief moment of security in his arms, and to tell him whatever her mother had made her practice saying.

Quiet always followed the storms. Moody moments of silence where Lavinia seemed not to notice Janay's presence. The little girl would rise on her own, feed herself, and stay well out of her mother's path as Lavinia moved in some other space she shared with no one but the taunting voices in her own mind. The child didn't know which was harder to endure, her mother's rage or her mother's silence.

This was the first night the woman had smiled since Manroot had left them. Janay did not want to wipe the smile away with too many questions her mother had no intentions of answering. They both heard the car horn blowing, which made Lavinia smile even more as she raced to finish get dressed.

The front door opening and closing surprised both of them. Lavinia's hand tightened around the hair brush she was pulling through the length of her hair. Janay sat up excitedly. Joy burst forth as her father entered the room filling the doorway with his large body. As Janay rushed into his arms, Lavinia sank back into the chair, the smile flying off her face.

"Daddy!" the little girl squealed, jumping up and down excitedly. "Oh, Daddy!"

Manroot's smile was forced as he lifted her small person up into his arms. Hugging her warmly, he pressed his full lips against her face, then laid her gently back down upon the bed. Janay smiled excitedly, grateful that she would not have to fall asleep alone. She didn't care if her mother left now because her daddy had come home. Turning his back toward her, Manroot stared at his wife, his expression harsh.

"Where you think you going?"

Lavinia shrugged, dropping the hair brush onto the dressing table. She did not answer.

"I asked you a question."

Lavinia stood up, turning to face Manroot. "I was going dancing. I was going to meet my girlfriends and we were going to go dancing."

"And what about Beauty? Who was going to look after my baby?"

Lavinia heaved an annoyed sigh. "Your baby was going to be just fine," she said, her tone less than enthused. "I was putting her to bed for the night and Miss Hannah was going to keep an eye on her for me."

"Who's that man sitting downstairs waiting for you?"

Lavinia turned away, the lie evident upon her face. "I don't know what you are talking about."

Gripping her arm roughly, Manroot spun her back around, pointing his finger in her face. "Don't lie to me. Nigga' say he was waiting for you before I kicked his ass," he shouted, his voice suddenly scary.

Lavinia's look turned defiant, malice filtering across her face. The duo eyed each other angrily, their growing emotions thick with hostility. "Go to hell," she spat, raising her hand and striking him across the face.

Manroot pulled his palm to his cheek, bit his bottom lip, then without a second thought slapped the woman back, sending her to the floor. Janay pulled the pillows around her body, her eyes bulging with fear. She had never before seen her father hit her mother. It was her mother who would always raise a hand to swing pain upon another person. Her father did not know how to be so cruel. Something was very wrong and the child was suddenly more frightened than she could ever remember being.

Lavinia lay sprawled against the floor, holding her face in the palm of her hand. Her anger was suddenly overflowing. "You are such a big man aren't you, Manroot? You think you know everything, but you know nothing," she said, the words spewing like manure from her mouth. She shook the cloudiness out of her head.

"You're nothing but a cheap whore. I'm out working my ass off for you and Beauty, and you can't even be no decent wife. You out whoring around, leaving this baby here by herself, and you think I won't gone find out? This shit gone stop right now. I ain't having it. You ain't gone be disrespecting me like this. You ain't gone be mistreating my baby like this no more!"

Lavinia started to laugh. Sitting on that floor she was laughing until tears were rolling down her face. Pulling herself up onto her knees, she was still laughing. It was a malignant cackle that was dead of any true emotion, filling the room with its rankness. Grasping her by her hair, Manroot pulled her to her feet. Grabbing his wrist as she struggled to gain her balance, Lavinia continued to laugh.

"Go to hell, Manroot Tucker. You don't care about me. Only thing you care about is your precious name and your precious baby. You can go straight to hell. You don't own me. I will do just what I want to do and you can't stop me, Manroot. You are not man enough to stop me."

Janay cringed as her father slapped her mother to the floor again, pulling the woman back up by her long strands. The little girl started to cry.

Lavinia continued to laugh, spewing bitter bile with each breath. "I won't stop. I won't. Did you know I have slept with all your friends, Manroot? Did you? I've slept with them all and they were better than you. All of them. Even Beauty knows they were all better than you. What do you think about that? I'm going to make sure she knows, Manroot. I'm going to make sure she knows that you are nothing.

"You are no man, Manroot Tucker. You are less than nothing. I'm going to find Beauty a new daddy. Maybe I'll get her a new white daddy. I'll show her what a real man is. She is my child and I am going to make sure that you never see her again." Lavinia spat her last words in Manroot's face, spewing a vile concoction of venom and saliva together.

It was the laughter that pulled the little girl from her hiding place behind the oversized pillow and brought her to her feet. It was the laughter that commanded her to race from the room to the kitchen drawer. The cruel cackle lifted the large carving knife into the child's small hands and guided her back to where her parents stood arguing. It was Lavinia's cruel chortle wrapped around her threats that pushed the knife toward where her parents stood.

Manroot did not hear his daughter's screams before Lavinia fell forward against him, her eyes bulged in surprise. He'd been oblivious to the small child before his wife clutched at the front of his shirt, mouthing his name. It was only when he let the woman go, dropping her to the floor beneath his feet could he even begin to comprehend the horror.

It was silence that fell from Lavinia's mouth as he picked her lifeless body up from the floor and laid her back against the bed. Side by side, Manroot and Janay stood staring at the woman whose biting words were now as dead as the rest of her. Manroot felt his legs suddenly give way beneath him, dropping his large body to the floor. The child gasped for air, the knife in her hand falling at her father's side. Throwing herself against him, her tears rolled uncontrollably as she sobbed into his lap.

"Don't leave me, Daddy," the girl wailed into his chest, blood spattered against her hands and down the front of her night clothes. "Don't let her hurt me no more. Please, Daddy, don't let Mama take me away."

****

The Tucker siblings gathered at their father's home. Eloise tucked her niece and daughter into their grandmother's bed and lay beside them until they both drifted off toward sleep. Even as she slumbered, Janay clutched nervously at her yellow blanket, her small hands gripped tightly around the delicate yarn. Dark dreams played cruel games behind her eyelids and every so often Eloise would have to draw a calming hand up and down her spine.

Downstairs, Chauncey and Titus paced the wood planked floor as Manroot told them what he had done. Daddy James leaned against the stone fireplace, his own life suddenly drained as he tried to comprehend the story his son had shared just hours earlier. That story had been the truest version of the evening's events. The version that only he, Manroot, and God would ever be privy to. The old man made no effort to listen to the story Manroot now told his brothers, the story that was as far from the truth as Manroot would ever be able to get.

"I ain't running," Manroot whispered to them, sneaking a glance toward his father. "I ain't gone run."

James inhaled, breathing in deeply. It had happened, just not as he had predicted it would. Now nothing would again be the same for any of them. He moved to stand by his son's side.

"Law gone be looking for you, boy. You want me to take you down to the sheriff?" he asked.

Manroot shook his head. "I'll go alone."

James nodded again. "You gone need you an attorney. Chauncey will go get Duke Waters and tell him what done happened. He knows he'll gets his money so shouldn't be no problem."

"Daddy, we can get Manroot up North before they come looking for him. These folks gone be ready to hang him once they find out. They ain't gone take to him killing no white woman, even if she was trash," Titus said.

Manroot bit his lip, rising to his feet. "Don't ever call Lavinia trash again. I don't want Beauty to hear none of you calling her mama names."

"What you care for? That woman done you wrong and everybody knows it," Chauncey said, staring at his brother.

Manroot shrugged, meeting his father's eye. "I care." He sighed again. "Daddy, take care of my baby for me. Beauty don't understand."

James nodded. "Baby gone be fine but understand this, boy. I can't be bringing her to no prison to see you. I don't ever want that child to see her daddy behind no bars."

Manroot nodded. "Don't want her to see me there neither. Man can't be no real man locked up in the jail and I want my baby to remember me right. I don't ever want her to remember what done happened. If she don't see me, she can forget. All I want her to remember is me like I was when I was home with her and she was safe. She needs to forget everything else."

Rising from his seat, he hugged his brothers, holding onto them tightly. Wrapping his arms around his father, he held on as sobs rose from his midsection. Catching himself, he lifted his head from the patriarch's shoulder and wiped his eyes with the back of his hand.

"I got to do this for Beauty," he whispered to his father. "I got to do right by that baby."

James watched as his youngest son walked out of his house for the last time, Chauncey and Titus on his heels. Then dropping to his knees, he lifted his voice up in prayer and asked the good Lord to guide them.

No one saw Manroot again until the day of his trial. They'd heard the vicious rumors and talk that filled the small town, but Manroot had left strict word that they were not to come see him. His attorney kept Daddy James posted on the case, always preceding his reports with the words, "The news ain't good."

On the first of April, when they led Manroot into the courtroom, handcuffed and shackled, his family barely recognized him. Manroot had suffered many a beating since the night he'd walked into the local constable's office and confessed to the crime. His dark face was battered black and blacker, his eyes and lips swollen grotesquely, but still he stood with his shoulders back and his head held high.

There was no further testimony after Manroot professed his guilt. He was quickly sentenced to life in prison with no chance of parole, just missing the death penalty thanks to Duke Waters and much of Daddy James' money. The courtroom cheered when they led him away. Some of the same faces that had offered words of support and encouragement were there to celebrate the fall of the Tucker name. His family stood shoulder to shoulder as they led Manroot out of the courtroom and only he saw the tear that rolled off his father's face.

As James eased his way down the courthouse stairs, his children following closely behind, he tipped his hat low on his head and pulled his suit coat tight around him. Others on the steps whispered behind their hands, smirks and laughter pulling at their mouths. It was okay though, because whether they knew it or not, Manroot had won. He'd escaped the noose that many had wanted to wrap around his throat, and though his life was no longer his own, they'd not been able to take the breath of life away from him. They could burn their crosses on as much of his land as they wanted, but his son lived, and his grandchild was safe, and that was enough for him.

MIRROR, MIRROR ON THE WALL....

****

I sobbed. Reaching for my grandfather, I brushed my tears into his. Darkness had settled firmly around us, the incandescent moon barely reflecting enough light to guide us. In the distance, the faint flicker of headlights pulled in, or maybe out, of the driveway.

"Do you remember anything, Black?" my grandfather asked, clasping me around the shoulders.

I shook my head no.

"You will. It will take time, but you need to remember. You need to finally let it go for good."

I stared at him, having no understanding of what it was I was supposed to be remembering. "Just tell me, Daddy," I implored, wanting him to ease the burden of discovery so that the hurt of it all would finally disappear.

Everett paced nervously behind us. "Let's go inside, Daddy James. It's getting cool out here. We can continue to talk inside once everyone leaves."

Daddy James continued to stare at me. "She feels safest here. It's easier for her to remember someplace she feels safest."

Everett leaned a hand against Daddy James' shoulder. "She feels safe with you no matter where you are."

We both looked up at him, the cool air drying the moisture against our cheeks. The last sliver of sunlight had disappeared from the vast fields behind us, a blanket of darkness filling the space. I was suddenly fearful of the dark and I could feel myself shaking as I reached for Everett's hand. He braced his feet firmly as he pulled me to my own. My grandfather followed slowly behind us as we made our way back toward the two-story farmhouse. Back inside, Everett politely excused the last of our guests, emptying our home of well-wishers. The kitchen had been returned to me spotless, no evidence of any intrusion save the last few pieces of fried chicken that lay against a ceramic plate and a homemade pound cake wrapped tightly in aluminum foil.

I sat down against the hearth of the fireplace, curling my body up against the red brick structure that filled the large wall. My husband came to sit beside me.

"Do you know what it is my grandfather wants me to remember?"

Everett dropped his gaze only briefly before returning his eyes to mine. "I only know what you tell me," he answered, his eyes saying so much more.

As Daddy James joined us, dimming the lights in the room, my ghosts walked in and sat beside us. Their hands were icy as they wrapped themselves around me leading me back to another time and another place.

I could hear a voice in the distance and I knew it was mine. The words spilled out into the open air, ringing in my ears. The tonality of my voice was strange, not sounding as though it belonged to me. I talked on though, the words coming easily, the apparitions pulling at them one by one, dancing to my intonation. I had heard their story, and their story was my story. Reaching for Daddy James, I told it from the beginning.

****

I could not have been more than three years old when I knew my mother did not love me. She didn't even like me. It wasn't only that she told me with regular frequency, but she showed me on a daily basis. There were no warm hugs wrapped in her arms. No gentle kisses against my forehead or cheeks. She said little to me and insisted I say even less to her. Joy was in my daddy's arms or my grandfather's. With the men who lumbered like giants above me, there was security and comfort. There was nothing from my mother.

Even at that tender age, I knew it was my fault that she didn't want me. Something I had done when I was smaller, maybe. Perhaps I'd cried too much when her head ached, or I might have soiled her favorite dress with some foul baby mucus. I was not sure what, but I knew that it had to have been something so serious that it had ripped what little love she may have had for me from her heart.

The day was dark, the sky filled with ugly clouds waiting to cry rain upon the dry soil. I walked slowly in front of her as she prodded me forward. It was too hot to move and I wanted only to be picked up and held. I whined, knowing that the look she'd tossed me had forbidden it. Then I stopped, throwing myself against the sidewalk, kicking my feet in rebellion. I watched my mother as she stepped over me and continued to walk away, the bags of groceries weighing down her arms.

"Mama!" I cried. "I tired. No want to walk no more. Want my daddy." And on she'd walked, continuing without me. I screamed against the sidewalk, oblivious to the stares and heads that shook in my direction. She'd left me there alone and I whined and cried louder, beating my small fists against the cement. "Mama," I screamed, the intensity of my cries shaking my body.

I felt the sting of the switch first, the freshly snapped branch wrapping around my legs. The pain was blinding as the thin green wood fell against me for a second strike. Then I saw her, anger warping the curvature of her face. "Get up," she hissed, striking a third blow. "Get up, now!" The switch continued to fall, welting the tender flesh along my back and legs. I struggled to my feet as my mother continued to beat me.

"Now walk," she commanded, pointing me toward home. I ran ahead of her, the switch starting to draw faint lines of blood from broken skin. Up the back stairs and into the kitchen I ran, tripping over the groceries in the doorway. It was Miss Hannah's voice that stopped her arm from swinging. The old woman's admonishments broke the stupor Lavinia walked in. I welcomed the scratchy voice that usually asked questions I dared not answer, appreciated the soothing words that brought the beating to an end.

When the door was finally closed behind us, I cried against her lap as she told me how ugly I was with the bruises against my skin. My daddy wouldn't love me, she'd said, brushing her hand against my hair. He wouldn't love me when he heard how bad I'd been and what I had made her do. She'd not tell, she'd whispered, if I promised to be good. She'd make the ugly go away if I promised to behave.

"I promise, Mama," I swore in a little girl's voice, the pledge shining in my eyes. I would have promised her anything, unable to bear the thought of my father not loving me.

I heard his laughter first, the deep baritone vibrating throughout the small rooms of our home. Rising from my bed, I raced into the living room toward the laughter that had warmed the cool morning air and pulled me from my sleep.

Manroot sat on the sofa with Lavinia in his lap, one arm wrapped over her shoulder, and the other hand lost somewhere beneath her dress. They giggled happily together, neither having heard me enter the room. "Daddy," I yelled excitedly, racing to where they sat and throwing myself into his chest. "Oh, Daddy!"

Lavinia rose in irritation as my father pulled me into his arms, kissing my face. "My beautiful girl," he sang in a sing-song voice. "How's my sweet baby?"

"Fine," I beamed barely noticing my mother as she made her way out the room. "Want to go with you, Daddy."

Manroot laughed. "Daddy ain't going nowhere, Beauty. Daddy is staying right here, for now."

I continued to beam. "You love me, Daddy?"

Manroot laughed again. "Daddy sure does. Daddy loves his Beauty best of all."

Behind us Lavinia cringed in anger, then stormed into her bedroom. Her man had come home, she thought, but once again he'd not come home to her.

It was birthday number six that approached with the new moon. Promises of new clothes, and toys, and cake, and candy, hung in the air like thick clouds against the bluest of skies. Neighborhood children had been invited to join in the festivities and I anxiously awaited the gifts wrapped in bright paper and bows that would fill the corner of the room with surprises meant only for me.

My daddy spun me high in the air, reveling in the laughter that shook my every muscle. Even Lavinia lifted the edges of her lips in kindness, a smile replacing her usual frowns. The calm before her storm.

"Daddy hugged me tightly the next day. Told me he loved me best of all, and as I watched him climb into his shiny car and spin the tires down the road, the torture began."

I choked back the pain, jumping quickly to my feet. Everett rose to wrap his arms around me. Daddy James hung his head into his hands.

"No more," I gasped. "No more, not now."

Daddy James nodded, tears rising like mist in his dark eyes. "I'm so sorry, Black."

His words echoed in my ears as I raced from the room to the security of my bed. Later, as I lay beside Everett, my head pressed against his shoulder, I thought of the time right after my mother's death, when Manroot had disappeared from my life like a sweet dream lost too soon to a morning sunrise. Daddy James bought me new shoes.

I had liked my new black, patent leathers with the thin ankle straps. If I looked closely, I could see my distorted reflection in the tops, darkening my color more like my Daddy's. I didn't like the white dress though. Aunt Eloise picked out the dress, insisting that it was only proper that I wear white to my mama's funeral. I had wanted a yellow one, and if they had only let me see my daddy, I could have asked him to get me a yellow dress the color of summer buttercups, with a wide skirt, lots of lace, and a big white bow. I heaved a low sigh as I drifted back in time.

****

I didn't understand this funeral thing. I only knew that I wanted my daddy and everyone kept whispering about him never coming back. I knew my mama was on her way to heaven to go see God. Daddy James had told me that the angels were coming to guide her to her heavenly home. He let me pick out the pretty white box that mama was going to travel in for the trip and he let me pick the pretty flowers that would go with her. I imagined that it might be real pretty up in them clouds on the way to see God.

Leaning a little closer to my granddaddy, I wondered why Aunt Eloise was crying so hard. Maybe since it was my mama's funeral I was supposed to be crying, too. I didn't want to though. I just wished my daddy would hurry back from the jail to come get me. I was tired of people patting me on my head and whispering every time I walked into the room. I was also tired of eating all the cold fried chicken people kept bringing to Daddy James' house. I wanted me some Jell-O. My mama always let me eat Jell-O whenever I wanted.

My mama looked real pretty laying there in that box. Someone had done her makeup different, kind of soft and sweet, not the bright reds that mama had liked so much. The ugly scar on her cheek that she'd hated so much was still there, but with the new makeup it was almost as if it had disappeared from sight. The black and blue bruises inflicted by my father were also gone, covered beneath the white of the powder foundation and the glow of rouge on her cheek. Mama had a new dress on, too. It was cream colored with itsy-bitsy flowers in shades of pink, yellow, and orange. It had a high neckline with lace around it, and long sleeves that fell down to her wrists. It was nothing like the other dresses mama used to wear. I thought my mama looked sort of happy lying there. I guess she must have been pretty excited about going on the trip with God.

I leaned up to whisper into my grandfather's ear. "Daddy James, why don't mama open her eyes? Don't she want to see what it look like when God come to get her?"

The man smiled at me faintly, lifting his finger to his lips to hush my noise. Pulling me onto his lap, he hugged me close and whispered back. "Your mama can see real good, baby. Now sit quiet. We'll be going home very soon."

I was thankful that this would soon come to an end and my life could go back to the way it was with my daddy home to take care of me. I even managed to squeeze out a tear when the nice preacher asked everyone to pray for me and my daddy. Later on, back at my granddaddy's house, more people came and patted me on the head. Aunt Eloise was dipping up more fried chicken than I would ever care to see again. My cousin Candy was commissioned to keep an eye on me.

Giggling quietly, we settled our small bodies beneath the kitchen table, watching legs pass beside us as people whispered their last condolences and made their way out the door.

"Thems is Miss Edna's legs. See her shoes? She got ugly shoes," Candy proclaimed. "I ain't never gone wear no old lady shoes like that."

I nodded my head, tilting my own new patent leather footwear from side to side. "Candy, when my daddy coming to get me?"

Candy looked at me foolishly. "Your daddy ain't never coming back, stupid. He gone to jail. My mama said he ain't never gone see freedom again. Mama say if he hadn't been so stupid over that white woman he'd be free now 'cause your mama won't no good. My mama said you daddy won't nothing but a fool and he got just what he deserved." She nodded her head firmly.

Tears rose to my eyes.

"Why you crying? It's the truth. Besides, your mama ain't never done nothing for you anyway. Everybody know that. My mama said so."

Hitting her in the face, I scooted from beneath the table to go find my granddaddy. Behind me, Candy's wails rang in my ears, echoing about the room.

Daddy James stood outside on the front porch with Uncle Titus. I threw my small body against his, the tears pouring down my face, as I repeated my conversation with Candy. The man said nothing as I cried against his shoulder, the dampness of my tears settling into the fabric of his white cotton shirt. At that moment, Aunt Eloise burst onto the porch, misery in tow, berating me profusely for having slammed Candy.

"Enough!" Daddy James bellowed, silencing us all. Candy and her mother both pouted as I burrowed my face into Daddy James' neck.

"Daddy, Janay ain't had no cause to hit Candy. That girl needs her butt smacked for being so damn rude." My father's sister cut her eye in my direction as Candy nodded in agreement.

Daddy James rolled his eyes. "If anyone needs smacking, it be Candy. She knows better. Janay ain't nothing but a baby, and Candy had no business talking grown folks' business in front of her. And you, Eloise, didn't have no business talking grown folks' business in front of Candy for her to repeat. No matter what you want to think, Manroot was still your brother, and Lavinia was a Tucker."

Eloise sucked her teeth. "Nothing ever changes does it, Daddy. I'm always the one that's wrong, ain't I?"

No one responded. Titus lifted his eyebrows, tossing an icy stare at his sister.

Turning on her heels, Eloise dragged Candy back into the house, storming through the foyer toward the kitchen. Titus exhaled.

"What we gone do, Daddy?"

James took a drag off his cigar, blowing the smoke into rings above my head. "We ain't gone do nothing. Law got your brother dead to rights. He gone have to pay for this."

Titus nodded his head slowly. He reached a hand out to rub his palm against my back, giving a quick tug on my ponytail.

"Go make your sister and that brat of hers feel better. I'll be in shortly," Daddy James commanded.

Titus nodded, leaned to give me a quick kiss, then stepped inside, closing the front door behind him.

Daddy James rocked me slowly, humming a deep tune into my ear. His warm arms were comforting, reminding me of my daddy. I lifted myself up to look into his eyes. Behind us, the sun was beginning to set in the distance. Fireflies were starting to rise above the tall grass to dance against the dark sky.

"When my daddy coming?"

Daddy James sighed heavily. Sitting down upon the metal glider that rocked us back and forth, he chose his words carefully, almost as if he needed to test them against his tongue before he spoke.

"Janay, I ain't never gone lie to you. No matter what, I will always tell you the truth. You understand?"

I nodded, tightening my grip around his neck.

"Manroot ain't gone come back. What your daddy did was wrong and now he gone be punished. I'm gone be your daddy now. I'm gone take care of you and you gone stay here with me. Now, ain't no reason for you to do no more crying. We ain't got no time for tears."

I nodded, not fully understanding what he was trying to say.

"I need you to be a big girl for me. You and me, we need each other now more than ever, okay?"

"Okay," I whispered faintly, not quite sure that it really was.

"Does my daddy still love me?" I asked.

The old man nodded. "Manroot will always love you. You's his baby girl and he loves you more than anything else."

I leaned my head against the old man's chest. "Will you make me some Jell-O?"

I could feel his chest rise and fall against my cheek as he chuckled softly.

"Yeah, and I'll show you how to make it for yourself, too."

I smiled.

"You ready to go inside now, Janay?" he asked, lifting me to my feet.

I nodded, slipping my hand into his. "Daddy James, don't call me Janay," I said as we headed inside.

He stopped short, bending down on one knee to look into my eyes. "What do you want me to call you?"

I shrugged, not quite sure, just knowing that my birth name didn't quite fit.

"What was it your mama and daddy used to call you?"

"Mama and Daddy called me Beauty. Mama said I was a black beauty 'cause I was black like Daddy and a beauty like her."

The man nodded. "Do you want me to call you Beauty?"

I thought about it briefly, twisting my hand beneath his as I did. "No," I said finally, wanting to leave the nickname my parents had for me with them. "No," I repeated, shaking my head. Wherever it was that they had disappeared to, I still needed a piece of them both that was special just between us three. My grandfather and I needed something special for just the two of us.

"Call me Black," I instructed. "Just call me Black."

Daddy James nodded his head slowly, agreement found in his gaze as he guided me through the door of my new home. "Let's go inside, Black. Time for both of us to get some rest."

****

The nightmares began in my grandmother's bed, following me from room to room, and mattress to mattress. I did not like to sleep unless I was wrapped tightly against my grandfather's body, secure beneath the weight of his arms. His presence made the dark dreams disappear. On far too many nights my cries and shouts pulled him from the warmth of his own bed to my side and only when I was confident that he'd chased the boogie woman away was he able to claim any rest for himself.

It was always the same nightmare. A room of silence roared thunderously in slow motion. Lavinia's hand would reach out to slap me as I fought for air. Her laughter would ring in my ears, an evil shrill that burned right through my body. Manroot stood off in the distance, tears flowing from his eyes. As I reached for him, he'd drift out of my grasp. I'd be running after my daddy, desperate to reach his side. And behind me, Lavinia would be laughing, blood gushing from the scar on her cheek, dripping over her face and into her hands. Those hands would always catch me, beating bloody palms against my skin. Then my daddy would be gone and there'd be nothing left but my bruised body soaked in my mother's blood.

It was November. The November after my daddy had gone away. The morning air was crisp, wind blowing chills through the old house. A fire burned in the hearth, the flames crackling with vibrant color. Shades of red and gold flickered against the dried logs that filled the brick enclosure, and I felt as if I could lose myself in the warmth of that color. Daddy James sat in his chair, sipping a cup of hot coffee. For whatever reason, I picked anxiously at a scab on my knee, rocking myself back and forth.

"What's wrong, Black?" Daddy James asked, watching me closely. "Why you so quiet?"

"Want my Daddy," I said, rocking myself steadily.

Daddy James inhaled deeply, setting the cup onto the table at his elbow. He nodded his head slowly.

"Want my daddy," I repeated as though he'd not heard me, over and over until the chant echoed about the room. "Want my daddy. Want my daddy. Want my daddy. Want my daddy...."

Daddy James let me rock for some time before he moved to lift me from the floor and pull me up onto his lap, wiping the tears out of my eyes. He hugged me tight against him, pressing his lips against my forehead. The chant had turned into a mournful hum twisted between my low sobs.

"Shhhh. Hush now, Black. It's all right. Hush now, baby," Daddy James whispered softly.

"Want my daddy," I whispered again.

"Manroot is gone, Black. I can't bring him back to you. I wish I could, baby. I wish I could."

"I was bad. My daddy don't love me no more."

Daddy James shook his head vehemently, lifting my face toward his, his fingers cupped beneath my chin.

"Your Daddy will always love you. You didn't do anything wrong. It was a bad thing that happened, but it happened because of Manroot and Lavinia, not you. You hear me?"

I nodded slowly.

"Manroot will never stop loving you, Black. Never."

That night, when I laid my head down to sleep, Lavinia told me otherwise, her blood splashing the truth across my face.

****

Sunlight skittered across a bright blue sky as I skipped about chasing the dark shadow that seemed to forever elude me. Auburn hair fell in a disheveled spray against my shoulders as dry dust spun small clouds against my sandaled feet. In the distance, I could hear Daddy James calling me from the front porch, but I ignored him, knowing he wanted only to pull a wooden hairbrush through my tangled mane. I did not want to have my hair combed.

As I heard his booming voice step off the porch, rounding the corner of the white washed house, I raced toward the cornfields, diving between the line of tall stalks. Lost between the thick rows I knew I could lose myself for hours before he would come to search for me. There was nowhere either of us needed to be today. It was Saturday and the biggest chore before us was the combing of my hair. And, I did not want to have my hair combed.

There was no greater playground than the land that surrounded the family home. Large fields lay patient beneath my feet as I skipped past freshly sprouted watermelons and danced around protruding rows of string beans, turnips, and collard greens. The warm July air was clean and fragrant, washing my senses with a simple pleasure. There was nothing better than to be outdoors with the dirt splashing between my toes.

Cutting across the back fields, I raced toward the pig pens and the litter of piglets wallowing in a pond of cool mud. If I'd had half a mind to I would set them free, but that would bring Daddy James running to pen them back up while he threatened to tan my bottom. I was in no mood to be yelled at so I ran my hand along the wire mesh instead, brushing my palm against their pugged noses. The chickens dashed about, clucking noisily as I pranced between them. I knew they found my presence irritating but I did not care. They were intruding on my domain, so let them be annoyed!

Spinning in circles, I could feel the laughter spilling out of my insides, frothing over the thin lips that were like my dead mother's lips. I found great happiness in being nine years old and able to run wild on land that was all mine, doing as I pleased. As I dropped to the ground, throwing handfuls of dirt above my head, I was as content as any one child could possibly be and I had my Daddy James to thank for it.

My name against his lips pulled me from my state of childish bliss, bringing the bright sun to blind my view.

"Black. You hear me calling for you. You come on here and let me do your hair. Come on, right now."

"I don't wanna come, Daddy James."

"Girl, you best bring your hips in this here house so I can do your hair. If you don't, I'm gone call your Aunt Eloise to come do it for you."

I sucked my teeth as I pulled myself up from the ground. "Don't want to get my hair combed. It hurts too much."

"I don't want to comb it either. Think about what I have to go through doing it, but it's me, or Eloise. Your choice."

I sighed heavily, dragging my small frame onto the porch and into his large lap. "Definitely don't want Aunt Eloise," I pouted, scratching at a row of mosquito bites along my arm.

"I swear child. Folks would think I don't let you near no water as dirty as you are."

I giggled, rubbing my cheek against the spiky growth of hair on Daddy James chin. "I ain't dirty. I'se natural."

"Naturally dirty." Daddy James grinned as he pulled the brush slowly through the tangle of knots. I winced as he pulled gently, separating the mess into smooth strands.

"You're a tender-headed child," he said as he always said when he brushed my hair. "Tender-headed is what you is."

The chore was not as uncomfortable as I made it out to be. In minutes, Daddy James had the dust brushed out of my hair and the long tresses braided into three neat plaits. Bright red ribbons were tied neatly around the ends. I looked civilized once again, instead of the "savage child" my Aunt Eloise claimed I was.

"What do you want to do today?" Daddy James asked, pushing me from his lap onto the seat beside him.

I shrugged.

"Want to go fishing down at the pond?"

"Can I go swimming too?"

He nodded, shrugging his shoulders. "I suppose so."

"Okay," I beamed, racing him to the barn and the old fishing poles he kept hanging on the side wall. Hand in hand, we made our way to the south side of the old property, whistling and humming as we strolled beneath the summer sun. Perspiration beaded up against Daddy James' forehead, raining in thin streams down his cheeks. Tiring of my sandals, I kicked them off as we walked, not bothering to stoop down to pick them up.

"I ain't buying no new shoes, Black. You best remember where you leaving that pair back there."

I nodded, knowing that tomorrow they'd be right beside my bed when I awoke, just like they always were. Daddy James would retrieve them, he always did.

We sat with our poles dangling in the water. We rarely caught any fish in the cool liquid, but we still enjoyed the quiet moment together down by the water's edge. When I grew bored with dangling the thin string into the dark pond, I dropped the pole to the ground, threw off my clothes, and flung my naked self beneath the wet blanket. Daddy James shook his head hopelessly.

The water was cool as I splashed about aimlessly. On the edge of the shore Daddy James sat with his back against an old oak tree, his knees pulled up toward his chest. As he stared out over the dark pool, he hummed softly.

Rushing out of the water, I dropped low to the ground, the green grass tickling my flesh. My giggles cradled the warm air around me and the sudden rush of cool air felt exhilarating.

"Girl, put something on before I skin your tail. How many times I got to tell you that you can't be showing your nakedness like that. You a girl and girls can't be running 'round showing they stuff."

"Why not?"

"Because it ain't decent."

"Why not?"

"Because I said so, that's why. Now, put your clothes on."

I rolled my eyes at Daddy James, screwing up my face in a pretend pout. We'd had this conversation so many times that it had started to grow old.

The damp clothes back on, I cuddled up next to my grandfather, stretching my body alongside his. We sat together quietly having no other desire than to enjoy each other's company. The pond was our special place where nothing ugly could find its way into our minds. The afternoon ticked away slowly.

"Daddy James?"

"What?"

"Why can't I go see Manroot?"

Daddy James cut his eye at me, nodding his head slowly. "I done told you before I don't think no little girls should be going down to that prison. It ain't proper."

"Barbara Jean Hinton goes to see her daddy at that prison. She done gone to see him four times already with her mama and he in there 'cause he done kilt two men."

"Well, I ain't Barbara Jean Hinton's mama 'cause if I was she wouldn't be going to no prison to see nobody."

"Well, I think I should be going to see my Daddy."

Daddy James leaned his body forward dropping his chin into the palms of his hands. He pulled his thick fingers through his graying hair.

"When your daddy left for Angola he and I made a pact. We promised each other that no matter what, you would never see him behind bars. Girl start seeing her daddy behind some prison walls and she start to thinking that it's okay for the men in her life to be in that kind of a situation and it ain't. It's not right and I won't have you thinking that it's okay. Manroot's in there 'cause he done wrong and he's paying for his crime. Part of his punishment was giving up the right to see his family whenever he chose. Besides, it ain't like Louisiana just round the corner.

"Now, I'm only gone tell you this one time. You don't ever chase after no man in no prison. A man in jail can't do nothing for you. Nothing. A man call you from the jail house, you run. You turn around and run fast. I don't care if he is your daddy or my son. He can't do nothing for us and there's not much we can do for him."

I let the silence swell between us, not sure if I should say what was on my mind. When Daddy

James leaned back against the tree, I twisted around to look him in the eye. "Don't my daddy need to know we still love him?"

Daddy James returned my stare. "Manroot know we still love him. But your daddy didn't want you growing up being ashamed of him 'cause he's ashamed of himself. If you was to go see him in that place it would make him feel like he's even less of a man. He don't need that and neither do you. Prison done had to make your daddy harder than he already was, and Manroot was hard enough to start off with. You his only soft spot and if he goes soft in jail it could get him killed. Some things just best left alone."

"Do you go to see him much?"

Daddy James nodded. "Black, you know I do. You know I go when I can."

"Does he ask about me?"

"All the time."

"Next time you see him tell him I said hey. Tell him...tell him I miss him and I still love him. I'm gone write him a letter and draw him some pictures for you to take. Okay?"

"Black, I tell your daddy that every time I see him. Don't you ever think just 'cause you can't tell him yourself that he doesn't hear it. I tell him, and Titus and Chauncey tell him too. We let him know what you up to and you know you can write him as much as you want to."

I nodded my head, laying it in Daddy James lap.

"Me and my mama sure messed things up, didn't we?"

"Is that what you think?"

I nodded again.

"Can't blame your mama and sure 'nuff can't blame yourself. Lavinia did some things wrong 'cause she won't a happy woman. Unhappy woman can't help some of the things she does. You was just a baby. You didn't have nothing to do with what happened."

"Mama could be real mean. I remember that about her."

Daddy James brushed my brow, his callused fingers rough against my skin.

"Yeah, but she won't always like that. When your daddy married her and she had you in your grandmama's bed she was different. She loved you and she loved your daddy. Most important though was she loved herself. Once she stopped loving herself she couldn't find no happiness and couldn't give no happiness."

I lifted myself up off the ground suddenly tired of the conversation, an annoying pain throbbing in my side. Back at the water's edge, I stared deep into the clear moisture, searching the gravel and foliage below.

"I like the pond when it's still like this. You can see almost to the bottom."

Daddy James nodded his head in agreement, rising to stand by my side. I tossed in a small pebble that broke through the rested waters, disturbing the quiet of the surface. I suddenly saw my daddy being gone and my mama being dead being very much the same. My rested waters had been disturbed, the quiet of my surface rippling from the breach. Extending my small hand out to Daddy James, I guided him back down the hill. "Let's go get some Jell-O."

Creekton was as small a Southern community as one could find after crossing the divide of the Mason-Dixon Line. It boasted a string of family-owned businesses that lined the short length of Main Street, two Baptist churches— one black and the other white, and a motley cast of personalities whose bloodlines probably ran too close for anyone's comfort.

Everyone knew everybody else and no one's personal business was beyond public scrutiny and the horde of opinions married to it. In the barbershop, comments fell like rain as Daddy James sat in the oversized barber's chair to get his graying hair cut by Mr. Bill Pratt. I sat patiently, eavesdropping on some things I understood and others I didn't.

Mr. Pratt reprimanded two teenage boys, reminding them that this was the one Saturday of the month that a young lady was present. Both dropped their gazes to the floor, nodding their apology.

"Sorry about that, Mr. Pratt."

"Didn't mean no disrespect, Mr. Tucker."

My grandfather waved a hand. "None taken, son." He gave me a quick wink. "Just go easy with the rough language. My baby girl don't mind a good debate but her precious ears can't take that vulgarity."

"Yes, sir," the tall boy with the dark freckles said. His name was Darius and he looked me up and down and grinned.

The other boy slapped him on his shoulder and the duo laughed heartily, sharing a private joke between them. The two older men shook their heads.

"What you think about them riots in Detroit, Mr. Tucker?" Darius asked. "Wasn't that something!"

Daddy James' expression answered for him, clearly finding nothing to be impressed about. "A man standing up for his rights doesn't have to be about destroying his own neighborhood. Decent men built those businesses out of nothing. Them young boys tore them down without blinking an eye. And what did they accomplish? Absolutely nothing. Hundreds of black men were hurt, thousands more were arrested, and tomorrow the police will be right back giving black folks a hard time."

"H. Rap Brown said that if Motown didn't come around they was going to burn 'em down," the other boy professed.

Daddy James rolled his eyes, tossing Mr. Pratt a quick glance.

"Young blood, people who have the economic power and control don't care if you destroy what's yours or what belongs to another black man. You could cut your brother's heart out for what it's worth to him. And you can trust that he's gone shut you down quick if you even think about touching what he thinks belongs to him.

"What you need to learn is that if you want to make a difference, you have to do what's *not* expected from you. Folks already think you stupid, so you need to run circles around them in the classroom. When they call you lazy, you have to work ten times harder to prove them wrong. They say you'll never amount to anything. Give them a taste of what economic security can do for you. Own yours, help another black man own his and together you build an empire no man can tear down or take away from you."

The two boys looked bored by the man's comments. "How you get all that land you own, Mr. Tucker?"

"My great grand-daddy."

"Won't he a white man?" Darius asked.

Daddy James smiled, his eyes squinting ever so slightly. "They say he was."

The other boy sneered. "That don't say much for how you got yours, does it, Mr. Tucker?"

My grandfather eyed the boy carefully before responding. "It says more than you think, son. It took a smart, black woman to make sure all that land was passed down to her black babies. A black man owned it then, a black man owns it now, and one day, another smart, black woman will pass it right on down to her own black babies. Ain't that right, Black?"

I grinned back, nodding my agreement. The two boys shook their heads.

"But you being part white ain't hurt you none."

My grandfather shook his head. "Boy, when I look in the mirror, I see the same thing you and everyone else sees. A black man with dark skin. Ain't nothing about me look part nothing. And there ain't many of us left who can say we ain't got some white blood somewhere down our family tree. But I don't care how much white you think I got or you think someone else has, if we look black, we black. Ain't no one gone stop to ask us just how much white we have or how much black don't we have."

Mr. Pratt brushed the last strands of loose hair from Daddy James' shoulders. "Don't waste your breath on these young boys, James. Talking to them's like talking to a wall."

Daddy James shook his head as he stood tall, pulling his blazer back onto his body. "If we keep talking to them, Bill, one day, one of 'em might actually hear what we got to say and learn something." The man extended his large hand in my direction. "What you say we go get us some ice cream, Black? Then later on tonight we can drive over to Raleigh to the drive in to see that new movie with Sidney Poitier. What's it called again?"

"To Sir with Love," I said softly.

He nodded.

"What's that about?" Darius' friend asked.

"It's about a black man who uses his brain to command respect from a bunch of hoodlum kids," Daddy James answered. He laughed, the richness of it swelling thick in the early afternoon air. "What's that new song, Miss Aretha sings, Black?"

I laughed with him, the two of us breaking out into a bad rendition of Aretha Franklin's *Respect*.

The two boys shrugged, both eyeing us as we made our way out of the shop, still singing at the top of our lungs as we made our way down the street.

Once I stepped past the doors of New Fields Elementary School, the weight of my third grade world seemed heavier than normal. My understanding of the why and the who was embodied in the dislikes of Mrs. Barbara Lang.

Mrs. Lang was atypical of the Southern-belles who populated Creekton, polyester-princesses with condescending demeanors masked behind brilliant Colgate smiles, heavy Mary-Kay makeup, voluminous hair, and enough bible-thumping to irritate the Holy Father himself.

The tone of our relationship was clearly established on the first day of school. I arrived in my new blue-striped slacks, white blouse, and white, high-top, Converse All-Stars. Daddy James had made my favorite for lunch, ham and Swiss cheese on swirling, rye bread, which I carried in a brown paper bag. Tucked in the front pocket of my slacks, I had fifty-cents for a carton of white milk to wash down the three chocolate-chip cookies he and I had baked the night before. I had a new book bag with three #6-pencils, an oversized rubber eraser, and a bright red, three-ring binder with extra sheets of loose leaf paper. I arrived prepared, excited, and a lot nervous.

Mrs. Lang greeted her students at the door. Catrina Elrick stepped in before me, her blonde strands billowing past her shoulders. Mrs. Lang greeted her with a warm hug, welcomed her to the class, and pointed her to a prime seat in the front of the room.

I stepped forward, my biggest smile painted across my brown face. "Good morning, Mrs. Lang. My name's Janay Tucker."

The woman turned to stare down at me, her brilliant smile fading to a thin line. Her eyes narrowed ever so slightly, her nose twitching as if she suddenly smelled something sour. "I believe you're in the wrong room, dear. This is the class for those students who tested very high on that special test you all took last year. This is the *gifted* class."

"Yes, ma'am." I stood my ground still waiting for my hug and front row desk.

"Did you hear me, girl?"

"Yes, ma'am. This is my class. This letter says so," I answered, passing her the requisite class assignment sheet.

She scanned it quickly, the tense lines across her brow tightening further. She nodded her head slowly, dropping the paper as if afraid to have her hands touch mine. We both watched as the document fell easily to the floor beneath my feet. Clasping her hands together in front of her, her jaw tightened as she cast a gaze down the hall toward the other teachers who stood in their own entranceways and the mix of children skipping off to wherever it was they belonged.

"Well, you need to go sit down. There's an empty seat in the back row," she said, not bothering to look back in my direction.

My own smile faded, a heap of heavy suddenly dropping down against my narrow shoulders. It was clear that I was not welcome in Mrs. Lang's class. It became clearer as the weeks passed and my presence was continually disregarded. She would ask for volunteers to come finish the problems on the chalkboard. I waved my hand excitedly, having already figured out the answers in my head. Mrs. Lang picked Catrina and Peter McCary, not even bothering to glance in my direction. I had become use to being ignored, but I was hopeful none-the-less that one day she would actually select me to be the hall monitor, or collect the test papers, or pass out the special paper, or give the answers that none of the other children knew. And so my hand was always one of the first ones to be waved, my thin fingers shaking anxiously for attention. Eventually hope ran dry, every ounce of my spirit dissipating with it.

"What's wrong with you, Black?" Daddy James asked, as he pulled his Ford truck up to the front of the school, coming to a stop in the parent's kiss-and-go lane. "Don't you want to go to school? Can't be no smart girl without school, now."

I shrugged, my voice barely audible as I whispered my response. "I just want to stay with you, Daddy."

He eyed me curiously. "Someone bothering with you, Black? Do you want to tell me about it?"

And I did, not really wanting to understand what it was about me that made Mrs. Lang cringe with distaste each and every time she looked in my direction, but knowing that my granddaddy would have the answers.

He nodded his head slowly before responding and I imagined a tear had risen to his eyes, but it was gone as quickly as I had fathomed it. "You head on to class, Black. I need to go park my truck. I want to go inside to have a conversation with Mr. Daniels."

"The principal? Did I do something wrong, Daddy?"

He smiled, the wealth of it as magnanimous as his spirit. "You haven't done nothing wrong, Black. Mr. Daniels and I just need to have us a talk about my expectations."

I eyed him curiously. "Your expectations?"

"That's right. You remember when you was in kindergarten and that nice Mrs. Johnson use to have you memorize three of the alphabet each night and I use to make you memorize five?"

I nodded, smiling at the memory of learning all my letters before everyone else. "Yes, sir."

"And when you learned your times tables, I made you learn how to do division at the same time?"

"Yes, sir."

"Well, I set the standards for your learning. No one else. These teachers here do a fine job but you're too smart a girl to just sit around waiting for them to decide what you should be learning. I make that decision. I say what's too hard for you and I say when it's not hard enough. No one else. And I expect all these teachers here to know that. If they're not teaching you the way I want you taught then they're not meeting my expectations. And since my daddy built this school, and a whole lot of my tax money keeps this school running, my expectations will be met. Just like when I tell you what I want from you, I have expectations that you have to meet. Ain't no different."

"Yes, sir, Daddy."

"Go on in now. Daddy James'll take care of Mrs. Lang. You just behave and do your work."

I looked back over my shoulder to watch my grandfather pull his truck off to the side of the building to park. As I entered the classroom, I didn't bother to greet Mrs. Lang since I knew she had no intentions of responding. I took my seat, adjusted my papers against the desktop and waited politely for the morning bell.

Before the day was out, Mrs. Barbara Lang was no longer a teacher at New Fields Elementary School. The next morning, Miss Brenda Peters hugged me too and let me be the hall monitor for the day.

****

At least twice a month I was reminded that I had more fathers than any one girl would ever need to have. Every other Sunday, Uncle Titus and Uncle Chauncey would roll their colossal frames through the front door bellowing do's and don'ts faster than I could absorb them. Sometimes it was too much for my small person to take.

I'd always welcome their arrival with a beaming smile and damp kisses against their cheeks. They both reminded me of my daddy and I so missed his thick arms around me and the dark chocolate complexion that had tinted my own color a milky brown. Manroot Tucker had been the prettiest black man I'd ever known and I didn't think any other man was as pretty as him. Even Titus and Chauncey didn't compare to my daddy. Daddy James was the only one who came close.

People always joked that Titus and Chauncey were joined together at the hip. They always traveled together, side by side. You could never call one and not have the other following closely on his heels. Daddy James said it was because they were so close in age. Aunt Eloise said that was why neither of them had a wife because no woman knew how to take their being so close. She didn't know a woman who'd been able to come between them. It was almost unnatural she'd remarked on more than one occasion. Daddy James had said Aunt Eloise was just jealous.

Sunday was always family day. The brothers would show up in time for Sunday service and we'd all pile into one of the cars and head off to church. I'd sit squashed between them and Daddy James, unless it was fourth Sunday and I was forced to sit with the children's choir. I couldn't sing worth a lick but Daddy James insisted.

He also made me go to Sunday school which I considered a total waste of time. They never let you ask any real questions without it getting you in trouble with someone, and I knew how to ask more "why" questions better than anyone else. Most times, I spent the better part of the hour trying to keep Dabney Hill from pulling on my pigtails or Leanna Tibbs from making fun of my clothes. If Mrs. Winston, the Sunday school teacher, wasn't yelling at me for saying the wrong thing, I was trying not to fight in church. Either way it almost always meant a scolding or a spanking from Daddy James when we got back home, depending on the severity of my indiscretion.

After church, we'd go home for Sunday dinner. If Aunt Eloise didn't come over and cook, Daddy James would always do it before we left and the aroma of good food would meet our empty bellies in the doorway. We'd feast on meals of smothered chicken, fried catfish, pan fried steak, or slow roasted beef with a supporting mélange of fresh collards or turnip greens, macaroni and cheese, biscuits, and heavy, sugary desserts like sweet potato pie, peach cobbler, pineapple or chocolate layer cakes, or coconut-cream pies. Uncle Titus and Uncle Chauncey would play games with me until Daddy James tired of us all and sent me to my bed and them to their own homes. It had become a comfortable routine for all of us.

The Sunday that our routine changed was an ugly Sunday. The sky had darkened early, only a brief flicker of sunlight flitting across the early morning sky. It had stayed dark, blistered clouds anxiously waiting to burst overhead. The humid air became even heavier, a damp acrid scent of mildew blowing in the wind. The moment was foreboding as the onset of rain came before most had prepared to receive it. I could feel the bad news approaching long before it arrived at our doorstep. Then I saw the car pull into the drive, racing up the road toward the house. I slowly slipped into my Sunday dress shoes, a white pair of Mary Janes that pinched my baby toe if I stood too long. Taking one last glance in the mirror I ran my palms down the length of my dress, the yellow cotton shift painted with bright pink flowers.

There was a sudden quickening of muscle in my abdomen as a rush of panic set in, digging its heels in as if intending to stay. The voices in the foyer below echoed strangely, the greetings void of the usual Sunday morning laughter. As I raced below to see what was wrong, I instantly noted that Uncle Titus had showed up alone. The look in his eyes confirmed that something was seriously wrong. He lumbered about, his large body seeming heavier than usual. His head hung low on his shoulders and the warm color was drained from his face. The gray cast to his dark complexion was frightening. I bit back my questions as he and Daddy James whispered rapidly between themselves, stealing an occasional glance in my direction as I eased into the room, coming to a standstill in the doorway.

I so wanted to ask where Uncle Chauncey was, but I instinctively knew better. I could tell they hadn't a clue as to his whereabouts either. The worry seeped out of Daddy James' pores, dripping into his eyes. The twitch around his mouth became pronounced as he chewed on the end of a toothpick, scratching his fingers against his pant leg. When I could take no more I crept between them and reached out my arms to be held.

"Black, you need to go pack some clothes. I'm gone take you to Eloise's for a few days."

My expression was incredulous. "No," I whined. "Please, Daddy, don't leave me, please," I implored, the fountain of tears turning on, water blurring my vision.

Daddy James bit his bottom lip. "I'se got to go Black, but I'll be back."

"No! Manroot ain't never coming back. Uncle Chauncey ain't never coming back, and if you go I ain't never gone see you no more either." The tone of my voice sounded strange as my shouting vibrated off the walls.

Daddy James and Uncle Titus both bristled, eyeing each other hesitantly. I stepped in closer, my legs moving on their own accord. Cold ran the short length of my spine as if an icy hand had suddenly touched me.

"Why you say Chauncey ain't coming back?" Titus asked, lifting me into his arms. "Why you say that?"

I shrugged my shoulders, my emotions sweeping between us. I had no words to explain it, but I knew that where ever Chauncey lay was where he would stay. It felt as if death had walked in and had whispered the news to me personally.

Daddy James pulled his fingers through his thick hair. He nodded his head slowly. "Can you do this by yourself, Titus? Get some of them boys to go look with you?"

Titus nodded his head yes, hugging me close against his chest.

Uncle Titus kissed my forehead, then stared into my eyes. "Is I coming back, Black?" he asked, his voice shimmering with anxiety.

I nodded. "Next Sunday we gone have fried chicken for dinner," I said quietly.

Titus nodded again. "I hate fried chicken," he said.

"Me too," I whispered in his ear. "Me too."

Daddy James and I sat in church by ourselves that Sunday, no other family by our side. It would be the first of many Sundays to come where there would be no other members of the Tucker clan to sit by our sides. The news of Uncle Chauncey's disappearance was whispered about quietly in the pews. Reverend Prescott prayed for Uncle Chauncey's safe return and the widow women who coveted Daddy James' attention all rushed to offer words of encouragement and support.

The pond became our sanctuary. Daddy James and I sat quietly by the water's edge, saying nothing to each other, but sharing volumes. There was a knowing between us as we waited for confirmation, the news coming to us four days later. As Daddy James held the telephone, his hands began shaking violently, barely able to place the receiver back onto the cradle. I hugged him tightly around the legs, wishing I could disappear into his side.

Reverend Prescott, Ollie Madison, and Joe Tate brought Uncle Titus home. The men had found Uncle

Chauncey's body down in the swamps behind his old house. The swamps that lay to the south of Creekton were Tucker property, and to this day most folks just say Chauncey died in his home. Although no one would ever know for certain what events led up to his death, and most didn't really care, we knew that whoever or whatever had ripped the breath from Uncle Chauncey's soul had done so viciously, the crime upon his person as violent an act as anyone could possibly imagine.

I saw Daddy James cry when they bought Uncle Chauncey's body for him to see. Though they tried to shield me from his grotesque form, I saw my Uncle Chauncey, his broken body bent awkwardly in the back of the pickup truck. His warm brown skin had turned ashen and swamp things crawled up and over his badly battered eyes and face. His body lay twisted, shattered bones protruding from swollen flesh. Daddy James cried for Uncle Chauncey, falling to his knees to pray. I cried with him, everyone else's gaze turned toward the heavens and all I could do was wipe my grandfather's tears against the back of my hand.

That night, Uncle Chauncey walked through my dreams, his vibrant smile guiding his path. He stroked my forehead, dropping brightly colored flowers above me, and when Lavinia tried to come, to steal the sweetness of Uncle Chauncey from me, he held me tight and sent her away. I picked yellow flowers. Bright shades of lemon and saffron interspersed between white roses. We buried him that Sunday and Uncle Titus ate Jell-O with me and Daddy James.

****

Birthdays came and went with minimal acknowledgement. Although Daddy James tried to make the occasions as festive as possible for me, each birthday served only as a bitter reminder of all that I had lost, all that I struggled to escape from. At the tender age of eleven, I no longer believed in Santa Claus, or the Easter Bunny, and the Tooth Fairy was a figment of everybody else's imagination. There was nothing that I longed for other than my father's return, though I had long since given up hope of ever seeing him again. I wrote to him faithfully though, filling him in on all my doings and sharing my days with him as best I could.

It was the week after my birthday that his first and last letter arrived addressed to me. Daddy James had held the white mailer at arm's length, balancing it precariously against his fingertips. Caution registered on his face as he debated with himself over whether or not he should give it to me. I settled the dispute when I pulled the letter from his hand and proceeded to tear at the seal, ripping it open and pulling at its contents. Plain white paper folded neatly in half dropped out on my lap. I reached a hesitant hand out to pick it up, unfolded it carefully, then began to read the neatly printed words aloud. Daddy James dropped himself into a seat beside me, resting his chin in his hands on top of the kitchen table.

"My dear Beauty, how are you? I am as well as one can be under the cir...". I leaned toward Daddy James, pointing at the word on the page.

"Circumstances."

"...under the circumstances. I'm sorry that I can't be there for your birthday, but I promise to blow you a kiss from here just as you are blowing out the candles on your cake. I have gotten all your letters and I thank you for writing me. I am sorry that I cannot answer them all but I am not much of a writer. I am glad that you are being such a sweet girl for Daddy James. He loves you very much and he is very proud of everything you do. I do not want you to waste any more paper on writing me. You should be doing school things and having fun. Life is too short for you to be letting it pass you by. I know that all of this has been very hard for you to

understand and I am sorry for that. What's important though is that you go on and make a good life for yourself. Daddy James will help you do that since I can't. Continue to be a good girl for Daddy James and remember that I am always thinking of you. Love, your father, Manroot Tucker."

Daddy James sighed, then yawned, stretching his body upwards. He nodded his head slowly, then rose from the table, pulling the fixings for dinner from the refrigerator. I reread the letter again and again, until I'd memorized each and every word. By the time I'd finished twisting the page between my fingers, Daddy James had two pots simmering, and was putting on the third pan for the meat. I watched him closely.

"He's not going to write me anymore, is he?"

Daddy James shrugged his shoulders, not bothering to lift his eyes from his vegetables. "Can't rightly say. Can't say what Manroot gone do or not do."

I nodded. "He don't want me to write him anymore. He said that."

"He said you need to be worrying about being a kid and doing kid things and not waste your time worrying 'bout him. That's what he said."

I bit anxiously at my bottom lip, sliding the letter back into the torn envelope. The sweet aroma of highly seasoned meat tickled my nostrils. Standing, I pulled two plates from the pantry and began to set the table. Endless thoughts of my father raced through my brain. When the table was set for dinner, I made myself comfortable in my chair, continuing to read my father's letter over and over again, hoping to find the hidden message, the sliver of hope I believed to be painted between the lines. Daddy James watched me out of the corner of his eye, finally setting the food onto the center of the table.

"Ain't you done with that letter yet?" he finally asked, taking the seat beside me.

I shrugged my shoulders slightly, not bothering to respond.

"Put that paper away, Black and let's eat before this food get cold."

"Yes sir," I answered, sliding the letter onto my lap.

I could feel the older man watching me as he chewed his food methodically, savoring each bite. Although I knew the stew beef and vegetables to be delicious, they tasted heavy in my mouth as I attempted to chew each fork full. Everything around me felt heavy.

"He's not coming back, is he, Daddy James?"

Daddy James laid his fork down against the table. "We done told you before your daddy ain't coming back. He's in jail for the rest of his life. We can't change that."

"What's gone happen to me?"

Daddy James sat back in his chair, the front chair legs lifting ever so slightly off the floor. "What has been happening with you for the last two years?"

I shrugged again.

"Have you been fed?"

I nodded my head yes.

"You got a roof over your head?"

I nodded again.

"I take you to church every week?"

"Yes, sir."

"Then I guess that's what gone happen to you. I'm gone feed you, keep this here roof over your head, and make sure you get to church every week. Your daddy mailing you one letter don't change none of that."

My gazed dropped to the table. Daddy James reached out his hand and lifted my chin up, resting my gaze upon his.

"I'm gone keep taking care of you and loving you just like always, Black. So, you stop worrying. Daddy James gone take good care of you. Hear me?"

I smiled a weak smile and nodded, one hand reaching to finger the letter in my lap.

There could be no denying that I missed my father. I missed the knowing that comes between a man and his child. I felt that there was a well of emptiness deep in my heart and no number of promises would ever again make it whole.

I watched my grandfather as he focused on the food upon his plate, his mind wrapped around thoughts of Manroot, and me, and the shift in our existence that had brought each of us to this point. Daddy James loved me. I had no doubt of that. Reaching for my own utensil, I pulled a forkful of vegetables into my mouth and began to chew, allowing the letter in my lap to slip slowly to the floor.

****

I adored Candy Alexander. I thought having her as a cousin was as close to getting a big sister as any girl could ever hope for. When Daddy James announced her visits, I'd cross the days until her arrival off the calendar, rushing through my chores as though it would rush the new day in. At fifteen, being so much older than me, Candy had no tolerance for my eleven-year-old presence. No tolerance except to send me to fetch a cool drink for her when she was hot or to pick up her side of the room when she knew Daddy James would come to inspect how well we'd done.

That all changed the summer of 1969. Candy Alexander was beaming with smiles when she walked into the room we would share for her annual five week visit. She hugged me real tight, kissing my cheek, telling me how much she'd been looking forward to seeing me. I reveled in the attention my older cousin lavished on me. Candy had become my new best friend.

We both heard the door close behind Daddy James as we sat on the bed peering through Candy's teen magazines. I watched as Candy jumped excitedly off the bed to run to the window.

"Where he say he was going?" she asked, smiling in my direction.

"Down to Mr. Jessup's to see about getting him to do some work for him. He'll probably be gone a good while. You want to play a game or something?"

Candy looked back out the window, fingering the buttons on her blouse as she peered out the curtain.

"Janay, you ever kiss a boy before?"

I giggled. "No. Why I want to do something fool like that? Daddy James would whoop me good if he ever caught me messing with some boy." I giggled again.

Candy sat back down on the bed beside me. "Want to play a new game? A secret game?"

"Sure," I answered, the excitement spilling out of my voice.

Candy smiled sweetly. "Got to promise to never tell anyone. If you tell, you'll go right to hell, Janay Tucker. You'll go crazy just like your crazy, honky mama did, and some man will break your neck just like your crazy daddy done her. Promise me!"

The excitement had dimmed when Candy mentioned my mama and daddy in the same breath as the word crazy, but I shook my head anxiously, not wanting to dispel any enthusiasm Candy had for including me in one of her secrets.

"Cross my heart and hope to die," I swore, crossing my hands atop my chest.

The smile grew sickeningly sweeter as Candy slowly unbuttoned the row of ivory buttons against her checkered blouse. A snow-white bra lay against the cocoa skin, the round of her small breasts protruding along the laced edge. As she pushed the cotton fabric up to expose the youthful tissue I stared in awe. "Touch me just like this," she instructed, taking my hand and placing it against her breast. Pulling my hand back, I moved away from her ever so slightly.

"Don't be a baby. You wants to play or not?"

I shook my head.

Candy hissed. "If you don't play this game with me, Janay Tucker, I ain't gone never play anything else with you again. I ain't gone pretend you my baby sister no more and I ain't gone come see you when you go crazy like your dead mama!"

The look across her face was cutting as she eyed me angrily. Grabbing my hand she placed it atop her skin guiding me on how to manipulate the soft dough between my small fingers. I watched her face as she tossed her head back, licking her lips lightly. "Ummm," she hummed. "That feel real nice. If you had some titties I'd show you how nice it feels," she said, reaching her hand beneath my shirt. I winced as she lightly pinched the flatness. I pulled my hand away.

"You did that real good. She inched closer, leaning her face against mine. When our lips touched, I could feel my breath slipping away, the air frightened out of my lungs.

"Kiss me back," Candy ordered. "Kiss me hard."

I felt myself slipping away as Candy pulled me on top of her, twisting her lips against mine. Wanting Candy to like me was motivation for anything I thought as I moved my mouth as she moved hers, shuddering when she pushed her tongue past my lips, licking the front of my teeth. She pulled away, breathless.

"They call that a French kiss. You put your tongue in each other's mouth, back and forth like a sword fight. Here, you try it," she said kissing me again.

I tried it, giggling at the thought of our two pink tongues dueling against each other.

"Knew you'd like it," Candy said. "Want to play some more?"

I shrugged my shoulders, more curious now than anything else. Candy once again fingered her nipples. "Kiss me here," she said pointing at the protruding, dark chocolate kiss between her fingers. "Give it a French kiss with your tongue."

I did as I was told and as I peered past Candy's chest toward her face I watched with amazement as her face twisted with pleasure. Candy liked what I was doing to her. Candy like the way I was playing her game. I reached up to take the other nipple in my hand, squeezing it ever so slightly. Candy's body jumped beneath mine.

I'd counted to a hundred when Candy finally sat up, brushing her hand against my cheek. The smile grew syrupy as Candy rose from the bed to peer once again out of the window. When she was sure there was no sign of Daddy James returning up the road she pushed her shorts past her knees and took off her panties. I stared at the dark patch of hair between her legs.

"Take of your shorts," she said, coming to lie back on the bed beside me.

I hesitated as Candy's fingers danced back and forth between her legs. "It's okay," she said, "I'm just gone show you the rest of the game."

As Candy pushed my shorts and underwear down to the floor I could feel the tears swelling in my eyes. I inhaled sharply not wanting Candy to see them fall.

Candy sat up on the bed, spreading her legs off the edge. "Sit like this," she instructed, easing my legs open ever so slightly.

"What's between here and here," she asked, touching one thigh and then the other.

I pointed at a spot on the bed between my open legs.

"Nope," she grinned. "What's between here and here," she asked again, moving her hands higher up my thigh.

I pointed to the spot between where her fingers had touched, my hand brushing against my flesh.

"Nope. What's between here and here?" Candy touched the crease of inner legs.

Pointing to the bed one last time, my breath quickened.

"No, this," Candy said, rubbing her fingers against my private parts. The feeling was electric as she tickled and taunted my virginity.

"Now you do it to me," she said.

"...between here and here?" I asked, touching Candy as she'd touched me.

"This," she said coyly, pointing to the bedspread.

I swallowed. "No, this," I whispered, pushing my fingers into Candy as she'd just done to me. Candy giggled, pushing her pelvis against my hand. I pulled my hand away, wiping my fingers against the bedspread.

Candy lay back with her eyes closed and her legs spread open farther.

"Next time when we play I'll show you how to do some more stuff," Candy said. "I'll do it to you too."

I nodded okay, wishing a silent prayer that there would be no next time for Candy's secret game.

Candy kissed me again, pushing my shirt up and out of the way.

"You better hope you get some titties. Boys ain't gone like you if you ain't got no titties."

My eyes fell to Candy's breasts, then back to my own washboard of a chest. Candy pushed me back against the bed, pulling my legs lengthwise across the soft mattress. She kissed one flat nipple, then the other, opening my legs with her hands.

Her voice came in a husky whisper. "Just keep rubbing until it feels good. Don't stop until it feels good, okay?" Lowering her pelvis over mine, Candy pushed against me, up and down, and back and forth. Before long, the warmth traveled across my lower extremities, the intense sensation overwhelming. Just as the warmth turned to burning, and the burning to an explosion, Daddy James called our names from the stairwell below, the door slamming behind his entrance.

As Candy and I jumped out of our skins, grabbing for our clothes, she whispered between gritted teeth. "If you tell anyone, Janay Tucker, you gone die just like your mama, crazy!"

I nodded my head foolishly, then raced down the stairs into Daddy James' arms and the chocolate-swirl ice-cream in his hands.

Each and every time Daddy James was gone for any length of time Candy wanted to play her games. By the end of her five-week visit, I'd even come to look forward to the explosion of warmth between my pre-pubescent legs. But for the very first time, I was also grateful to see Candy go.

The following summer Candy didn't come at all. The news of Candy's pregnancy reached Daddy James even before it had reached the girl's mother. Although the words of support Daddy James spoke were kind in their tone, Aunt Eloise did not accept them as such. Her own disappointment in her daughter's predicament pulsed through her like a fever spoiling everything around her. It was when the insult to her injury became far too much for her to bear that Aunt Eloise snapped, her anger lashing out at Daddy James.

"You think this is my fault, don't you?" Aunt Eloise spat, rising in anger.

The lines in Daddy James' face tightened as he set his mouth in a tight grimace.

"Don't you?" Aunt Eloise shouted.

Daddy James crossed his arms across his chest and his legs out in front of him. "Be careful what you say, girl. Don't let your mouth write no checks your butt can't cash."

The tears brimmed out of Aunt Eloise's eyes. "You have always blamed me for everything. You blamed me for having her. You blamed her for not being no perfect grandchild like that beast of Manroot's. I ain't never been able to do nothing that you ain't found wrong."

Daddy James shook his head, reaching a large hand out to pull Eloise back onto the thinly padded kitchen chair resting in front of him. His tone was soft, but firm, as he held his daughter's gaze with his own. "Listen to yourself, baby girl. You know better than that. You know that all I have ever wanted was for you to show some respect for yourself, and this family, by doing right. I expected you to teach that child of yours the same values your mama and I tried to teach you and your brothers. The mistakes you made were your own, but you have never owned up to one of them. And you have never tried to do better."

Daddy James took a deep breath before continuing, his eyes still resting on Eloise's face and the tears that ran down her full cheeks. The tone of his voice could not have been softer.

"You're standing in my house, raising your voice at me like I put that piece of trash at your door and told you to sleep with him. Now he done gone and got you and your daughter pregnant and you still want to blame me instead of finding fault with what you've allowed that man to get away with. He's been laying up with Candy with no respect for you at all, and then Candy's out in the streets flaunting it. Your own child disgraced your home."

As the look of shock and surprise registered on Aunt Eloise's face, Daddy James instantly regretted the words that had spilled out of his mouth. Aunt Eloise jumped to her feet, spun around, and vomited into the kitchen sink as Daddy James sat back against his own chair, and dropped his head into his hands. The pain sweeping through Aunt Eloise swept up and over Daddy James' shoulders as he reached out to offer comfort to his daughter.

"Don't you dare," Aunt Eloise spat, shaking his arms from around her shoulders. "What a filthy lie! Candy ain't pregnant for Lionel Jasper. I'm having Lionel's baby. Me. My child wouldn't do that to me." The tears poured down her face and into Daddy James' hand as he reached out to caress her cheek. Daddy James could only shake his head as the truth of all he'd said flooded Eloise's body, consuming her spirit. Falling into her father's arms, Aunt Eloise sobbed into his shoulder, the beginnings of her pregnant belly just visible beneath the sweat clothes she wore.

When Aunt Eloise left, she held onto the porch rail for a brief moment, pausing to stare up at her father. Neither spoke a word, there being nothing else between them to say. Eloise swiped a palm across her swollen eyes. Daddy James reached out a callused palm, placing it gently atop her shoulder, squeezing it lightly. Aunt Eloise stepped out into the yard, climbed into her car, and left.

The news of Candy getting herself pregnant by her mama's boyfriend, a burly, red-faced man named Lionel Jasper, proved too much for Aunt Eloise to bear. Her own disappointment and embarrassment destroyed her spirit, ripping any love for life from her. The baby boy that Daddy James named Louis Elliott Tucker died with his mother during an intense labor that left my grandfather weeping for his only girl child and her stillborn son. Neither Candy, nor Lionel Jasper showed up for Aunt Eloise's funeral when we buried her and her baby next to Uncle Chauncey, the sweet scent of blooming lilacs and freesia wafting through the air.

Two weeks after her mother's death Candy gave birth to a baby girl that she named Precious Alexander. I'd not been privy to the conversation between Candy and Daddy James when he went to see her and his great-granddaughter at the hospital. I only knew that Daddy James agonized over it for months after, most especially when Candy and her baby left Creekton, not even bothering to come say goodbye.

****

Tossing and turning in my bed, I thought about the suffering that goes along with someone dying. When the lives of loved ones are lost, it changes time, as though the hands of a clock are torn from its center, twisted and turned about, then replaced. Time ticks on, but nothing else remains the same. Daddy James and I suffered through Uncle Chauncey and Aunt Eloise dying. There was no more that we could possibly do. I clung to Daddy James, and he to me, and we walked each other through the days and nights, which in my young mind had seemed longer than usual.

After Aunt Eloise's funeral, Uncle Titus moved himself away, stopping to linger first in Tennessee, and then Mississippi. His last letter had come from some small town in Maryland where he'd found work and was settling down for the moment. He felt responsible for Uncle Chauncey's death, blamed himself for not being there. Blamed his going to see some portly woman with large breasts who lived down on the edge of town. It had been one of very few times he'd not asked Chauncey to go with him.

Blaming himself tore Uncle Titus up more than having Chauncey dead did. We'd watched as he let it eat away at his soul and everyday a small piece of him was gone from us until there was very little of him left at all. Daddy James was the one who finally told him to pack his bags and leave. Creekton held too many memories for Titus and guilt kept forcing him to hold on to all of them. We sent him off, and when he returned home, he came back in a mahogany casket lined roughly in cream-colored satin.

The day we got word that Uncle Titus had suffered a heart attack and had succumbed to its stagnant malady began my summer of ugly. Laughter no longer danced in the fields as I sought solace in moods of black and melancholy. Dark dwelling places of misery became my constant companions as the sun outside shimmered without me. I found no splendor in living and overwhelming silence swirled within my thirteen-year-old mind.

Daddy James' heart had grown heavier and heavier with each child he'd lost, and there was nothing I could do to lift the weight from his spirit. Being unable to help, I found myself adding to his burdens. I was not his child, I thought, as putrid words spilled out of my mouth, tainted curses of an adolescent's rude and nasty behavior.

Hope was found only in the letters that I continued to write to Manroot, my scribbly handwriting on yellow-lined paper. I cried my eyes on those pages, ink seeping with teenage uncertainty and anxiety. The line of my handwriting ached for his feathery kisses against my cheeks and the weight of his arms around me. He never answered though, unless it was just a brief paragraph scrawled at the bottom of a note to Daddy James, and then his words were always the same. *He loved me. He missed me. Be a sweet girl for Daddy James.*

I'd ask insignificant questions about what he was doing and if he'd made any friends. I'd even been so bold as to ask if he missed my mama. When there were no answers, I figured not only that he didn't miss her, but that he didn't miss me either. I figured I must have been too painful a reminder of my mother and the curses she'd cast upon us.

I didn't miss my mama. I didn't miss the condemnations that rang in my ears, the screams that thundered through my head. I didn't miss her because she came regularly, continuing to punish me for having been her child. I could no longer find any comfort in the fleeting memories of the woman who had on rare occasions smiled a sweet smile at me as she brushed her hands against my hair. The few soft songs that she had hummed in my ear when it stormed, when I was afraid of the thunder, had faded into silence. The one or two memories of Lavinia that were faintly warm for me, fading snapshots in black and white, were few and far between and I no longer searched hungrily for them.

As age, puberty, and the inevitable passing of time fought for control over my body, everything about me began to change. The nonexistent breasts that had been a source of much concern bloomed to a full 34C-cup brassiere. Seemingly overnight, baby fat shifted to long, lean legs, full hips, and a pencil-thin waist. I didn't recognize the young woman who stared back at me from the mirror. There was no longer any comfort in my own skin. Sometimes I would stand and stare at my own reflection and question why God was pushing my body in the directions it was going.

What had I done to bring this curse upon myself? What had been my crime?

With each new day I couldn't help but wonder what difference a mother's presence would have made. Would Lavinia have made it better, bringing some understanding so that it didn't feel so unnatural? Would she have been there to share her maternal wisdom and engage me in mother-daughter activities, or would our conversations still be filled with her slaps and my screams?

Insult to injury were the old men down at the corner who sat around drinking warm beer all day and telling lies about jobs they were not planning on going to and women they would never marry. They had started whistling and calling my name every time I walked by them. It made me nervous and there was no one to explain to me why. I felt awkward and ugly and I longed for the little girl who'd felt safe and secure in her little girl body. Sometimes I even wished for Aunt Eloise to be there to tell me what to do and how to do it.

When the boys at school started to act strangely toward me, I crawled farther into my shell, wanting nothing more than to be able to steal away into a hole and disappear. Had I been able to just sit on the front porch and rock the time away, everything would have been all right. But I couldn't and things weren't. I wanted to trust that Daddy James would do whatever was in his power to make things well. Since he trusted God, I couldn't help but hope that I would somehow benefit from the shelter of that umbrella. Whatever was happening to me didn't feel as if it was going to stop and if I had to put my faith in anyone, Daddy James would win hands down. I knew Daddy James would keep me as safe from harm as he could, but I still wished for my daddy to come back and call me Beauty.

His footsteps creaked against the wooden steps of the back porch. Peering out the back window I watched as Daddy James brushed his work boots against the floor mat, his hand paused against the doorknob. I marveled at how old he suddenly appeared. The gray had thickened throughout his hair, blending the few dark strands away into nothing. He smiled half a smile as he eased inside the doorway, pushing the latch closed behind him.

"Is everything all right?" he asked, lifting his eyebrows in my direction.

I nodded my head yes, my hands swimming beneath the soapy water in the kitchen sink. Newly washed dishes lay drying on the countertop to my right.

He nodded, reaching into the refrigerator for the plastic pitcher of cold water. "I'm tired tonight, Black. I think I'm gonna go to bed early."

I cleared my throat, reaching for a dishtowel.

"Daddy, I need some money, please."

He turned toward my direction, a half-full water glass clasped firmly in his hand. "Money for what?"

"I need to buy me some stuff."

"What stuff?"

I heaved a heavy sigh. "Just some stuff from the drugstore."

Daddy James pulled out a kitchen chair and sat down, his fingers still wrapped around his glass. He pursed his lips as though to whistle, blowing warm breath past his lips instead. "What kind of stuff, Black?"

Humiliation tempered my emotions. "Girl stuff. Just some things I need," I said quickly, impatience tainting my tone.

The man nodded his head slowly. "Don't play games with me, Black. I give you everything you need and there's not much you want that you don't get either. But I don't give my money away on *stuff* I don't know about."

I shifted my weight awkwardly, moving from one foot to the other. "Sanitary pads. I need to go buy myself some sanitary pads." My voice was hardly a whisper as the words spilled quickly out of my mouth.

Daddy James nodded again, the muscles in his face barely quivering. "You done got your monthly?"

I nodded, the color creeping rapidly into my cheeks.

He continued to nod glancing down to the watch on his wrist. "You need me to take you to the store now? They should still be open for another hour or so."

I shook my head no. "I'm okay until tomorrow. The school nurse gave me some for tonight. I'll go to the store right after school."

Daddy James rose to his feet, pushing in his chair. "I'll leave you some money on the table in the morning," he said, heading out the door.

I turned back to the sink, wishing for a hole in the floor that I could drop into.

Daddy James called out to me from the stairwell. "Is you feeling okay, Black? Nothing hurt you, does it?"

"No, sir, I'm fine."

I could feel him nodding his head. "Hot tea always made your grandma Lucy feel better when it was her time of the month. Lots of hot tea. I'll make you some if you want."

"I'm fine, Daddy, thank you."

As his footsteps faded off into the distance, tears sprang to my eyes. The moment had almost been as bad as having the offending curse drop in Mrs. Moss's math class right before fifth period history. I'd struggled to hide the telltale signs behind a cable-knit sweater wrapped tightly around my waist, barely making it to the nurse's office for assistance. And while I'd thought the world was lost to me, Daddy James had barely batted an eyelash, wanting to do nothing more than make me feel better with a cup of tea.

We were in the elbow of an Indian summer, the daily temperatures reaching record highs for the autumn of the year. Outside, the fragrance of newly cut hay and green grass filled the air, and the two new horses my grandfather had won at auction were grazing out in the pastures. Daddy James and I had finagled a day of hooky, him passing the chores off to a newly hired farm hand and me staying home for school in honor of *Taking Your Child To Work* day. Together we sat watching the horses from our seat in the center of the pond.

With every move either of us dared to make, the rickety rowboat beneath us rocked from side to side, and so we both sat still and silent, staring out to the fields where the two Palominos grazed lazily. Sweat poured down Daddy James' face as the sun above us painted both our complexions from dark to darker.

My grandfather shook his head, swiping at the perspiration that lined his brow. "This is crazy, Black."

"No, it's not, Daddy. It's hot, but it's nice out here. There's a nice breeze blowing."

"So, what are we sitting here for again?"

I sighed, angling my body around to look into Daddy James' face. The boat waved threateningly and Daddy James reached to grip the side.

"We're supposed to be talking without any disruptions. This is supposed to be our chance to share things with each other that we might have been afraid to before or just didn't think we should say. We're supposed to be communicating our feelings."

Daddy James chuckled. "Oh, I thought this was going to be like them tea parties you use to make me sit through when you were little."

"Daddy!" Exasperation filled the air around me.

"So talk then. What do you want to talk about?"

"I don't know," I said shrugging my shoulders upward.

A flash of annoyance crossed the old man's face and he heaved a deep sigh. "We really don't have time for this, Black. Now, either make your point or we can get out of this boat and go get some work done." He shifted his gaze back toward the horses. "Let's talk about you, then. What is it you think I've never communicated to you?"

I noted the faint touch of sarcasm that coated his words. I rolled my eyes skyward. "Please don't tease me."

"I wasn't teasing. Obviously you have something on your mind and I'm just trying to get to the bottom of it so I can get out of this boat before I have to swim back to shore."

The expression gracing the old man's face made me laugh as I shook my head from side to side. "Do you ever wish I'd been born a boy, Daddy?" I finally asked, trying to be serious.

"No. Why are you asking?"

"Sometimes I wish I'd been born a boy. Boys have it easier."

"Not really. Boys have the same troubles you girls have."

I sighed, lowering my gaze to my lap as I twiddled my fingers against my lap. "Billy Joyner tried to kiss me. When I told him no he pulled my tube top down in front of the whole class during assembly."

"Pratt Joyner's boy Billy?"

I nodded, taking a quick glance up to meet my grandfather's gaze.

"What you do when he done that?"

"I punched him in the face and bloodied up his nose. His mama said she was gone call you. She said it was my fault. Said I was teasing Billy and that made him do what he done."

"Do you believe that?"

"No, sir. I didn't do anything to Billy to make him act like a fool. He done that all on his own."

Daddy James nodded his head slowly. The boat floated over the surface of the water, moving only with the light breeze that blew through the air. "That's your body, Black. Don't any man have the right to be putting his hands on your body without your permission. You did right. Billy or any other boy put their hands on you the wrong way you bust them as hard as you can, then come get me. Don't you worry none about that boy's mama. She don't have to call me 'cause I will be calling her. I'll set her straight about that bad ass child of hers. I promise you he won't be putting his hands no place they don't belong when I'm through."

"If I'd been born a boy wouldn't nobody be putting their hands on me like that."

Daddy James sat silent, not responding.

"I don't like being a girl, Daddy. It's too hard," I whispered.

"Nothing comes easy, Black. A boy turning into a man is just as hard. Different maybe, but just as hard. I guess if your grandma Lucy or your mama were around it would be easier for you to understand all the changes you're going through. I might not be able to explain it all like they probably would, but don't you ever forget that you can ask and tell me anything and you don't ever need to be afraid."

"Daddy?"

"Yes, Black?"

"Can we go buy me a larger bra?"

Daddy James smiled. "Black, you think you got enough stuff to be putting into a bra?"

"Daddy!" My look was incredulous as I blushed profusely.

My grandfather laughed. "Yeah, girl, we'll go as soon as you get me out this here boat. And while we're at it we should probably get me a new shotgun."

"A shotgun?"

"Yeah, for all them fresh boys I'm gone have to put some buckshot to."

I grinned, and the ocean of water beneath us washed joy from my grandfather's heart to mine.

There were twenty-seven students in Mrs. Holloway's eighth grade homeroom class. Twenty-seven of us preparing to graduate from the middle school up to the newly refurbished Creekton High School. There were sixteen girls, eleven boys, nine blacks, seventeen whites, and me, the biracial kid who was considered too black to be white and too white to be black. I was the anomaly that didn't quite fit in anywhere.

The devil himself didn't know what evil was if he'd never had the privilege of spending one school day with a group of teenaged girls. The epitome of cruel came embodied in hip-hugging jeans and tee shirts that pulled taut against newly acquired bust lines.

"Oreo! Oreo!" The chant vibrated across the schoolyard.

I ignored the taunts. I always ignored them having grown use to the abrasive jeers that had come with relative frequency since the first day of kindergarten. Brenda Mallory led the pack, the young woman's bite as vicious as her bark. She stood six inches taller and some twenty pounds heavier than the rest of us. Most of the girls and even a few of the boys were scared of her and rightly so. Brenda could be more vicious than a rabid dog on the attack and no one wanted to be on the receiving end of her torment.

Everything about Brenda was dark, from the tightly curled locks of her black hair, past the deep ebony tone of her complexion, to the very depths of her angry personality. I had no clue what haunted Brenda but I'd sensed early on that whatever it was had painted her spirit a deep, dank shade of bitter and unhappy.

"You think you cute, don't you?" Brenda hissed, reaching to tug harshly on my ponytail. "Think you cute with your white girl hair."

I rolled my eyes in defiance, silence my only other response. Our gazes were locked tightly, one waiting for the other to show an ounce of weakness.

"Well, you ain't. You ain't nothing but a dirty half breed," Brenda quipped, looking to the girls who stood in servitude at her side. "Is she cute, Elaine?" she asked, her gaze resting on last week's victim.

Elaine Purdy, a too-thin redhead with overly large eyes, ears, and a bust line that rivaled most pinup models, shook her head, the appendage bobbing against her neck like a loose hinge. There was sadness in her eyes as she looked at me. We both knew if she didn't respond to Brenda's liking, the girl would turn on her without taking a second to blink.

Brenda shouted. "What did you say, Elaine? I didn't hear you."

"She ain't cute," Elaine said, shrugging her shoulders as she pushed her hands deep into the pockets of her denim jeans.

Brenda grinned, the wide smile punctuated with ugliness. She spun around her heels, headed toward the school lunchroom. "Janay thinks she's too cute to eat lunch with us, so ain't no one gonna eat lunch with her today. No one," she commanded as the others followed like sheep behind her.

I heaved a deep sigh, watching as they left me standing alone. I watched as they entered the building one by one. Elaine was the only girl to turn back, tossing a quick glance over her shoulder, her gaze meeting mine ever so briefly before she too disappeared inside.

****

Without even looking I could feel his gaze caressing me, long even strokes that ran like a cool breeze up and down the length of my teenage frame. Out of the corner of my eye I could see the Reverend Robert T. Prescott watching me a tad too closely. Reverend Prescott's stare was always a tad too close. A woman knows what a man wants when his longing seeps past the crystal of his eyes, glazing them ever so lightly. And I knew exactly what the good minister wanted as my gaze met his and held it. It had become a dangerous game Reverend Prescott and I played, this touching with our eyes. A game the good Mrs. Prescott would not find to be remotely entertaining.

I knew that if I stood there for any length of time he would find his way over to my side to lean just a whisper away from me, much too close for anyone's comfort. I had successfully avoided the attention of Reverend Prescott on each and every occasion I was made to be in his presence. With each passing Sunday, the task became more daunting. I also knew that it would take quick thinking on my part to continue to do so tonight. I had heard my name being called more times than I cared to count and I knew that the good Reverend Prescott was doing all in his power to volunteer my services for some function that would inevitably force me to be alone with him.

Now, I had no fear of what Reverend Prescott might or might not do were we to be alone. In fact, I knew fully what his intentions were if we were ever to find ourselves secreted away from prying eyes. What I feared most was that I would take too much pleasure in the kind of attention the Reverend intended to offer. Lusting after the church's pastor was one thing. I knew that I was not the only one who found the attractive black man to be easy on the eyes. Many of the church sisters sought the good minister's attention with batting eyelashes, skirts that fit a hint too tight, and the pretense of a problem that only his good ministry could help them resolve. Acting on that lust though would be something very different and it would definitely make for Thursday night gossip at choir practice. I did not dare put myself into the position of having to explain my behavior to Daddy James. I was hopeful that Sister Olivia Bradsher was going to be my saving grace this particular night.

"Janay," she called out, coming to stand by my side. "How are you doing, baby?"

"Just fine, thank you," I responded, giving her my full attention.

Sister Olivia shook her head from side to side. "Reverend Prescott was just saying that you would be the perfect person to help organize our Youth Day program this year."

I smiled politely as she continued.

"Reverend Prescott thought that it would be a wonderful idea for you to become more involved in some of the church's activities. Your grandfather already does more than his share and you need to set an example for all the younger girls who look up to you for guidance. What you think about that?"

I brushed my hair out of my eyes. "Well, I'm very flattered. I surely would like to, but with my school schedule, and work, and taking care of Daddy James, I'm not sure I'd be able to do the program justice. It might be wiser to ask someone who has more time to put into it. It was very nice of Reverend Prescott to think of me, though."

I could feel the warmth of Reverend Prescott's hand against my shoulder as he came to stand by my side. I smiled politely, a faint shiver running down the length of my arm.

"Is Janay being uncooperative, Sister Olivia?" he asked, grinning broadly.

Miss Olivia giggled lightly. "Not Janay, Reverend. Deacon Tucker has raised her right. She's a sweet, sweet girl."

Reverend Prescott nodded, his hand squeezing ever so lightly. "I agree, Sister. I'm one of Janay's biggest fans."

Smiling politely, I turned to face Reverend Prescott, extricating myself from his grasp. "Both of you are too kind, Reverend, but I was just saying to Miss Olivia that I don't think I would be able to help with the Youth Day program and do it justice with all my other commitments."

"Nonsense, Janay. I keep telling you that you need to give as much to your church as you do to everything else you're involved in. I think you would do a fine job with the program. In fact, why don't you come by my office tomorrow afternoon and we can discuss it in greater detail."

I smiled weakly, the wheels spinning excuses, one behind the other, in my mind. At that moment

Daddy James made his way over to my side, as Reverend asked for the second time about me meeting him the following day.

"That shouldn't be no problem, pastor. Janay can come right after school," the old man said, his head bobbing his approval.

I nodded my assent, forcing a wider smile across my face as the other two stood staring at me. Reverend Prescott winked his eye.

"Well, Black, you ready to head home yet?"

"Yes, sir," I nodded, grabbing my grandfather's large hand. "Good-night, Reverend. Good-night, Miss Olivia," I said, fighting not to look Reverend Prescott in the eye.

"I'll see you tomorrow, Janay," Reverend Prescott responded, as he shook hands with Daddy James. Reaching out to squeeze my shoulder one last time, his eyes whispered at me brazenly, blowing a chill straight down my spine.

White Rock Baptist Church had been organized in 1906, in the home of Mrs. Margaret Faucette, following a series of house-to-house prayer meetings conducted by her second husband, Reverend Jessie Faucette. The building itself was a grand, white-brick structure that sat on a six-acre tract of land donated to them from my great-great-great grandfather. The church's name had come from the large, white flint rock that had been found in the front yards during the start of excavation. Some fourteen pastors, and close to two million dollars later, the church now boasted a reconfigured chancel, improved lighting, refurbished cedar pews, a state-of-the-art audio-visual system, new baptismal pool, a grand piano, a Moeller-Letourneau pipe organ, and magnanimous stained glass windows.

Reverend Prescott's grandfather, the church's eleventh pastor, had initiated the original changes to White Rock's two-room sub-structure. Reverend Prescott, Jr. had taken it to the next level, his visions a direct reflection of his own swollen ego and inflated sense of self-worth. Reverend Robert T. Prescott, III, had amassed wealth and prestige for the institution that would have put the efforts of both his kin to shame.

I had dragged myself into his office that afternoon, the smile across my face fading as the church secretary, a portly woman with dimpled cheeks and over-processed hair, passed by me, heading for the church's parking lot.

"Gots to go run some errands for the pastor, Janay," Miss Cotton smiled as she gave me a quick hug. "Shouldn't be gone too long."

Reverend Prescott stood watching from the doorway. "Janay and I'll be just fine, Sister Cotton. Not to worry. You just take your time."

Sister Cotton waved a quick goodbye as she scurried down the short length of corridor and out the side entrance. Reverend Prescott's gaze glistened as he reached for my arm, locking one hand against my forearm and the other around my shoulder.

"So, how was school today, Janay?" he asked sweetly, tilting his head slightly as we walked into the office sanctuary.

"It was fine, thank you, sir."

He nodded, still holding tightly to me. "I'm thrilled to be working with you. You're one of our most promising young ladies. We're all very proud of you."

I smiled ever so slightly, finally pulling out of his grasp and dropping into one of the cushioned chairs in front of his desk.

"Why don't you come sit here on the sofa with me," he said, gesturing toward the small floral loveseat that sat against the rear wall.

"This is fine, sir. I can't stay long. Daddy James is expecting me."

The man smiled a wide smile as he sat himself down, crossing his legs evenly. He clasped his hands together in his lap. Reverend's voice filled the small room. Its deep vibrato seemed to caress the lemon-scented air, coating the walls with its husky sensuality as he began to explain what would be required of me. His tone was even and controlled, just shy of being mellow, a bedroom bass that was as far removed from his preacher's persona as one could ever imagine it being. Had he ever used that tone for Sunday sermon, every woman in the congregation would have lost her religion.

I nodded my head as he continued to speak and responded as required, my answers limited to yes's and no's. My gaze flitted between his face and the clock on the wall as I wished for Sister Cotton to knock on the door announcing her return. Reverend's stare was burning, the heat of it lighting a low flame beneath me that I had no control of.

The man came to his feet, easing himself behind me. His hands dropped down against my shoulders, his fingers gentle kneading the tense flesh. Leaning to whisper into my ear, he called my name, and told me what a beautiful girl I was. No one had called me beautiful since my daddy.

Reverend Prescott whispered a lot that afternoon, offering religious rhetoric to explain his perverse version of the birds and the bees, and how God had shown him personally how I could best serve him by serving the good Reverend's many needs. When Sister Cotton's knock finally sounded against the closed door, it couldn't have come too soon. Reverend Prescott smiled again, the bend of his full lips gliding over pearl-white teeth. "We were just finishing, Sister," Reverend said as the woman pushed open the door and stepped inside. "I think we're off to a great start. Don't you, Janay?" he said, squeezing my shoulder gently.

I nodded again, my head still bobbing up and down. "Yes, sir."

Sister Cotton grinned. "That's some good news. I'm sure we'll have a nice program for the congregation. It's good to get our young people so involved. You'll set a good example for them, Janay."

Reverend Prescott winked again as he guided me toward the door, his arm draped casually across my shoulder. "We should meet again tomorrow, Janay. We'll decide on your committee, help you start planning your agendas, setting up your meetings and get you rolling. I'm sure by the end of the week you'll be able to take charge all on your own."

My mouth opened and closed like a guppy out of water, sucking in air. No sound escaped as I struggled to respond.

Sister Cotton smiled again. "We'll see you tomorrow, Janay. Give your grandfather my regards, dear."

"Yes, ma'am," I finally managed as I hurried out of the room.

Days later, the man's kisses were cool sprays of mist as the light stroke of his hand trickled up and down the length of my sixteen-year-old body. It was not supposed to feel so good I thought, trying to let reason intrude upon my rising emotions. As I felt his lips brush against the curve of my breasts, down the flat of my stomach, toward my quivering thighs, I shuddered, all control lost. If I were not already headed for hell, I had surely opened the door and begun my descent down the path toward purgatory, I thought. Although I had most enjoyed the beginning flirtations with Reverend Prescott, this was very different. This felt too good to be right for anyone.

Somewhere in the distance, I could hear someone moaning. It was a low hum, rising from some dark place into the open air. As my back arched toward the ceiling, I realized the sounds were coming from my own mouth, rising from the pith of my midsection. Reverend Prescott was kind enough to silence the loud echo with his own lips pressed against mine.

I watched as he shed his clothes, his honey-brown skin beaded with perspiration. Reverend Prescott had an athletic body, taut muscles stretching over large bones. He didn't look a day close to his forty-plus years, his chiseled features and picture-perfect smile giving him the magnetic aura of a big-screen movie star and not a Baptist minister.

The sofa that supported my body seemed to grow smaller and smaller as I suddenly wished I could shrink and disappear down between the cushions. How had I gotten myself into this predicament? Better still, how was I going to get myself out of it?

Reverend Prescott breathed heavily into my ear, the length of his body pressed against mine. As he pulled anxiously at my clothes, panic set in, anxiety sweeping from the top of my head to the bottom of my feet. I pushed against him, summoning all the strength I could find to shove him away. But when he whispered my name down the length of my neck and his hands warmed the cold chill against my flesh, weakness wrapped my arms around him, pulling him close instead.

A ray of sunlight peeked through the stained glass window of his office as Reverend Prescott penetrated the virginal cavity. It was a blue angel who hovered in disappointment above us, the expression that graced her face seeming to voice a mountain of displeasure. Tracing the line of light along the colored glass with my mind's eye I lifted myself above the heavy weight that dripped of sweat against my chest, ignoring the faint trickle of blood that splashed against my thighs. At that very moment, if I'd possessed an ounce of belief in prayer, I would have said one for Reverend Prescott who I thought needed it more than I ever would.

The scandal rocked the congregation. When Daddy James came home that Wednesday night from an emergency meeting of church elders, I could see the disappointment painted across his face. He sat sullen in his favorite chair, a faded brown rocker that had worn skid marks against the wooden floor. I was too afraid to ask what was bothering him, but I had to know what was being said.

He sat staring into a raging fire, a tobacco-filled pipe pressed to his lips. There was an unnatural twitch around his left eye and every so often, he'd brush at his face with the back of his hands as though fanning away a fly. The curiosity was overwhelming.

"What's wrong, Daddy?"

His eyes met mine, then drifted back into the fire. I sat down beside him waiting for him to speak. Guilt swept through me and I debated whether or not

I should just go ahead and confess. Fear was raging a vicious battle in the pit of my stomach.

"What was the meeting about?"

Daddy James sighed, then reached out a wrinkled appendage to stroke the top of my head.

"Seems Reverend Prescott done gone and got into some serious trouble. The church voted to remove him as pastor tonight. In fact, he should be leaving town soon if he ain't already left."

I bit my lower lip. "What did he do?"

Daddy James paused, his gaze falling to the flicker of fire that burned in the fireplace. "Reverend forgot that he's a man of God who's supposed to be doing God's work. And we folks all forgot that he ain't no savior. He's just a man."

"He sinned?"

My grandfather shook his head. "What he done was a crime, Black. An out and out crime. A sin can be forgiven. A crime has consequences and Reverend is facing them consequences now."

"But he's done so much for the church, hasn't he? Can't the church forgive whatever it is he's done?"

His gaze met mine. "If the church lets this go, Black, then that says we care more about the building and the money than we do about the virtue of our young people. Ain't no man I'm gone pray beside is ever going to trade his daughter for no church building or bank account. Not while I'm a deacon on the board. And not while I have something to say about it."

I asked again. "What did he do, Daddy? Please tell me."

"You know that Bean girl? Arnetta?"

I shook my head yes. Arnetta and I were in the same gym class and I think we'd even had a sewing class together once.

"Well, Arnetta's gone and got herself pregnant. She says Reverend Prescott is the baby's daddy and he confessed to spoiling her."

I sat stunned, disbelief dripping off my brow. "Reverend Prescott's been messing around with Arnetta Bean?"

Daddy James shook his head yes. "Now, I don't want you saying nothing to your little friends at school. You don't need to be disrespecting Arnetta. It ain't her fault. Reverend Prescott took advantage of her."

I inhaled deeply. "It's not like she couldn't have said no. She could have told someone." There was an edge to my voice that I did not recognize.

Daddy James eyed me curiously, leaning forward in his chair. "Would you have told someone, Black?"

I met his stare with my own, then turned to study the fire. I shrugged my shoulders, pushing the tight muscles up toward the beamed ceiling. "I don't know."

Daddy James' eyes scanned the lines of my profile, sketching his own mental picture of my reflection. I exhaled, pushing anger and jealousy past a subtle pout.

"Did Reverend Prescott ever get fresh with you, Black?"

I shook my head from side to side, still reading the reds and golds that danced in the fireplace. "No," I lied.

"Are you sure?"

I flipped a quick glance at Daddy James' face, not wanting to meet his eyes. "I said no."

Daddy James sat back in his chair, his expression edged in ice. "Well, I hope I done taught you better than that, Black. Don't you let no man disrespect you. If you needs to be laying up with some man then you makes sure he willing to marry you first. If you don't want to hear it from me, you learn your lesson from Eloise. I don't need to tell you again 'bout that trash she went and laid up with, come back home here with Candy like she was something common. Then Candy going off and doing the same thing."

I pushed the wisps of hair out of my face, behind my ear. "I said no. I ain't been laying up with nobody." My tone was bitter, coated with deception. Daddy James could hear it in the inflection of my words.

Daddy James slammed his fist against the mahogany table by his side. I jumped, turning to stare up at him. "Don't you go shaming me, Black. I won't have it," he shouted, wagging his index finger at me like a loose hinge. "Don't you go shaming this family like Eloise and Candy done. You too special for that."

Storming to his feet Daddy James bounded out of the room and through the front door. In the distance, I could hear his old pickup truck thunder down the dirt road, headed toward the parsonage. The quiet in the room grew louder, rising off the walls like a thick morning mist. The warmth of the fire was all-inviting as I inched closer to feel the intense heat against my skin.

The anger inside was overwhelming as I thought about Reverend Prescott, and Arnetta, and the baby that would soon be coming. I thought about me and the Reverend and the promises I knew to be lies the moment they'd fallen from his mouth. I suddenly felt about as special as the flavor of the month down at the local ice cream parlor. Daddy James had taught me better, I just hadn't acted like it. Pulling the gold crucifix from my neck, I stared at it only briefly before tossing it into the flames.

I had never known such loneliness as when Daddy James had nothing to say to me, barely raising an eye in my direction. Silence walked a slow path between us, the words shared only polite greetings as we passed through each day. It would have been easier to have had my heart ripped crudely out of my chest.

Three days passed before my endurance ran dry. On the fourth day, I rose early. The sky was still dark, enveloped by thick, luminous clouds. Tossing on a pair of old jeans and a tattered tee shirt, I followed behind my grandfather as he made his way out the front door to tend to the animals. He only nodded in my direction as he pushed a bucket of feed into my hands and pointed me toward the hen house. His hum was soft, barely audible over the morning sunrise.

I worked hard that morning, harder than I had worked in a very long time. By the time all the animals were fed and their enclosures cleaned, I had missed the morning bus to school, but I didn't care. Daddy James stood up on the porch as I walked toward the house, tears tottering at the edges of my eyes.

Daddy James lowered his body to sit on the upper step, clasping his large hands in front of him. He rocked slowly, an easy motion of body muscle sliding to and from. His head, more gray than black, waved in unison, a carefree bob at the end of his thick neck. My tears no longer tottered, spilling freely, like water from a tap. I cried against his knee and only when there were no more tears shaking my body, did I feel his heavy palm brushing the hair from my brow. Reaching to be held I cuddled against his chest and I asked for his forgiveness.

"I'm so sorry, Daddy. I didn't mean to shame you. I swear I didn't."

Daddy James nodded, biting against his lower lip. Lifting my chin, he stared into my eyes. "All my children have made mistakes. It is only when they don't learn from them that I'm ashamed. Why didn't you come to me, Black? Why didn't you tell me 'bout Reverend Prescott bothering with you?"

I dropped my gaze to the dirt beneath my feet, embarrassment wrapping around me.

Daddy James nodded, lifting my chin back into the palm of his hand. His eyes met mine, his look, like a soft tissue, wiping the embarrassment away. "Black, you've grown to be a beautiful woman. There's gone be men who will do and say anything to be laying up with you. You've got to be smart enough to know when they care about you and when they don't. That means you've got to know that what you have is worth waiting for and if a man truly loves you he will wait for you. You don't be giving yourself away to any man who just happens to ask for it. Do you understand?"

I nodded my head yes. Daddy James pulled me down to the step beside him. We sat side by side, neither saying a word, listening to the pattern of each other's breathing. Daddy James finally broke the silence.

"Do you ever pray, Black?"

"No," I answered honestly. "It has never worked for me. I guess I just don't know how to do it right."

Daddy James nodded his head slowly. "You should pray. Prayer can work miracles."

I shrugged my shoulders. "I use to pray that my mama wouldn't be so mean to me, but it would only get worse. Then I use to pray that Manroot would come back home and he never did. I prayed that Uncle Chauncey would be okay and he wasn't. God ain't never answered none of my prayers. God don't care nothing about me."

"God loves you, Black."

I shrugged again. "He sure has a funny way of showing it, Daddy." I wiped away a tear with the back of my hand.

"You still miss your daddy, don't you?"

Rising, I reached out to squeeze Daddy James' hand. "You're my daddy now. Manroot's been gone too long to be anybody's daddy."

Inching past his hulking frame, I leaned down to kiss his cheek before heading toward my room and a hot shower. "I love you," I whispered into his ear. "I love you very much."

"Loves you too, Black," Daddy James answered. "I love you too."

****

Sleeping soundly beside me, Everett shifted his body slightly, wrapping his arms tighter around my body. Outside, moonlight danced a slow drag with the dark sky, the duo moving in sync like age-old lovers. I'd laid awake for hours, afraid to close my eyes. I couldn't help but wonder if Manroot would come to see me in my dreams. Would he be waiting with Lavinia, the cold flow of their blood curdling in my screams? I heaved a deep sigh, easing myself closer into the gulf of my husband's warmth.

Everett snored softly, sleep deeply pressed into the creases along his brow. His mouth hung open ever so slightly, drool puddling at the edges of his lips. His body felt good next to mine and just for a moment I wished him awake, his hands exploring the length of my body, erasing the memories from my mind.

Had Manroot known about Everett? Had he heard the tales that had bought this man into my life and by my side? I wondered just how much Daddy James had bothered to share. Rolling onto my side I continued my trip down memory lane, wondering just how much information about my life my father had been privy to.

I had hated high school. I'd detested the constant struggle to fit in and feel as though I belonged. I did not belong. Everybody knew it, whether they said so or not. I'd not been like other girls who'd had their mama's or grandmama's at home with them and whose daddy's weren't in jail. My parents and the circumstances of their lives placed me outside the cliques and friendships that had seemed to be everyone else's birthright.

Lifting my body out of bed each morning to drag myself to school expended more energy than I possessed. I did it though, detesting the snickers behind my back and my peers who made me feel irrelevant. I was counting the days till graduation, knowing that it would soon be over and I would be able to put it all behind me.

It had been Daddy James' wish for me to leave Creekton and go away to college after graduation. I personally had no desire to leave the farm. I didn't want to leave the land that was mine. I was nourished by the scent of rich earth that greeted me each morning. The swelter of sunshine that gleamed across the green crops filled my spirit with joy. And I didn't believe I could bear to be away from Daddy James. He and I had never been apart and I was terrified that if I left him, he might not be there when I returned. No, come hell or high water, I was not leaving Creekton.

Every morning Earl Bingham would be waiting by my locker, a full grin plastered across his goofy face. Earl and I had been best friends since fifth grade. He and his parents had moved from the center of town to the large farmstead that bordered the vast Tucker acreage on the west end of town. In fact, Earl had been the only friend I'd ever really had. Daddy James and Earl's daddy were both members of the same Masonic lodge, and the camaraderie between the two families went way back, even before Earl and I had been born.

For years I towered over Earl, until the summer between ninth and tenth grades, when Earl sprouted wings and soared sky-high on lean, lanky legs. He was basketball player tall, but exceptionally thin, his too lean frame just pounds shy of being fragile. Thick, coarse curls lay tight against his skull, his large head appearing too heavy for his neck and body. For years, Earl had been awkward and clumsy, and then seemingly overnight, like a butterfly fleeing its cocoon, Earl had blossomed into a secure, confident young man who moved with the grace of a gazelle.

I loved Earl like a brother. We had grown up laughing, falling out into fits of giggles over episodes of *I Love Lucy*, which was Earl's favorite, and *The Carol Burnett Show*, which was mine. Saturday mornings were reserved for Don Cornelius and *Soul Train*, the volume on his television set or mine breaking sound barriers in one of our living rooms. Daddy James would make pancakes, chocolate chip or blueberry, depending on the moon. Earl's mother always cooked French toast with powdered sugar and strawberries during the summer and peaches after the onset of fall.

As Earl and I had both approached adolescence, Earl and his daddy had fallen out and Daddy James had been there to support my friend as much as he'd supported me. I questioned why Earl's daddy had treated him so ugly and Daddy James had said some men couldn't handle knowing their sons had a little sugar in their blood. Earl's daddy had felt that there was something seriously wrong for Earl to prefer books and art over sports and automobiles. My grandfather loved Earl none the less.

Earl and I were both too odd to run with the popular crowds, but had enough family clout to not be total outcasts with the really unpopular kids. We'd found a secure niche with each other and the fit was comfortable. Neither of us questioned the other's motives and there was a level of contentment between us that we had not been able to find with the rest of our peers.

Earl's smile was in full force when he greeted me that Tuesday morning. For the first time, in a very long time, I'd not found any comfort in it. In fact, it had quickly worn on my last nerve and I silently wished him away. Anxiety had been pulling at my insides for most of the morning and I sensed something or someone was going to upset the balance of my existence. Daddy James was my only family who had not been snatched from me and I was panicked that I was going to return home to find his body lying dead across the kitchen floor, rigor mortis setting into his limbs.

"Hey, girl. What's up?"

I rolled my eyes. "Earl don't you have some place else to be?"

He continued to grin. "My, my, my, ain't we in a mood today."

I shrugged, sifting through the mess of books and papers that littered the small metal cabinet. "Sorry."

"Guess who I just saw registering in the front office?"

I shrugged again. "I don't know. Who?"

"Wayne Tanner."

I looked up quickly. "Wayne Tanner? But he goes to Central High, doesn't he?"

Earl shook his head. "He's transferring. Starts today. Him and his mama down in the office filling out the papers."

Everyone knew of the infamous Wayne Tanner. He'd been the star basketball player for the opposing high school. He was stereotypical of many young men who longed for promising college careers and possible NBA success. Wayne stood out over all the others because not only was he a gifted talent and a strong athlete, but he had a want for stardom that exuded an energy that could not be missed. Wayne had already staked his claim for celebrity and anyone who'd met him knew it.

Wayne's daddy was a doctor and his mama had been some kind of beauty queen in college, the two having graduated Morehouse and Spelman Colleges at the top of their respective classes. Dr. Tanner had built a thriving medical practice in Creekton, heading up the town's growing hospital. His mother served on more non-profit boards and fund-raising committees than anyone could keep track of and both were constant headlines in the state's who's who of the black elite. Wayne came from what Daddy James called good stock.

Every girl in Creekton had a crush on Wayne Tanner, myself included. Wayne was a tall, burgundy boy with long legs and a muscular frame. Thick, black hair curled in loose body waves on top of his head and deep dimples caved in the crest of his cheeks. He walked with a self-assured swagger. His thin lips pulled into a slow, sweet caress of a smile and his dark, deeply set eyes were mesmerizing. The boys called him the King of Cherry Hill because it was rumored that Wayne had broken in more virgins than most of them would ever be able to count.

I nodded my head slowly, then shrugged my shoulders. Turning my back on Earl, I pretended to be uninterested. "Yeah, well, don't make much difference to me."

Earl's smile transformed into an all-knowing smirk. "Yeah, right. Girl you best get your foot in the door first if you want to catch you some Wayne fever."

"Why you got to be talking stupid for? I am not interested in that boy."

My friend chuckled. "Well, you should be. It ain't like I'm gone marry you once we get out of this place."

"I sure don't need nobody to marry me," I quipped, slamming the locker door for emphasis.

Earl said nothing, falling into step beside me as we ascended the steps to the second floor classroom and history with Mr. Bernard White. On the other side of the closed door, Mr. White's icy stare and our classmate's giggles and smirks greeted our tardiness. My embarrassment was quickly dispelled as the door behind us opened to usher in the illustrious Wayne Tanner.

The silence that greeted his arrival danced in midair, spinning a pirouette beside the faintest of giggles. As Earl dropped comfortably into his seat, my legs would not allow me to bend to mine as my knees locked in place. Spinning around to face him as he walked in, I found myself focused on the tiny black mole that kissed the right side of his chin. His lips were pulled into a broad grin as he passed his admittance papers to Mr. White.

Wayne Tanner was beautiful. My full attention had been captured by his presence, held hostage by his enigmatic smile and air of confidence. His gaze was illuminating, piercing everything in its view. The pale yellow sweater and oversized jeans I wore suddenly felt too small as Wayne looked me up and down, then peered past me to appraise the other girls in the classroom. Mr. White's booming voice pushed the quiet out of my head, spinning my slow motion into warp speed.

"Miss Tucker, is there a problem? Miss Tucker...?"

Widespread laughter slapped me to my senses as I tripped over my own feet into the wooden chair. "No, sir," I whispered, shaking my head vigorously.

Earl looked back over his shoulder, a pencil eraser perched between his teeth. His grin continued to annoy and I flipped him my middle finger. In the seat on the other side of the room, Wayne leaned back in the wooden chair, the chair legs tottering uneasily beneath him. At one point, I thought he'd winked at me until Tanya Williams started giggling softly on my other side. Sighing heavily, I dropped my head into my book and pretended to be interested in the text Mr. White had instructed us to read.

Knots twisted heavily in the pit of my stomach. I felt as though I was going to vomit and I looked anxiously toward Earl whose comforting smile calmed my nerves. He'd known since forever that I'd had a crush on Wayne Tanner, a crush rivaled only by my love for Sidney Poitier and Billy Dee Williams. It was wasted energy spent on too many daydreams and fictitious rendezvous.

Unfortunately boys like Wayne had but one interest in a girl like me. Girls like me, who lacked the confidence to look them in their eyes, and respond to their catcalls and whistles with coquettish wit or spirited humor, only drew their taunts and laughs. Girls like Tanya Williams with her cafe au lait complexion and permed bob, who wore form-fitting skirts and silky blouses, were better suited on the arm of a boy like Wayne.

Tanya's face was always meticulously dressed, the makeup impeccably applied. I wore no makeup, the offending blushes and creams detrimental to my crystal complexion. There also had been no one to show me how to apply the delicate colors across my cheekbones and over my eyes. Even the simplest of lipsticks penciled lightly across my lips appeared harsh. I had made the attempt only once and when my grandfather had laughed, the chuckles rising from his mid-section, I knew my efforts had been fruitless. As he'd wiped the color from my cheeks with a soft washcloth, thoughts of my mother reached out to slap me and I swore never to make that mistake again. Makeup and I were not to be partners. I understood this. Others would just have to accept it.

The end of class could not come fast enough. As the bell sounded in the distance, Wayne and his entourage of new followers headed out the door toward the back ramp where the in-crowd socialized between classes. Earl sidled up beside me shaking his head. My look told him not to utter one word about the likes of Wayne Tanner.

"You going to Spanish?"

I shook my head. "No."

"Why not?"

I shrugged my shoulders. "Don't feel like it. I'm going home."

Earl shook his head and finger at me. "Girl, you better watch yourself. You keep cutting class like you doing and you won't be going nowhere. Shoot, we only got another few months till graduation. Sides, you know that woman gone have a fit if you skip out on her again."

I shrugged again, not really caring. Mrs. Solomon, the illustrious language instructor from the Midwest, and I had not taken to one another since the very first day of class. It had become a battle of wills between us. It was her intent to force me to sit in agony through her classes as she pitted my skills or lack thereof against the students she favored most. It was my intent to insure she had as few opportunities to do so as I could possibly get away with. Thus far, I was ahead on our game, outscoring her at least two to one.

Earl shook his head, rolling his eyes. "So, what you gonna do?"

"I'm going home," I responded, tossing my books into the bottom of my locker. "I don't feel so well."

"I'm gone call you later. We need to talk about this."

"Yeah," I muttered under my breath as he headed off to class. "You call me."

Thirty minutes later I lifted legs of lead weight up the front steps into the house. The fear that consumed me was tangible, a blanket of dread that draped heavily across my shoulders and around my body. I'd not inhaled since passing the rusted mailbox down at the edge of the road. It was Daddy James' booming voice that blew breath back into me.

"Black, what you doing home from school so early for?"

I inhaled deeply, filling my lungs with air. Tears dropped against my cheek. "I didn't feel well so I came home."

"What hurts you?"

I patted my fist between my breasts, the tears spinning into a low sob. "It all hurts, Daddy."

Daddy James nodded his head slowly, lowering the newspaper he was reading to the table. Hanging my head I cried loudly as Daddy James sat watching me. The twitch over his eye started to jump softly. Chewing his bottom lip, he didn't move, making no motion to console me. We both lost track of time and it was not until the elderly man lifted himself from his seat to place the tea kettle onto a flaming burner did either of us realize any time had passed at all. As he reaching around me to pull two large mugs from the cupboard, I heard a low whistle blow over his lips. After dropping the cups onto the table, he pulled out one of the wooden chairs and guided me into the seat. His hand tapped awkwardly against the top of my head, his lips brushing quickly across my forehead.

"We all needs us a good cry every now and then to make it feel better. How you feeling now?"

I shrugged, watching the black of his hands as he filled the two cups with hot water, cream, and spoonfuls of honey. My own hands were a pale contrast beside them.

Daddy James nodded his head. "I cried yesterday and you crying today. I sure hope we both all cried out now."

"You cried?" I asked, lifting my eyes to stare into his.

He nodded yes, pulling the hot mug of tea to his lips. Steam rose from the sweet fluid as he blew cool breath over its surface. "Needs me a cry every now and then too."

"Why did you cry, Daddy?"

Daddy James' hand shook lightly as he placed his cup gently against the table, running his thick index finger along the rim. "Was thinking 'bout your grandma and all my children. Was thinking 'bout how much I miss them all. Thought that was as good a reason to be crying as any."

I nodded my head understanding.

"So, what are you crying 'bout?"

I inhaled again, dropping my gaze to the tabletop. Water brimmed at the edges of my eyes once again. My mouth opened, then closed, as I sputtered like a fish out of water gasping for oxygen. I finally sighed, inhaling deeply to fill my lungs with aroma of our kitchen, relishing the faint scent of nutmeg and cinnamon that had seasoned the apple pie served for dessert the night before. I bit down against the edge of my tongue. When I looked back up into Daddy James' face, the question mark still hanging in his eyes, a gale of melancholy blew thunderously past my lips, filling the room with seventeen years of grief and depression. When I was done, Daddy James and I cried again, tears melding one into the other. Hours later, when we saw the hilarity of our reflections in the large window pane over the back door, the laughter followed, and I suddenly felt as if things could actually be better for me down the road.

Earl lay across the handmade quilt that adorned my twin bed, his size twelve Converse-clad feet hanging over the foot board and off the end of the small bed. I sat curled up on the pillow, a paperback book splayed open in the curve of my lap. I was posed, pretending to read as Earl drew a charcoal pencil across a sheet of white paper, sketching an image that was supposed to be a likeness of me. He would scratch a series of blunt lines, one behind the other, occasionally lifting his gaze to stare up into my face. For a brief second I met his gaze, then dropped my eyes to peek at what he'd drawn.

"That doesn't look nothing like me," I said grinning.

Earl stuck his tongue out in my direction. "No, it actually looks better than you do. Had to help you out a bit."

"Shut up."

"Truth hurts."

I lifted myself from my seat to stand before the full-length mirror that hung against the back of my bedroom door. I studied my reflection as my friend watched me. "Do I really look bad, Earl?"

He laughed, shaking his head from side to side. "Don't play. You know you look good. But you need to take your hair out of the butt tail you keep wearing and maybe put a dress on every now and then. Most days you look like you wearing Daddy James' clothes."

I glanced down to the button-up, plaid, flannel shirt and oversized jeans that I wore, then shrugged. "You think Wayne Tanner would like me if I fixed myself up some?"

"He'd probably like you fine if you didn't. But we won't ever know 'cause I know you ain't never gone say nothing to him. He don't even know you exist."

"I looked stupid in class yesterday. Did you see how I tripped when he came in the room?"

"Everyone saw you trip, Black. But that was yesterday, tomorrow can be different."

"I wish I was more like Tanya and them other girls."

"You're better than that lot and you know it."

"But they know how to talk to the boys, and did you see how Wayne was looking at her?"

Earl rolled his eyes. "I thought he was looking at me." He reached a hand up to fluff the Afro on his head. Not all the boys be looking at you trashy girls."

I tossed him a look that said I didn't find that funny and he laughed, bemused by my annoyance. My hands reached for the elastic band that held the strands of my hair at the nap of my neck and pulled it loose until my hair fell down past my shoulders. Earl shifted against the bed, leaning up on his elbow to stare harder.

"See, you'd look better if you loosened up some."

At that moment, the bedroom door swung open and Daddy James stepped inside. He eyed Earl, and then me, then nodded his head slowly as he opened the door wider.

"What's going on in here?" he asked, his stare resting on Earl.

I shrugged again. "Nothing, Daddy."

"We were just hanging around, sir," Earl said as he sat up quickly.

Daddy James nodded again.

"Daddy, do you think I'd look better with my hair down?"

My grandfather came to stand behind me in the mirror, studying the reflection that I'd been staring at. Without responding, he turned back toward Earl, reaching for the sketchpad in the boy's hand. His gaze moved from the drawing, to me, and back again.

"Very nice, Earl."

"Thank you, sir."

"You still looking to go to art school after graduation?"

"Yes, sir."

"You need to talk to Black. I ain't heard her say nothing about going to college. What kind of influence have you been?"

Earl stared hard, not sure if my grandfather really wanted an answer.

Daddy James chuckled softly as he passed the drawing back to Earl. He directed his comments in my direction. "You need to be thinking about your education, not your hair. Your looks aren't what's going to take you places. You might be a real beauty queen today, but one day you gone be old and gray just like me. Then your looks won't mean a thing."

"You might be old and gray but you still look good, Daddy."

My grandfather cut his eyes in my direction, a smirk gracing his face. "I do now, don't I?"

I grinned. "Earl said I need to fix myself up so I can find me a husband 'cause he don't plan to marry me."

Daddy James laughed loudly. "Is that right?"

The color drained from Earl's mahogany face as his mouth dropped open, surprised that I'd say such a thing in front of my grandfather. He stammered, searching for words. "I...I mean...I didn't..."

Daddy James laughed harder. "That's okay, boy. I wouldn't marry her either. Black can't cook a lick. You'd go hungry."

Earl tossed me a look of sheer exasperation, embarrassment still gracing his face. I stuck my tongue out at him, then laughed with my grandfather.

Daddy James crossed back to the door, reaching for the knob to close it behind him. "Earl, you need to be out my house before dark and get them feet off that quilt. Black's grandma Lucy made that quilt and I know your mama taught you better."

"Yes, sir."

Earl hurled his pencil in my direction as the door closed behind my grandfather.

"You're not funny," he hissed just before breaking out into laughter. "You know your granddaddy scares me to death."

"Daddy James wouldn't hurt you, boy."

"I know, but I sure 'nuff don't want to do nothing that might disappoint him. Daddy James has been good to me. Better than my own daddy."

A look of sadness crossed my best friend's face and as I watched him turn back to his drawing, I couldn't help but let the memory of my own daddy wash over me.

****

The ringing telephone pulled me from the comfort of my rocking chair, off the front porch, and into the foyer. Daddy James followed, standing in the doorway, waiting to see if the call was for him.

"Hello?"

"Hey, is this Janay?"

"Yes, it is." My expression was one of confusion as I struggled to identify the voice on the other end of the line. "Who's this?"

"Hey, this here's Wayne. Wayne Tanner. How are you doing?"

I inhaled sharply suddenly afraid I'd drop the telephone to the freshly waxed floor as nervous energy shook my body. I swallowed hard, searching for my voice, my gaze flitting between my grandfather's face and the telephone.

"Hey? You still there?"

"Yes...yes. I'm sorry. I'm fine. How are you doing?"

Daddy James eyed me curiously, then turned, and headed back out the door. I watched from the window as he eased himself off the porch, heading toward the fields.

"I'm good. Look, I don't mean to be bothering you or nothing, but Mr. White thought that you might be able to help me."

"Help you? With what?"

"I gots to pass this history class or I ain't gone graduate. My mama and daddy say I need to get me a tutor and Mr. White said you'd be the best one to give me a hand. I'm willing to pay. I've got to graduate. I plan on going to Chapel Hill to play basketball next year."

"Is that the only reason you want to go to college, to play ball? Did you get a scholarship or something?"

"No. But I like ball, and I'm good, and if I decide I want to go pro, Carolina's one of the best places to showcase my talent."

"Sounds like a waste to me. Carolina has a great academic program. One of the best."

"Maybe, maybe not. You gonna help me or what?"

I nodded my head into the receiver, a smile pulling at my lips. "I guess so, but you don't have to pay me nothing. I don't mind giving you a hand."

"Thanks. I'd really appreciate it. Do you think we can start tomorrow?"

"Sure. I can come to your house if you want or you can come here?"

"Why don't you come here so my folks know I really done got me a tutor. I got a car so we can come right after school, if that's okay with you?"

I nodded again, clenching the receiver tightly within my palm. "That's fine. I'll ask my grandfather to come get me so you won't have to bring me home."

"Whatever. Won't be no problem either way. Well, I guess I'll see you tomorrow. Bye, Janay."

Replacing the receiver, I broke out first into a broad smile, then into a panic and sweat. How would I ever survive being alone with Wayne Tanner? Pulling the telephone back into my hand, I dialed Earl. When he answered I begged him to come over. When I was assured he was on his way and that I had nothing to worry about, I raced toward the fields to share my news with Daddy James.

The next day, the lengthy ride to Wayne's home was a quiet one. He had stopped trying to make conversation when we'd passed the intersection between Route 70 and Interstate 86. I assumed it was difficult to maintain a dialogue with someone who would only answer "yeah", "uh huh", and "I guess".

Perspiration painted my palms and I nervously pulled them back and forth over the skirt I wore. The black leather mini and matching vest were borrowed items from Earl's older sister's closet, being more feminine than anything I owned. The fit was flattering, but left much to be desired in the way of comfort. The afternoon heat was intense as I felt the puddles forming under the black pantyhose I wore. The bright sun had turned my hair a golden brown with very blond highlights and the full mane fell in wet wisps against my neck and back. Pulling it back into a ponytail, I twisted it into a tight bun, knotting the thick strands into a neat roll. I could feel Wayne watching me out of the corner of his eye.

"I like your hair. It's real pretty."

I smiled slightly. "Thanks."

"You got white in you or something?"

I cut my eye in his direction, my lips pulled into a thin line.

"I mean you got really good hair. I can tell you don't ever have to put no perm in it or nothing to get it straight. Besides, you got a lot of yellow in your skin."

I shrugged. "My mama was white."

He nodded. "Is it true what they say? Did your Daddy really kill her?"

I inhaled deeply, my chin dropping to my chest. My grip tightened against the edge of my skirt. "Is that what they say?"

He nodded, flipping his gaze back and forth between me and the road. "Yeah. They say he shot her dead, then carved her face and body all up into pieces."

I shook my head slightly. "Well, he didn't do all that."

"But he killed her?"

"That's what he's in jail for. Look, maybe this wasn't such a good idea. Maybe you should just take me home and find someone else."

"I'm sorry. I didn't mean nothing. I was just being nosy. I didn't mean to get you upset getting into your business like that. But damn! Folks be saying some crazy stuff 'bout you and I just wanted to know the truth. You so quiet and all it's hard to know what's going on with you."

I nodded, turning to stare at him, trying to decide if I wanted to be angry. Realizing I had nothing to be angry about, I shifted back into my seat and sighed. "It's okay. It happened a long time ago. I don't remember it anymore."

He nodded. "You going out with that guy Earl?"

I laughed. "No, not like that. Earl and I are friends. He's like my brother."

Wayne smiled. "They say you two are like an old married couple."

"'They sure have a lot to be saying about me, don't they?"

Wayne laughed. "They sure 'nuff do, girl! They sure 'nuff do!"

We talked easily for the balance of the ride, conversation finally flowing smoothly between us. As we pulled into the driveway of his very large, very brick home, a wave of nervous energy pierced my stomach but the emotion was instantly relieved when

Wayne's mother answered the door. I instantly liked Wayne's mother. Mrs. Lenora Tanner met us in the entrance wrapped in a salmon-colored gabardine pantsuit with matching ballerina flats. Shoulder-length hair in midnight black framed a perfect oval face. Her makeup was tasteful, a simple touch of color on her tan cheeks and a brush of gloss against her lips. Large, diamond studs neatly pierced each earlobe. She extended a perfectly manicured hand in my direction to welcome me, her wide smile a canvas of picture-perfect, pearl-white teeth.

"Oh my!" Mrs. Tanner gushed. "Aren't you the cutest thing. What's your name, dear?"

"Janay, ma'am. Janay Tucker."

"Well, welcome to our home, Janay. I do hope this son of mine isn't going to be too much of a nuisance. He refuses to study. Only wants to play basketball."

Wayne rolled his eyes. "I study," he muttered. "I just don't like it."

Mrs. Tanner turned to kiss her son's cheek. "Why don't you take Janay into the living room so you two can get started. I'll go get both of you something to snack on. Your father should be home shortly, and then you and Janay can let him know how much we are going to owe this young lady for saving your rear end."

Wayne nodded as his mother squeezed my hand one last time before exiting the room. "Don't pay her no never mind," he said as he turned toward the living room.

I followed behind him. "She's very nice."

He shrugged. "Yeah, mom's pretty neat. My older brother Everett is her favorite, though."

"Now, Wayne you know better," Mrs. Tanner interrupted, a tray of crust-less ham sandwiches, two glasses of sweet tea, and a plate of oatmeal cookies in her hands. "Don't pay him any attention, Janay. I love both my boys the same and they know it." After setting the tray down, she reached to tousle the curls on Wayne's head. Wayne grinned.

"So, Janay, were you born here in Creekton?" Mrs. Tanner asked.

"Yes, ma'am."

"Where are your parents from dear?"

"My father was born here also. My mother passed away when I was six." I cut my eye over toward Wayne, then dropped my gaze to the floor.

"Oh, my. I'm so sorry to hear that, dear."

"I live with my grandfather, James Tucker."

She searched her thoughts momentarily, then nodded, an intrigued expression crossing her face. "I've heard of your grandfather. Your family has a great deal of history here in Creekton."

I nodded slightly, unable to help but wonder what else she had heard.

"Well, I look forward to meeting Mr. Tucker. But don't let me hold you two up any longer. This boy here needs all the help he can get. If you need me, I'll be in the kitchen. We're having chicken for dinner. Would you like to stay?'

"Thank you, ma'am, but I don't want to intrude. Maybe another time."

Mrs. Tanner smiled sweetly. "I hope so. Perhaps your grandfather might even be able to join us."

Nodding my head, I smiled back.

It took no time at all to realize that Wayne's problem was one of simple laziness. His mother was right. He just refused to study. After an hour and a half of repeating myself over and over again, I grew weary with the task and told him so.

"Wayne, you are never going to get this if you keep paying more attention to what's going on with basketball than what's been written in this here book. You don't need a tutor, you need to sit your butt down and do some reading."

He laughed. "I know that. I surely didn't need you to tell me that."

I rolled my eyes. "Then what do you need me for?"

He smiled, lowering his head ever so slightly. "I need you to go out with me." His tone was flirty and teasing.

I looked up, surprise registered on my face. "Excuse me?"

"Friday, there's a dance over at Central. I need a date."

My mouth dropped open. Wayne laughed.

"Don't looked so shocked. Didn't you think I'd want to go out with you?"

"I never really thought about it," I answered, trying to appear nonchalant.

"So, is that a yes?"

I shrugged, a smile pulling at my lips. "Sure, I guess so."

Wayne grinned widely. "Cool. Pick you up at 7:oo."

I shook my head. "So, what are your going to do about the history?"

"Study I guess. It'll be easier with you around to do it with me."

At that moment, the front door opened, welcoming Ellis Tanner, MD. A nicely aged version of Wayne's face smiled into the room, waving his hand in our direction.

"Hey, Pop."

"Good evening to you, too. And hello there," Dr. Tanner smiled warmly as his wife rushed into his arms. A pang of jealousy pinched my side. Was this how family was supposed to be?

"Did you meet Wayne's new tutor, dear?" Mrs. Tanner questioned, nodding her head in my direction.

Dr. Tanner shook his head, then extended his hand. His skin was soft and damp, not like the solid, warm flesh of my grandfather.

"Hello, sir. I'm Janay Tucker."

"It's very nice to meet you, Janay," he said politely before turning his attention back to his wife. "How soon before dinner will be ready?"

"Thirty minutes at most, dear."

He nodded. "I'll be in my office. I've some calls to make. Has Everett called?"

Mrs. Tanner shook her head no. "Ellis, it's still early. He'll call after dinner, you know that."

The two walked out of the room together, still chatting between themselves.

"Your folks are nice."

"Yeah," Wayne shrugged, before dropping back onto the sofa. "They're not bad."

"Everett's your brother?"

Wayne nodded his head yes. "My perfect, older brother. He's away at college. He's a senior at Morehouse. He's studying to be a minister or something stupid like that."

Looking nervously around the room I could not think of anything else to say, noting Wayne's sudden silence.

"Well, my grandfather should be here any minute to get me. I can wait out on the porch so you can go eat with your folks."

Wayne rolled his eyes. "What? Your grandfather won't ring the doorbell or something?"

"No, I just don't want to be in anyone's way."

He shook his head at me. "Don't be stupid. You don't have to be waiting on no porch." He kicked his feet up on the glass tabletop. His high-top sneakers were well worn. I didn't think his mother would appreciate him putting his feet up on her coffee table, but I didn't comment. At that moment, I heard my grandfather's heavy footsteps against the porch stairs.

The doorbell rang as I hurried to gather my books and papers. Mrs. Tanner appeared out of nowhere to answer the doorbell. Towering above her, the old man greeted her politely, first introducing himself, then asking if I was ready to leave. I smiled when I saw him standing there, his cap clutched in his hands, perspiration beaded upon his forehead. His gray hair shimmered in the light.

"Mr. Tucker, we surely appreciate Janay being able to help our son. She is truly a delight. Would you two care to stay for dinner?"

"That's very nice of you, but we can't stay."

Mrs. Tanner nodded, patting me against the back as I came to stand by Daddy James' side. "Well, perhaps another time then. Janay, I hope we'll see you again soon."

"Thank you, Mrs. Tanner, and it was very nice meeting you."

As we eased into Daddy James' pickup truck the old man grunted, flipping his cap back onto his head.

"What's wrong, Daddy?"

"Nothing at all. They was nice people if you like them high society types."

I rolled my eyes. "They were very nice."

Daddy James cut his eyes in my direction and grunted again. "I'm sure they are especially when they want something they think you got."

"What could they possibly want from me?"

Daddy James pushed out his lips in a full pout, then curled his lips. "Girl, if you was two shades darker than them folks I don't doubt they would have some concerns about you being too near they boy. I done met his daddy before and I know them kind. Light and bright make you alright, dark and darker make you not they type. Thems the kind of black folks that like things a certain way. They expect folks to act a certain way and they won't risk being embarrassed by folks who don't act right in their eyes. They're not like the rest of us average Joes. I imagine they won't take kindly to you being the granddaughter of a dirt farmer."

"I don't believe that."

"Uh huh. Well you ain't gone be doing nothing but tutoring him no way so we won't worry 'bout it."

I bit my bottom lip. "Wayne asked me to go to the dance with him on Friday. I said I would."

I could see Daddy James' grip tighten against the steering wheel. "You don't be telling no boy you going nowhere 'till you get my permission first. You know that."

Silence filled the car, fogging up the windows with discord. Daddy James finally cleared the air. "What time is this dance?"

"It'll be over by eleven."

"You tell that boy to have you home by eleven-thirty and I'm telling you now, don't be laying up with that boy like you ain't got no good sense."

Nodding my head, I bit down on my lower lip, fighting not to grin. I was going out with Wayne Tanner.

I wore a dress. Earl picked it out, Daddy James approving the twenty-eight dollar Alexander's purchase. It was a simple blue and white, sleeveless, A-line shift that buttoned up the front. Large, white hoop earrings and white sandals completed the ensemble. After much goading from my friend, I'd left my hair hanging against my shoulders, my crowning glory more of an enigma than anything else. For as long as I could remember I'd been ridiculed and teased by the other girls for the silk-like waves perceived to be "good hair", supposedly representing the depths of my "cute-ness" and the lack of my "blackness". All I knew was that the strands tangled unmercifully when washed and hung like oiled rope if not washed daily. I'd grown to despise the nuisance of it, wishing I could shave my scalp bald like Manroot and my Daddy James. But Wayne had complimented my tresses and so I allowed Earl to pin curl the strands and finger wave the top into a style that made me look much like the image of my mother in one of the family photos.

My grandfather had smiled his approval as I'd eased into the kitchen, spinning in a slow circle awaiting his appraisal.

"Don't you look pretty!" Daddy James exclaimed, his head bobbing against the thick line of his neck. "Yes, indeed. Pretty as a picture."

"Thank you. Do you think Wayne will like the way I look?"

My grandfather shook his head. "Don't much matter, Black. As long as you like how you look. You comfortable in them clothes?"

I nodded. "This dress feels fine."

"Then you ain't got nothing else to worry about. You'll be the prettiest girl at the party if you feel good."

I smiled as my grandfather leaned to hug me, wrapping his arms tightly around me, his full lips pressing against my forehead. At that moment the doorbell chimed, announcing Wayne's arrival.

Daddy James stared down at me. "Remember what I said to you, Black. Don't you let that boy disrespect you."

"I won't, Daddy. I promise."

The old man followed as I rushed to the door. Wayne stood grinning on the other side. He wore black jeans and a bright white dress shirt that was opened down to his breastbone. He greeted me warmly, then extended his hand in greeting toward Daddy James.

"Good evening, Mr. Tucker."

Daddy James nodded as he shook the appendage, his grip just shy of bruising. His gaze searched the driveway behind Wayne's head, resting on the gray Lincoln Town Car parked in front of the house. "You driving tonight?" Daddy James asked.

"Yes, sir. That's my father's car. He's letting me use it this evening."

"What time is this dance over?"

"Eleven o'clock, sir. And if it's okay with you, Mr. Tucker, there's a group of us going over to the diner right afterwards for a bite to eat. Would it be okay if Janay went with us? I promise I'll have her back here by midnight."

Daddy James pursed his lips, looking from Wayne, to me, and back again. "I thought the Creekton diner closed at ten?"

I shook my head. "Daddy, you know Mr. Tillman doesn't close up until late on Fridays."

He cut his eyes at me and said nothing. Wayne and I stood waiting, the boy tossing me a quick look as if I might be able to move my grandfather's decision along any faster. The old man cleared his throat and then spoke.

"Drive like you got some sense. I expect you to bring my child back home here just like you taking her. You understand me?"

"Yes, sir."

"Have her home by midnight. Not one minute past or this'll be the last time you'll be taking her anywhere."

"I will, sir. I'll take good care of her."

Daddy James nodded as I reached up to embrace him. "Thank you, Daddy. I'll see you later."

"You kids have a good time."

The old man stood in the entrance watching as Wayne and I descended the porch steps, Wayne holding the passenger door for me as I eased myself inside. He waved one last time in my grandfather's direction before moving to the driver's side of the car and taking his seat. As we pulled out of the driveway, Wayne chuckled under his breath.

"Your grandfather's a piece of work, isn't he?"

"What do you mean."

"Man acts like I'm gone steal you away or something."

"He's just protective."

The boy grinned. "I guess he should be as pretty as you are. You sure look good tonight. You're a real beauty, girl!"

I grinned back. "Thank you."

The boy winked and I felt as if I'd fallen headfirst into heaven.

The Central High School gymnasium had been elaborately decorated in the school's colors. Crepe paper streamers in red and white hung from the ceiling, were wrapped around chair legs and had been tossed sporadically over the few tables that lined a back wall. There was a beverage table which sat to the right of the retracted bleachers, a large punch bowl, and stacks of plastic red cups being monitored by a requisite number of teachers and parents acting as chaperones.

Wayne's arrival was met with much noise, students cheering and clapping as we eased our way inside. Wayne held my hand, pulling me along behind him as his friends welcomed him back and he greeted them all in turn. From the doorway to the entrance of the gym, we were bombarded and the discomfort of so much attention was pulling at my fragile nerves. As if sensing my discomfort, Wayne wrapped a protective arm around my waist and pulled me close. He leaned to whisper in my ear, his low tone and warm breath causing me to quiver.

"You just smile sweet," Wayne said, giving me a quick squeeze. "You're my girl tonight. I promise you'll have a good time."

I could only nod as he guided me to the dance floor, the loud beat of the music dictating the mood. I danced. Before that night I had only danced alone in the privacy of my bedroom or with Earl as we'd copied the young people who displayed their skills down the Soul Train line. I danced as if I'd been born to do it and Wayne danced with me, his pleasure inked in the deep cavity of his grin.

The night flew by and before I knew it the bright lights filled the space, an adult voice announcing the end of the event over a loud speaker. The music was still playing as students began to move toward the exit. Heatwave was singing, *Always and Forever* spilling out of the speakers. The low, sultry tune vibrated with seduction through the warm evening air. As he pulled me back toward the center of the room and the dance floor, Wayne laughed when

I eyed him curiously. He drew me close to him, pressing the line of his body against mine, and together we moved in a slow drag, no other couples sharing the space beside us. Although conscious of the many eyes that watched us, at that moment, Wayne Tanner's gaze locked with mine was the only thing I remembered.

It was not long before Wayne and I were officially an item. I wore his letterman's jacket, drove his new truck, and fell at his side at the snap of his finger. I felt as though I'd been transported into the realms of nirvana, the bliss of being chosen by the crown prince himself as consuming as anything else could ever be. Girls who barely knew my name now stopped for conversation and when they whispered, it was about how lucky I was to be Wayne Tanner's girl.

Puppy love spread like poison ivy, a raging itch that should not have been scratched. I floated on clouds lined with naiveté, drifting hopelessly in a self-indulging wanderlust. Wayne commanded my full attention, beckoning my favors with the pretense of a pout, feigned displeasure, and his ever-wandering eyes.

A week before graduation, Wayne was invited to participate in an exhibition basketball game. Arranged by his mother to raise monies for a new playground at the elementary school, it was also a forum for her to show off her son's athletic prowess. Six professional bench warmers from the state's professional basketball team, friends from Mr. Tanner's alma mater, had been invited and Mrs. Tanner pulled out the stops to make this the event of the year. Wayne strutted like a pretentious peacock over the attention he was getting from everyone.

That Friday afternoon when I'd gone looking for him, I'd found him down in the gymnasium, Brianna Horton, Tanya Williams, and Felicia Dawes draped around his shoulders like three, flannel-lined, winter coats. Wayne barely acknowledged my presence with a nod of his head as he whispered into Tanya's ear, sending her into a fit of giggles.

I sucked in air, biting back my anger. Brianna and Eloise rose sheepishly, waving hello and good-bye as they exited the large recreation center. Tanya rose reluctantly, cutting her eye in my direction, before kissing Wayne on the cheek, and wishing him luck. The eye exchange between her and I was venomous as she pranced past me, a smug smirk across her face.

"Hey, baby, what's up," Wayne chimed, stretching his long legs across the bleachers beneath him.

"Maybe you should tell me. What was that all about?"

Wayne shrugged. "Don't be having no attitude now. You know them girls don't mean nothing to me."

I studied him, not knowing anything of the sort. "Your mama said that we should meet her and your daddy by four o'clock."

Wayne nodded. "You mad at me?"

"Do you care?"

Wayne reached out and grabbed my hand, pulling me down onto his lap. "Don't be stupid. You know I care. Don't like it when you get mad with me."

His hand felt warm against my back, the other playing with the edge of my shorts. "So, when I win tonight, how do you think we should celebrate?"

I shrugged again, trying to ignore the reddish-brown fingers creeping up my thigh. Catching his hand in mine, I kissed him quickly. "I think your mama has plans for you tonight."

Wayne heaved a loud sigh, poking out his lips. "Maybe and maybe not. Why you keep avoiding the subject? We been going out for a long time now and you still holding out on me. Brother can't be waiting but so long. If you don't want me, just say so, 'cause I don't need to be wasting my time here."

I closed my eyes not wanting to start the conversation that always ended with angry words between us. "Wayne, please don't start. You know I want you."

"Then you better start showing me." Wayne leaned to brush his cheek against mine. "Girl, you know what you do to me," he whispered into my ear, his breath hot against my neck.

I shook nervously as he took my hand and placed it over his crotch, rubbing my palm against the rise of flesh that pressed against the front of his pants. "You know you make me want you bad."

"Don't do that," I said with a soft giggle, pulling my hand away. "Someone might see us."

Wayne grinned. "You like that don't you?" He pulled me closer, wrapping his arms tightly around my torso, leaning to whisper into my ear. "Baby, I promise I won't hurt you. I'd never do anything to hurt you. I just want to show you how much I love you. I want to see just how much you love me. I know you can understand that."

I nodded ever so slowly as he continued, his words almost pleading.

"I know it's scary the first time, but I swear to you I'll do everything I can to make it special for you. I want to make love to you, Janay. I need to make love to you before I go crazy. You're driving me crazy with your beautiful self!"

I sighed, still nodding. This conversation had been repeated between us far too many times to be counted. I had not found a way to tell him that I was nobody's virgin, sensing that the knowledge would move the relationship where I didn't want it to go. Wayne thought that my not having dated before him made me an innocent luxury for him to conquer. It was his intent to be my first and I didn't know how to burst his bubble with the news that I no longer had a bubble for him to burst. I also had no intentions of sleeping with him, having sworn to myself that I'd not abuse my grandfather's trust.

Confident that he'd been convincing, Wayne smiled eagerly. "We're gonna celebrate for real tonight. You and me. I can't wait to be with you, Janay."

My head continued to bob foolishly against the end of my neck as we made our way out of the gym to meet the elder Tanners. It was later that evening that Everett Tanner pushed into the seat beside me, extending his hand. He stood as tall as his younger brother with the same broad shoulders, dimpled cheeks, and wavy, baby silk hair. His complexion was different though, more mahogany than rosewood. I shifted my position on the bleacher to make room for him.

"Hey, what's the score?"

"Forty-two to thirty-eight. We're leading," I responded. "Wayne's got three personals on him though."

Everett nodded. "That boy always did play too rough."

I shrugged my shoulders, not bothering to answer.

"So, you're the girl my baby brother is sweet on, huh?"

I shrugged, my thin shoulders jutting skyward. "And you must be Everett?"

"Yes. It's nice to meet you. I've heard a lot of good things about you." He smiled brightly.

I could not help but smile back, studying him out of the corner of my eye. He resembled their mother more than Wayne did. I liked his face, the warmth from his eyes flooding over his features.

"So, it must be pretty serious between you two, huh?"

"Why do you say that?"

"Mama says you've lasted longer than all the others. Wayne doesn't usually stay with any one girl for any length of time."

"Oh?"

"Either that or you're smarter than the others were."

I looked at him questioningly.

Everett chuckled. "It means you've told my brother no. I hate to be the one to say it, but Wayne's like most males his age, once he gets lucky, the girl gets dumped."

I blushed slightly, looking around to see if anyone else had heard him. The people sitting around us were too intent on the game to have paid our conversation any attention. Relief flooded my expression as my gaze fell back on Everett.

"I'm sorry. I didn't mean to embarrass you."

"You didn't, but I don't think you should be talking about your brother like that."

Everett shrugged. "Sorry, but I believe in being honest. It's one of my many bad habits."

I rolled my eyes, turning my attention back to the floor, where Wayne stood arguing with the referee. Even if you could not hear them, you could see that the words out of his mouth were ugly. You knew he'd been nasty even before they ejected him from the game, sending him back to the locker room.

Everett got up to follow. "Wait here. I'll go see if he's okay."

I watched as Everett made his way out of the bleachers, down the side of the gym and out the door. His parents followed closely behind, annoyance painted on their mother's face, anger on their father's.

When the game ended and the crowd flowed out of the gym toward the parking lot I still sat alone, waiting. Eventually Mrs. Tanner came to stand in the doorway, gesturing for me to join her.

"Janay, Wayne's father has taken him home," Mrs. Tanner said, heaving her irritation. "His behavior was totally uncalled for." She patted my shoulder. "If it's okay with you I've asked my son Everett to give you a ride home. I don't want your grandfather to be worried about you and I've got a house full of company I need to get home to." She lifted her hand to beckon at Everett. "Have you met my son, Everett?"

I nodded. "Yes, ma'am. That's fine. I can even call my grandfather if it's a problem."

"Oh, heavens no, dear. Everett doesn't mind. Besides, someone has to drive Wayne's car home." She smiled politely, turning her attention to Everett.

"Don't be long, sweetheart. Mr. Gibbons and Mr. Humphries have been anxious to speak with you about medical schools. This is a great opportunity for you to make some useful contacts."

Everett smiled, leaning to kiss his mother's cheek. "Yes, Mom. I promise I'll rush right back." I detected an edge of sarcasm in his voice.

We both watched as Mrs. Tanner bounced out of the building, stopping only to make conversation with Mrs. Rutt, the school's principal. I could read the apology for her son's behavior in her eyes.

Everett grabbed my hand and pulled me toward the door. "Let's get you home safe," he winked, still flashing a bright grin in my direction.

Pulling out of the parking lot, Everett played with the radio, switching the station from the intense beat of Kool and the Gang, to a softer jazz station. The change was a pleasant one and I said so.

"That's very nice. Wayne usually only likes to listen to that new rap music and loud rock and roll."

"Wayne and I don't share a whole lot of the same tastes or styles. You will find that my brother and I aren't at all alike," Everett said, still smiling. "In fact I'm not sure we even like each other."

I looked over at him curiously as he focused on the dark road.

"Why not?"

"We just don't agree on many things."

"That doesn't have to be bad."

"I agree, but Wayne doesn't see it that way."

I shrugged, not wanting to say anything negative about Wayne to his brother. "Wayne says you're studying to be a minister?" I said, changing the subject.

"Well, I'm actually studying philosophy and history. I am thinking about going into seminary after graduation to study theology. I'm not sure though. I don't know if I truly have a calling for the ministry."

I nodded. "I didn't think your family was very religious."

"They aren't really. My parents were both raised in very strict Baptist families but they've distanced themselves somewhat from the church. I'm sure they'll go back someday. Besides, they're still hoping I'll change my mind and go into medicine like my father."

I nodded again. "My grandfather's very religious. He doesn't miss a day in church if he doesn't have to."

"Do you go?"

"Only when I have to. Not nearly as much as Daddy James would like me to though."

"Well, everyone has to find their way through the door on their own."

I bit against my lip nervously, not sure what else to talk about. Everett beat me to the punch.

"I've met your grandfather. He's a great guy."

I looked up surprised. "You've met Daddy James? When?"

"My senior year in high school. Mr. Tucker came in to talk to one of the business classes. He was great."

I sat with my mouth open, shocked.

"It apparently wasn't too long after he'd lost one of his sons and he talked about his family and all of their accomplishments. He even talked about your father."

"Daddy James told you about my father?"

Everett nodded. "He wanted us to understand what could happen when we don't maintain control over our lives. He told us that your father had been a brilliant business man, negotiating all kinds of deals in New York and Chicago and how he'd helped the family business grow in even greater directions until he went to jail. Some folks think it doesn't take much to run a farm but when you're buying and selling produce or land, it takes a lot."

I was dumbfounded, not knowing whether or not to believe what Everett was telling me. "I never knew Daddy James ever did anything like that."

Everett nodded. "Well, he did. In fact, he's spoken at the school a few times that I've known about. Maybe not since you've been there though."

I nodded with him, still in a state of disbelief. I'd not noticed when he pulled in front of the old Farmers Market and shifted the car into park.

"Chocolate or vanilla?" he asked, as I stared at him stupidly.

"What?"

"Ice cream. What's your favorite flavor?"

"Chocolate."

He nodded. "Be right back."

I watched him saunter easily into the store, talking to a rotund girl with big eyes behind the counter. Moments later he was back with two oversized cones in his hands. I leaned over to open the door for him. As he slid inside and passed me a cone, the melting confection dripped onto the back of my hand. I jumped when Everett leaned in to lick the sticky flow from my skin.

"Sorry. I couldn't reach the napkins in my pocket."

I nodded. "No problem. Thanks for the cone."

Everett smiled his deepest smile. "Are you always so nervous?"

"I'm not nervous."

"Yes, you are. You look like you're about ready to jump right out of your skin."

"Don't be crazy. I do not."

"Uh huh."

"I don't."

Everett and that smile brightened the darkness around us and once again I could not help but smile back. When he pulled down the driveway and stopped in front of the house, I could see Daddy James' large body rocking on the front porch. A flicker of light burned in the end of a pipe. Everett jumped out of the driver's side to come open the door for me, then walked me up the stairs to greet my grandfather.

"Good evening, Mr. Tucker."

"Good evening," Daddy James said, rising to his feet.

"You probably don't remember me, sir, but my name is Everett Tanner. We met..."

"I know who you are, son. How are you doing?"

"Just fine, thank you, sir."

"How's school coming along?"

"Very well, thank you. My brother got into a bit of trouble with my parents this evening, and my mother asked me to bring Janay home. I hope I haven't gotten her home too late, Mr. Tucker."

Faint wisps of smoke rose from the end of that pipe as Daddy James shook his head. "No. It's fine. Your mama called to let me know. I appreciate you and your mama taking care of my girl for me."

Everett nodded. "Not a problem, sir. Well, good-night. It was nice meeting you, Janay."

I smiled. "Thanks for the ice cream," I said, waving as he jumped back into his car.

Daddy James stared at me as I watched Everett pull off into the darkness. Night sounds rose in the distance, the low hum of crickets and buzzing insects rousing for a long evening.

"Shame that Wayne boy ain't got good sense like his brother."

I ignored his comment. "How come you never come to the school to talk anymore?" I asked instead.

Daddy James sat back down into the rocker. "Figured you wouldn't want me coming round. Didn't want you to be embarrassed."

"Why would I be embarrassed?"

"'Cause I don't tell no lies about your daddy. I let them young boys know just what can happen when you take risks that don't make no good sense and you don't do right by people. Since you don't be telling your friends about your daddy I figured you wouldn't want me doing it whilst you was in school there."

I continued to stare off into the distance, the faint tail lights having long since disappeared out of sight.

Daddy James rose and headed inside. "Watch yourself, Black. Don't you forget them boys is brothers."

I looked over my shoulder as he closed the door behind him, only slightly taken aback by his comment.

"No, sir," I nodded, pulling the last of the ice cream to my lips. "I surely won't forget."

****

When I awoke, I heard Wayne's voice out in the yard with Daddy James. The discussion between them appeared intense as they stood facing each other. Wayne was animated, his hands dancing excitedly in midair. After splashing my face with water and quickly brushing my teeth, I jumped into an oversized tee shirt and a pair of shorts and headed outside. Daddy James nodded his head in my direction, ending the conversation abruptly, then turned toward the barn. Wayne came across the yard and up the porch to meet me.

"Hey, what you doing here so early?"

Wayne kissed my cheek, then brushed past me, heading inside. I followed behind him, glancing only briefly over my shoulder to see if Daddy James was watching.

"So, what's up?"

"What did you do with my brother last night?"

"Excuse me?"

"You heard me. What happened with you and Everett?"

"Nothing. He just gave me a ride home."

"Took an awful long time for him to get back. Must've been some ride."

I reached up to brush the hair out of my eyes. "Nothing happened with your brother, Wayne."

"I just told your grandfather that he shouldn't trust Everett around you. He came home last night talking 'bout how nice you were to him like you'd done something with him. I didn't appreciate that."

My eyes narrowed ever so slightly as I waited for him to elaborate. The look in his eye told me he was lying, but I wasn't sure why.

"Everett told you I did something with him last night?"

"He said a lot of things. You shouldn't have been leading him on."

"I didn't lead him on. He gave me a ride, we talked on the way, stopped for an ice cream, and that was it."

"Don't be so stupid. Don't you know some guys get the wrong idea when you act too nice around them?"

"I'm not stupid."

Wayne grunted. "I don't want you around my brother anymore."

My look was incredulous, reflecting how asinine I thought the conversation was, but knowing it wasn't worth pushing. "Anything else?"

We stood staring at each other, the tension thick. Wayne looked me up and down and I suddenly felt uncomfortable as he stepped in closer. His arms wrapping around my shoulders felt heavy and I fought against the sudden urge to push him as far away from me as I could.

"We didn't get to celebrate," he whispered, leaning to kiss me. "I had plans for us last night."

I kissed him back, wanting to dispel the anger between us. "We have time, Wayne."

Wayne nodded, brushing his hands up my back and over my abdomen.

"How long before your granddaddy coming back in?"

I laughed, finally pushing him away. "Don't even think about it. Daddy James catch us doing anything in his house and he'll skin us both."

Wayne heaved a heavy sigh. "So when then?"

"I don't know, Wayne."

The boy nodded his head, his eyes darting about in thought. "Go ask him if you can go for a ride."

"Where to?"

"I don't know. Just ask him."

Not wanting to argue, I headed for the barn and Daddy James who stood observing one of the horses.

"Daddy, can I go for a ride with Wayne?"

Daddy James continued to stare at the animal.

"Please?"

One eye darted in my direction, then over to Wayne. "No. You don't need to be going nowhere this early in the day."

I pushed my hands into my pockets, knowing better than to ask again or argue.

Wayne eased ahead of me. "Would it be okay if I stayed here with Janay for a while, Mr. Tucker?"

Daddy James grunted, then flipped his hand for us to get out of his way.

"Thanks, Daddy. We're gonna walk down by the pond."

Daddy James looked up briefly. "Act like you got some good sense, Black."

I rolled my eyes, nodded my response, and headed out the door.

Sitting at the water's edge, his kisses were intense, almost bruising as his lips raced over mine. Nervous, I kept looking across the fields expecting Daddy James to come bounding over the hill to catch us. Wayne rested his weight above me groping anxiously at my breasts. I found myself struggling beneath him.

"Stop, Wayne."

"Damn, woman. I want to do this."

"Daddy James might see us."

"That old man ain't gonna see nothing. We can see him if he's coming."

One hand pulled anxiously at my zipper. The other eased its way beneath my bra. He panted heavily in my ear, grinding his pelvis against my thigh. An uneasy moan passed his lips, then he cursed as a sudden spread of wetness eased through the fabric of his jeans.

"Now, look what you've done."

"What I've done?"

"Yeah, you. You get me all excited then you leave me hanging until I can't take it no more. Now you done made a mess."

He stood up angrily. "I can't take much more of this, Janay. If you want to be my woman you need to start acting right. I'm gone pick you up later. Be ready. My mama expects you to have dinner with us. She said she'd call to clear it with your granddaddy."

Nodding, I pulled my clothes into place as Wayne stormed toward his pickup truck and away from the farm. I don't know how long I lay staring off at the blue of the sky, mesmerized by the billow of clouds that floated carelessly across the royal background. I only knew that much time had passed as the sun had shifted in the sky. In the back of my mind, I composed a letter to my father, knowing that it would never make it to paper. I'd stopped writing Manroot. He never wrote back so I'd figured why waste the time. Daddy James had gone in March to see him and had reported that he was doing as well as could be expected. He didn't know when he'd make the trip again to see his son.

My thoughts drifted to Everett and I was wondering what had actually occurred between him and Wayne when Daddy James came up behind me, a fishing pole in each hand. I smiled, welcoming his company. We sat together for some time, neither uttering a word, just bobbing our lines in and out of the cool, blue-green water. Daddy James finally broke the silence.

"Mrs. Tanner called to invite us to supper."

I nodded. "Wayne said she was gonna call."

"You want to go?"

I shrugged, hunching my shoulders upward. "Are you coming with me?"

"I told her I couldn't make it but that you was welcome to go if you wanted. I gots to go over to the church tonight. She said she was gonna send Everett to pick you up 'cause Wayne has a meeting with his father somewhere first."

My eyebrows shot up slightly.

The old man continued. "But, I told her that won't necessary. I can take you there myself."

"Thank you."

Daddy James leaned back against the grass. "You know you asking for trouble with that Wayne boy. He ain't no good."

"I really like Wayne."

"Why?"

I paused, thinking about the question, realizing I really didn't have an answer. "I just do," I said finally, resting my head against my grandfather's side.

"You like Everett, too?"

"Yeah. He's nice."

Daddy James puckered his lips, chewing on the end of a toothpick. "Wayne don't like that you think his brother's nice. In fact, Wayne don't much like Everett. Not like he should. Jealous of him. Nasty jealous. He ain't been raised to do right by his blood."

I nodded my head. "Well, he doesn't have anything to be jealous of."

"Uh huh. So you say." Silence hung briefly between us before Daddy James continued. "When brothers start chasing after the same woman, someone bound to get hurt sooner or later. I don't want that someone to be you."

I laughed. "Daddy, Everett is not chasing after me. He was just being nice. That's all."

"Uh huh. You just think about what you doing. You hear me?"

I nodded, already contemplating the Tanner brothers.

Everett opened the door to welcome me. Daddy James beeped the horn then waved a callused hand in our direction before pulling off. I suddenly wished he had stayed with me or I'd thought to have gone with him. I could hear Mrs. Tanner bustling about in the other room and I called out to greet her.

"Hello, Mrs. Tanner. Can I do anything to help?"

"Hello, Janay. No, dear, just sit and relax. We'll eat as soon as that husband and son of mine get back. Is Everett still there?"

"Yes, Mom. I'm right here."

"Keep Janay company for me, honey. I've got my hands full at the moment."

Everett's smile was piercing. He led the way into their family room. Their house was large and immaculately decorated. Mrs. Tanner's tastes were a bit contemporary for the Southern-framed farmhouse, leaning toward bold geometric prints and overly bright solids, but it still felt homey inside.

"So, are you excited about graduation?" Everett asked, disrupting the silence.

I nodded. "Excited that it will soon be over."

"What are you planning to do afterward?"

I shrugged my shoulders. "Haven't decided."

He nodded his head slowly. "Have you thought about college?"

"No. I'm not leaving my grandfather."

"Is that what he wants?"

"What's with the questions? Why are you so concerned about what I'm planning to do?"

"Sorry. You're just a very bright girl and I would think your grandfather would want you to continue on in school.

I sighed, dropping into an oversized armchair. "He does. I don't. At least not for a while."

"What about my brother? What's going to happen with the two of you?"

I glanced up to study his expression. Surprisingly I'd not given any thought to his question. Wayne was going off to Chapel Hill in September and I guess I'd assumed that we would still continue along the path we'd been traveling.

"What did you say to Wayne about what happened last night?" I changed the subject.

"Nothing. I told him I stopped to get you an ice cream and took you home."

"He said you were talking like something else had happened between us."

Everett crossed to the other side of the room, taking the chair opposite me.

"Do you believe that?"

I thought about it only briefly before answering. "No. But he still said it."

"I think he was afraid something might have happened, but like I asked him, why would you have sex with me when you've never had sex with him?"

"How do you know I've never had sex with him?"

"I know my brother. And I think I know you, too."

The room grew silent again as I pondered his remark. My eyes danced around the outline of his face as we both reflected on each other, and Wayne. Our gazes locked and we held it tightly between us. Energy spun a fine web of longing that seemed to rise out of nowhere to encompass the two of us. Everett smiled ever so sweetly and in that brief moment I was reminded of all those things that were good in my world.

Daddy James had been right. I had to be very careful about what I did or didn't do. There was something secret spreading between Everett and me, and if I was not careful, its prickly growth could come back to sting us all.

I'd not heard Wayne enter the house as he bounded into the room bursting with energy.

"Hey girl," he said, sliding into the chair beside me, cutting his eye over at Everett. "What you two up to?"

I smiled, kissing him on the cheek. "Just talking about school and graduation." I smiled nervously over at Everett.

"Hmmm." Wayne cut his eye back and forth between us, then wrapped his arms possessively around me.

"Well, I'm here now big brother. We don't need your company anymore."

Everett laughed a low laugh, shaking his head. "No, Wayne, you don't," he said rising from where he sat. "Janay, I'll see you at the table."

As he walked out of the room Wayne flipped him a middle finger behind his back.

"Why'd you do that?"

He pouted angrily. "I told you to stay away from him."

"And how was I supposed to explain that to your mom?'

Slamming his fist against his thigh, he sucked his teeth. "If you love me, you better do what I say. I know what I'm talking about. You're too stupid to understand."

I bit my lip. "Don't call me stupid."

"Then don't act like it."

Mrs. Tanner strolled into the room, disrupting the waves of tension that permeated the air. "Let's eat you two. Dinner's ready."

Wayne rose, pulling me to my feet beside him. "Just remember what I said," he hissed under his breath. "You'll do this if you love me like I love you."

Later that night Lavinia stood laughing, her finger pointed indignantly as she raced across the fields behind me. I was tired of running, the strength in my legs giving way beneath me. My mother hovered angrily over me, blood dripping slowly from an open vein. She laughed and called me names, rude and ugly enumerations that flowed as swiftly as the blood that puddled around us. I wished her away, but she stood her ground, refusing to be moved by my tears. She yelled and I cried as she reminded me again that I was damned for all my sins. Her slaps and screams came like thunder and rain, the violence of her storm tormenting.

Daddy James shook me from the nightmare, the warmth of his palm pulling me from my sleep. Perspiration dampened my skin, and the bedclothes, reminders that Lavinia had been in control. Darkness still danced outside my window and as Daddy James headed back to his own bed, I sat wide-eyed and awake in my own. There would be no sleep that night. My mother had come to visit me.

"I think you like his brother," Earl teased. "You're always talking about him. You talk about him more than you talk about Wayne."

"I do not," I professed, dropping down onto the side of my bed next to my friend. "I love Wayne."

The boy rolled his eyes. "You love that being with Wayne has made you one of the popular kids. That's all you love."

I turned to stare at him, his words burning a bruise against my heart. "That's not fair to say, Earl. It's not like that."

He shrugged. "You have to admit that folks are a lot nicer to you since you started going out with Wayne."

I sucked my teeth, swatting him with one of the pillows pulled from the head of the bed. Even if my friend Earl was right, I had no interest in admitting it.

Earl dropped down onto his back, pulling his hands beneath his head. "You and Wayne do it yet?"

I shook my head. "He keeps trying but I don't want to," I answered, knowing what 'it' he referred to.

Earl nodded. "Daddy James will kill you if you do, you know that don't you?"

I shrugged my shoulders. "I know."

Earl cleared his throat, his gaze racing from corner to corner as he struggled not to look at me.

"What?" I asked, sensing there was something he needed to say.

"Promise you won't get mad."

"Mad about what?"

"Them boys was in the locker room and one of 'em was saying that Wayne was sleeping with Tanya."

I shook my head, a nervous laugh rising from my midsection. "Wayne wouldn't do that. He loves me. You know how them boys like to tell lies."

Earl leaned up on his elbows. "Well, you should know that's what they're all saying."

There was a moment of quiet between us.

"What else they had to say?" I finally ventured to ask. "I know someone had to add some details for you all to believe him."

Earl heaved a deep sigh. "They say that last week after the senior prom that after Wayne dropped you off here, he went and got Tanya and took her to the after-parties since Daddy James wouldn't let you go. Then that Saturday they all drove up to Charlotte to that new water park for the day and that Tanya was with Wayne. Said he had his hands all up under her clothes on them rides and that they did all kinds of nasty stuff in public."

I bristled as I took in the information. Daddy James had refused to give me permission to go to any of the parties after the prom, but Wayne had understood. In fact, he'd had a basketball event to attend that next day and had not seemed at all upset about having to go home early. He had been so understanding and attentive that I had barely given the ending to his night a second thought, assuming that we had both been on the same page, feeling the same way about the turn of events. I said this to Earl, attempting to dispel the rumors that said my boyfriend was a lie and a cheat.

Earl shrugged. "I wouldn't have been upset either if I already had plans to be with someone else."

"Wayne wouldn't do that to me."

"You sure about that?"

We both fell into silence for a second time as my friend sat staring at me. I didn't have an answer and the expression that painted my face told him so.

As I sat reflecting on the truth that I wanted to believe, convincing myself that there was no way Wayne Tanner would even imagine committing such a crime against me, I couldn't help but wonder how my mother would have handled it. Would she have ranted and raved at the man who'd wronged her so? Would she have sent him packing, cutting him into pieces with the sharp edge of her vicious tongue? Perhaps she might have shrugged her thin shoulders and ignored the he-said-she-said comments. I wondered if she had been there if I could have asked her for advice, her womanly wisdom shared with me. My gaze met Earl's and I smiled weakly.

He shrugged again, an easy smile returned. "Just be careful, Black. Don't let that boy make no fool of you. And don't give him no chance to be hurting your feelings. He ain't worth it, girlfriend. He sure enough ain't worth it. Besides, that brother of his is much cuter."

I flipped my hand in his direction. "I'm not studying Everett or them other boys. I'm telling you it's just jealous lies. Wayne loves me."

Outside the bedroom door, Daddy James stood listening, forming his own conclusions as he absorbed the conversation he'd been eavesdropping on. He hadn't much liked that Wayne boy from jump, and Earl's comments had only served to further cement his disdain. He thought about interceding, but knew to do so would serve no purpose other than to send his granddaughter straight into that boy's trap. He'd made that mistake with his own child, Eloise thinking that half a man was better than no man at all. He'd learned a hard lesson from that blunder and he refused to make the same error with his granddaughter.

He nodded his head slowly as he eased his way back down the stairs and into the kitchen. Time would be his saving grace, he thought, as he reached for the teapot that rested in the center of the stove. Patience would serve him well if he allowed it, he mused. As he listened to the two young people who'd come bounding down the steps in his direction, Daddy James knew that he had all the time and patience in the world if it meant protecting Manroot's baby girl.

It had been a good while since I'd finished washing the dinner dishes, but I still stood in front of the sink, my crinkled fingers playing in the sudsy water. My mind had disappeared out of the kitchen some time earlier, my thoughts rambling in the warm evening air. I'd gotten lost in my reflections of Wayne and the rumors that rode the carriage behind every path he traveled. I'd disappeared in the frustrations of not knowing what was true or false. I was so completely absorbed that I did not hear my grandfather calling my name until he'd had to repeat himself twice, his voice rising an octave the last time.

"Black, do you hear me talking to you?"

The cobwebs fluttered from my mind. "Sir?"

"Did you hear me?"

"No. I...was...I'm...sorry, Daddy..." I stammered, spinning around to face the man who stood staring at me from the doorway.

Daddy James shook his head. "Where were you just then?"

I shrugged. "Nowhere really. I just have a lot of stuff on my mind."

He nodded again, his head waving up and down slowly, concern piercing his gaze. "Why don't you come sit and talk with me a spell," he said, his tone commanding.

"Yes, sir," I answered, reaching for a dishrag to dry my hands against.

I followed him to the front porch, sitting down on the white oak swing that hung from the corner posts. Neither of us spoke as we settled down into the warmth of the evening air, watching the sun as it dropped from the sky and disappeared below the line of the horizon. A full moon had risen to take its place.

I waited for him to speak first, knowing that Daddy James would lead the conversation in his own time, more than likely moving it someplace I had no desire to go. As I took a deep inhale my grandfather strummed his callused fingers against the arm of the metal glider that supported his weight. He hummed softly, a quiet hymn filling the evening air. And then, just like that, he stopped, his gaze focusing his attention on me.

Daddy James cleared his throat. "Let me tell you a story, Black," he started, his tone as calming as his presence.

I leaned in as he continued.

"When I was a young man I didn't always do what was right. Some things I did I knew better about but I did 'em anyway. I used to know some young ladies that I didn't treat as nice as I should have. But being a boy I was kind of wild and my mama and your Grandma Lucy use to say that I was spoiled." Daddy James smiled.

"When I met your grandma I wasn't much older than you are now. We was both real young. Now I have to be honest and tell you that when Lucy and me started courting, I had me a couple of other girlfriends, too. I thought it didn't matter much as long as things was going my way."

I leaned forward with more interest.

"One day I was downtown with this girl who didn't have such a nice reputation. We was being fresh, hugging and holding hands and your grandma Lucy happened to catch us at it. Your grandma didn't know about them other girls and when she caught me, I could see the hurt in her eyes." He shook his head at the memory as he continued. "That was the first time I realized it was possible to actually break somebody's heart 'cause I sure 'nuff broke your grandma's heart that day."

"What did Grandma Lucy do?"

Daddy James sighed. "Miss Lucy walked right up to both of us just as sweet as you please and told me not to call on her no more. I tried to beg my way out of it, but your grandma wasn't buying none of it. She said, 'Mr. Tucker,' his voice changing as he mimicked my grandmother. 'Mr. Tucker, you don't deserve a good woman like me and I, sir, deserve a much better man than you. You aren't worthy of my love and a man like you could never be the father to my sons. My children will only have the very best example of manhood to follow.'" Daddy James chuckled ever so softly. "Your grandma made me look at myself different that day."

I smiled. "But she changed her mind. She forgave you and you got another chance."

He nodded. "Only because I changed my ways. It took a long time before she would give me the time of day. But I knew right then that I wanted a woman who was willing to demand the very best from me to be my wife. And your grandma wasn't going to accept any less from me or anyone else. She was special and she knew it. And she made darn sure that I knew it, too."

The space between us grew quiet again as I pondered his story and he fell into the haze of memories long since forgotten. After a few minutes

Daddy James came to his feet and turned to go inside. He stopped at the doorway, turning back around to stare at me. "If you don't demand the best for yourself, Black, ain't no man going to give it to you. Especially if he thinks he can get away with not doing right. You spending time with this Wayne boy now, and I'm sure you'll be spending time with other boys too. You just make sure they do right by you. You a special girl, just like your grandma. You make sure you demand the best for yourself. Cause a man will only do what you let him get away with. You remember that."

"Yes, sir."

He stepped inside the screen, closing it easily behind him. "Time for bed, Black. We've got us a long day tomorrow."

Descending the stairs in my ivory cap and gown, I spun a slow pivot in the foyer, glowing under the beam of my grandfather's smile. Daddy James shook his head majestically and the pride that gleamed from his eyes was painted in a kaleidoscope of colors around me. His hug was comforting, his broad arms expressing the sheer delight in being able to see his granddaughter graduate from high school. The tears rose gently to the edge of both our eyes. I had needed much love to get myself to this point and Daddy James had willingly parted with every ounce of it.

Wayne and I made the stroll across the football field hand in hand. I waved to his mother who stood clutching her husband's arm, the mist of her tears shimmering against her face. Daddy James stood beside them, his navy suit fitting him cleverly, but clearly looking awkward out of his daily denim attire.

We could not have asked for a more beautiful day to toss our tasseled mortarboards up into the sky, the edges of the commencement caps grazing the sunshine. The heat was pleasant, not at all unbearable, and a mild breeze blew faint scents of blooming flora against our cheeks. The icing on my cake came when I was able to hand the gold inscribed diploma to the man who'd loved me most and have him brush tears of joy against my cheek.

The celebrations were many as Wayne and I rode from one party to the next, but I was happiest once home, back on the porch beside my granddaddy, watching the sun drop down behind the edge of the vast fields as we both contemplated my future.

The next day Daddy James woke me early for church and I begrudgingly dressed and joined him. A visiting minister from Asheboro preached, his sermon entitled, *Weathering the Storm of Youth*, and I thought it hypocritical coming from a man who looked as though he'd obviously forgotten what it meant to be youthful. It was not until service was over that I noticed the Tanner family seated together in one of the rear pews. Wayne looked annoyed as he fidgeted with his tie. Everett sat with his eyes closed, a silent prayer whispering past his full lips. As the family moved to take their leave, Everett noticed us first, coming forward to speak.

"Hello, Mr. Tucker. Hi, Janay. How are you two today?"

"Good, boy. How are you doing?"

"Fine, thank you, sir. I just wanted to know what time you wanted me to start tomorrow?"

Daddy James cleared his throat, folding the church's neatly printed program in half and tucking it into the breast pocket of his suit jacket.

"Day starts early. You need to be there by five."

"No problem, sir. I'll be there on time."

I looked at Daddy James questioningly, just as Mr. Tanner and his wife came to shake Daddy James' hand. The chatter was brief and polite as Wayne glared behind them. Everett leaned to whisper into his brother's ear and Wayne responded with a look of pure hatred. I eased past my grandfather and over to Wayne's side.

"Hey, didn't know you were going to be in church today?"

"There's apparently a lot you don't know, or at least haven't been telling." His tone was cold, the words glazed in a thick icicle.

With his hand against my lower spine, he pushed me ahead of him, up the vestibule and outside, pausing at the top of the brick steps.

"Why didn't you tell me Everett was gonna work for your grandfather?"

"He is?"

Wayne shook head, his stare haunting. "You knew, don't pretend you didn't. I can't believe you'd do this after I told you to stay away from him."

"Wayne, I had no idea. Why don't you believe me? Why wouldn't I tell you if I knew?"

"Don't think I don't see how you and him keep looking at each other. You can play this innocent farm girl act all you want, but I'm not the one that's stupid."

Grinding my back teeth in anger, I looked over my shoulder, not wanting the harsh words spewing between us to be overheard. Our families were just reaching the entranceway, engaged in conversation with the pastor. I could see Everett watching us, his concerned expression too serious for so pretty a Sunday.

"I don't know what your problem is, Wayne, but I didn't tell you because I didn't know," I hissed.

Wayne grabbed my arm roughly and from the corner of my eye, I could see Daddy James bristle to attention.

"You just better remember—" Wayne started, just as Daddy James reached our side.

"Is there a problem here?"

I shook my head. "No, sir. There's no problem."

Daddy James nodded his head then leaned his mouth close to Wayne's ear.

"Well, boy, if we don't have a problem then you best take your hands off my child."

Wayne inhaled a deep breath, releasing his grasp on my arm. "I didn't mean nothing, Mr. Tucker, honest," Wayne stammered, tossing a glance toward his parents who stood oblivious by the minister's side. His eye met Everett's, his brother's stare condemning, and he bit his bottom lip.

Daddy James nodded his head slowly. "Let's go, Black. Time to head home."

I tossed Wayne an angry look, then slipped my hand into Daddy James'. Before heading toward the truck, Daddy turned to speak to Wayne one last time.

"I don't want to be seeing you on my land any time soon. You take some time to figure out what your problem is because if you ever put your hands on my girl like that again, you gone answer to me. Do I make myself clear?"

Wayne nodded as Daddy James turned his back on him, leaving my boyfriend to explain the remark to his parents on his own.

The ride home was anything but quiet.

"What was that all about?"

I shook my head. "It was nothing."

"Boy put his hands on you like that and you gone tell me it's nothing? I ain't gone ask you again, Black. What was that all about?"

I took a deep breath. "Why didn't you tell me you gave Everett a job?"

"I don't answer to you about who I do or do not hire. When's the last time you gave a hoot about what was going on with this farm? I done hired a dozen or more boys to work this land with me and you ain't paid a bit of attention. I hire Everett and now I'm supposed to tell you? Now, I asked you why that boy put his hands on you and I want an answer."

The tightness in my jaw hurt. I could feel defiance stroking my brain, but fought it. "He was mad 'cause he thought I knew about Everett and didn't tell him."

"And that gives him reason to be putting his hands on you?"

"He doesn't want me to be around his brother and he thinks you're doing this so me and Everett can be together."

Daddy James grew silent, his hands heavy against the steering wheel. He nodded his head.

"Well, maybe the boy ain't as dumb as I thought he was."

I looked over at the old man with disbelief. "Is that why you hired Everett?"

"I hired him because he wants to work and I need the help. Anything else was just frosting on the cake."

"Why?"

"I done told you. Wayne ain't no good. He ain't gone do nothing but hurt you. Now, Everett's a good boy. He's hard working. He respects you. Given half a chance you gone see what that boy feels about you and what you feels about him."

"Wayne's my boyfriend. I love him."

Daddy James rolled his eyes, screwing up in mouth in a bitter pout. "Well, you right 'bout him being a boy, but he sure' ain't no friend and you don't know who you loves."

"And you do?"

Daddy James cut his eye at me, his gaze chastising the tone of my voice.

"I know you better then you know yourself. Don't think that I don't."

"I'm not a little girl anymore, Daddy."

"No. But you ain't grown yet either."

I turned to stare out the window, concentrating on the cars whizzing past us on the other side of the road. Maybe he didn't consider me an adult, I thought to myself, but no matter how old I was, I had to know what I wanted for myself better than he did.

I couldn't help thinking that my relationship with Wayne cycled much like the blooming magnolia tree that grew sky high along the rear of the property. Daddy James had proclaimed it my Grandma Lucy's favorite and he spent much time beneath its dense, towering limbs. Every year it would bloom gloriously, extraordinary, showy, large white flowers coming to life under the bright rays of summer sunshine. The air would dance with the sweetest aroma that caressed and kissed you like a gentle lover and then as quickly as the flora blossomed, it and its leaves would die off, turning a horrid shade of dead brown. The foliage would take forever to decompose, stagnating as ugly against the landscape as it had preened so beautifully in its full glory. Wayne and I were like that, shining beautifully when we were at our very best and disintegrating when an act of nature bested us, interiors as ugly as our exteriors, and deteriorating far too slowly for anybody's good.

I heaved a deep sigh, the rise of summer heat burning my lungs with its rank humidity. Rolling onto my back, I pulled an arm above my head, adjusting the pillow beneath my neck. Maybe I was the problem. Perhaps Wayne was right about my behavior. He'd proclaimed his love and although I believed it, I was still reluctant to return the heart he'd handed to me so willingly. As much as I wanted to pull him close, I fought intensely to hold him at bay. I would be frustrated as well if the shoe were being worn on the other foot. Manroot had loved my mother deeply and she had held him at arm's length, proclaiming love with words that had nothing material to support them. I would not be my mother, I thought. If I claimed the affection Wayne offered so readily, I couldn't imagine things not getting better for us. I shook my head with determination, intent on what I had to do. Wayne loved me and I would not allow myself to hurt his heart like Lavinia had hurt my daddy.

****

Wayne called every day, apologizing profusely for what he had done. We'd spend most of the morning on the telephone while I'd spend the afternoon avoiding his older brother. It was two weeks before Daddy James permitted him to come to the house again, and even then, he made it clear that Wayne was not truly welcome.

"Hey there," Wayne said, syrup coating his throat. "I missed you."

I smiled. "Me too."

He peered over my shoulder toward Daddy James who sat rocking on the porch. "Hey, Mr. Tucker. How are you this evening?"

Daddy James rose from where he sat and walked into the house. Before closing the door, he called out to me over his shoulder.

"I want you in this house before midnight. You hear me, Black?"

I nodded. "Yes, sir."

Wayne and I giggled as we jumped into his truck and peeled out of the driveway. About a mile down the road, he pulled the pickup off to the side and turned off the engine.

Leaning over he kissed me hungrily, his hands searching the length of my spine. "Still ain't got my graduation present," he whispered, outlining my ear with his tongue.

I giggled again, excited to be seeing him. "And what's that?"

"You know what it is. I been waiting a long time, Janay. Don't make me wait no longer." His voice was almost a whine. As he kissed me again, I did not know if I possessed the fortitude to clash with him yet again, but for some reason, it still did not feel right and I needed it to feel right.

"Wayne, I can't sleep with you. I can't. It's wrong."

"What do you mean wrong? Don't you love me?"

"Wayne, you know how much you mean to me."

"If you love me you'd do this. I know you want to do it. I can feel it."

I shook my head. "I swore to Daddy James I wouldn't..." My voice trailed off into the darkness.

"Daddy James? He don't own you. You acting like a baby. When you gone do what you want to do?"

"Daddy James has always said that if a man really loved me he would wait."

"Haven't I been waiting? What else should I be waiting for?"

I closed my eyes. I had not wanted our reunion to be a battle. "Let's just go get something to eat. I've missed you. I just want to be with you. Can't we spend time together without it being a fight?"

Wayne's fist flew into the dashboard, scraping a layer of skin off of his knuckles. I found myself cringing in the corner against the door.

"Get out."

"What?"

"Get out. You can walk home from here. I'm going."

"Wayne, don't do this," I begged, tears rising to my eyes. Please, don't do this!"

"Get out!" he shouted. "It's over. I don't want to see you anymore."

I stood in a pocket of deep darkness as Wayne's truck disappeared down the road. The walk home was long, and the sky, which once enchanted me with its beauty, waned pale instead, the bright stars nothing but dim bulbs ready to fade into oblivion. I knew there would be no way to get past my grandfather without him seeing my tears and so I braced myself for the confrontation. He had only to look at me to know what had happened and he left me to sob alone on the front porch as he stood leaning against the doorframe, anger permeating his spirit. I heard him on the telephone with one of the Tanner parents, but I tuned out the words he spat into the receiver. Daddy James went to bed without a comment and when he awoke the next morning, I was still planted in the pine swing curled soundly asleep.

Everett brushed the hair out of my face, startling me from a restless nap. I lifted my body up uneasily, pulling my knees into my chest.

"What time is it?"

"Eight o'clock."

I rubbed the sleep from my eyes, pulling my hands through my tangled hair. "Where's Daddy James?"

"Went to get some supplies. Said he'd be back in an hour." Everett sat down beside me. "I heard what happened last night. I'm sorry. My brother can be a fool when he wants to be. He caught hell when he finally came home this morning."

"It was my fault. I shouldn't have made him angry."

"Don't you dare defend him. He was wrong. You didn't deserve that."

"You don't understand. I don't make it easy for him."

"Is that the line he's using now? You make it hard for him? He can't control his behavior because of you?" Everett sighed. "Even my mother knows Wayne isn't any good for you."

I pulled my legs in closer, leaning my head against the front of my thighs. Everett watched me, then lifted the hem of his tee shirt, and wiped at the edge of my mouth where drool had dried in a crusty film down my chin. His hands felt warm against my skin and I pulled away from the gentleness of his touch.

"I need to get a shower," I said, avoiding his eyes.

He nodded, grabbing my hand as I tried to ease past him. "He's not worth it, Janay. He's my brother and I love him, but he's not worth the hurt you're going through. If he loved you he wouldn't hurt you."

Pulling my hand away, I slammed the front door behind me and ran up the stairs to hide. From my bedroom window I watched as Everett made his way back across the yard and down toward the barn, disappearing inside to finish whatever chore had been left for him.

A long hot shower and a stomach full of food did nothing to ease the tension pulling at my being. I was angry. Although I did not truly miss Wayne, and was even beginning to believe what everyone else was saying about him not being right for me, I was angry that he had left me. Why were people always leaving me? What had I done to deserve to be left so coldly?

The water lay still across the pond. I'd always marveled at the clarity of the pond, no murky shadows dimming the wetness. Sunshine shimmered just so against the surface, sparkling like melting ice. The grass beneath my bottom tickled the back of my bare legs, edging the hem of my shorts. Plucking the thin blades, I tossed them into the humid air, the heat having risen to the brim of discomfort. Perspiration trickled against the length of my torso pasting the cotton tee shirt against my chest and back. I found comfort in the farm sounds that swallowed up my trepidation. Tranquility danced with me in the summer sun.

Everett approached hesitantly. His was a slow climb over the hill leading in my direction. He twisted a damp shirt in his hands. The steady work had thickened the muscles along his arms and across his chest, nicely offsetting the length of his solid limbs. I could not help but gasp with admiration.

When he finally reached the edge of the water, he dropped down beside me, extending his legs. "Hey."

"Hey."

"Want some company?"

"Don't you have work to do?"

That damn smile caressed me. "We're done. I was headed home, but wanted to make sure you were okay. Mr. Tucker said it would be okay to come check on you."

"I just bet he did."

Everett nodded. "Wayne called."

"Why?"

"Probably to apologize. He's good at that. Your grandfather refused to call you to the phone though."

"Good."

"You mean that?"

I shrugged. Everett leaned back on his elbows.

"Why do you waste your time with my brother? Don't you think you deserve better?"

I ignored him and returned to my grass plucking.

"Your grandfather thinks it's his fault that you are too trusting of men."

"He said that?"

"Not in so many words."

"You two seem to spend a lot a time talking about me."

He laughed. "I like talking to him. I like working on the farm with him. I think I might want a farm of my own someday."

I eyed him curiously. "What happened to your calling?"

"Nothing. I'm just as close to God and firm in my convictions about doing good and being an example for others."

"That's good I guess."

"I admire your convictions too. It takes a lot not to give in to the pressure, especially when you think it's love. The temptations can be hard to resist."

"Look, it has nothing to do with resisting temptation. Just...just stay out of it, okay?"

"Hey, there's nothing wrong with being a virgin. Some days I wish I still were. I think it would have been a great gift to give to the woman I've fallen in love with."

"I'm not a virgin." The declaration fell easily out of my mouth, no rebounding syllables jumping to slap my face. "I made a big mistake a while back and I promised myself and my grandfather that I wouldn't let it happen again."

Everett nodded his head and then I let the entire story come pouring out. When I'd finished, he still had not moved and there was no judgment of damnation peering past his eyes. For the first time, I felt as though the burden of guilt was fading, granting me absolution for my sin.

Sitting up Everett reached over and took my hand beneath his. "You are a beautiful person, Black. You've done nothing wrong but you want to take the blame for everything bad that has ever happened to you." His hand brushed along the curve of my cheek.

"Nobody calls me Black except Daddy James, and maybe my best friend Earl."

"I'm sorry. I didn't mean to offend you. I'm just so use to your grandfather calling you Black that if felt natural to do so myself."

I nodded, a faint blush of color rising to my cheeks. "It's okay. I like you calling me Black."

We both smiled. Everett got up to leave, brushing dirt from the seat of his jeans. I rose with him, pushing my hands deep into my pockets.

"Thanks."

"For what."

"For being my friend." I looked down shyly.

Everett cupped my chin to stare into my eyes. "Friends first. No matter what, you and I will always be friends first. Deal?"

"Deal."

Hugging my hand in his, we walked back toward the farm and Daddy James who sat rocking on the porch waiting for us.

I sat down against the bottom step as Everett pulled out of the drive, waving his hand in the distance.

Daddy James pulled a gnawed toothpick from between his teeth, tossing it over the railing out into the dirt yard. "That boy called here for you."

"I know."

"What you gone do?"

"I don't know."

"You've got a lot of decisions to be making."

I looked up to where he sat staring down at me, waiting for him to continue.

"That boy ain't your problem. You need to be deciding 'bout what you plan to do cause you ain't gone be sitting round here doing nothing but sucking up my air conditioning all day long."

"I can help work the farm."

Daddy James shifted his gaze, raising his eyebrows. "Why?"

"Well, you need help, don't you?"

"No. I needs for you to start making some plans 'bout going to school."

"I don't want to go to school."

"Why? What other big plans you got? You got a job maybe or a husband waiting to take care of you?"

I glared in his direction. "I don't need any one to take care of me. I can take care of myself."

"Well, you best start acting like it."

I got up and stormed into the house.

"Where do you think you're going?"

"I've got a call to make."

Daddy James rubbed a fist against his thigh, deep breathes rushing into his lungs. As he called out my name, I ignored him, dialing Wayne instead. Later that evening, as Daddy James slumbered heavily in a chair, I crept down to the edge of the road. Our arguing had been bitter. Daddy James had lectured and I'd responded with teenage indignation. I thought I was grown and would no longer be controlled. I fumed as I waited for Wayne to come get me.

The boy was all grin as he picked me up and sped away from the farm. "I knew you wouldn't let that old man keep us apart. You're my girl!" he exclaimed.

I smiled weakly. "Why'd you hurt me like that? Why'd you leave me alone on the road like you did, Wayne?"

Wayne grinned sheepishly. "Baby, I'm sorry. I didn't mean nothing by it. You just get me all worked up until I want to explode. I ain't never wanted nobody as bad as I want you, Janay. But I love you. You know that."

"Have you talked to your brother?"

He shrugged. "Forget him. I ain't said nothing to him since he jumped in my face all big and bad. He thinks he's so high and mighty. Boy's a punk."

"He's your brother."

"Yeah. But I don't plan on spending the whole night talking about the prodigal son. If that's what you had in mind I can turn around and take you back home right now."

I shook my head.

He grinned with satisfaction. "Good. 'Cause I got better plans for us, baby girl."

"Where are we going?"

"Secret place, baby. Some place where we won't be disturbed."

The ride seemed long although we only wound our way through town, up the main boulevard and down toward the elementary school. Wayne drove toward the back of the old brick building. Pulling his truck up alongside the dumpsters, he blocked any exit from the passenger door. Throwing the transmission into park and turning off the engine, Wayne cracked open the windows, then leaned to adjust the radio. The Commodores crooned seductively in the background.

"You scared?" Wayne asked huskily, playing with the buttons on my blouse.

I shrugged, studying the dark surroundings, the faint green glow from the radio the only light shining in the cab's interior.

Wayne kissed me, pressing himself so tight against me that I felt as though I was suffocating. I gasped for air, pushing my palms against his chest.

"That's it, baby. I know you want it," he muttered fumbling his hands against my pelvis.

"Wayne, slow down. Please..."

I felt the buttons pop on my shirt as he continued to kiss me, his lips like lead weight against my skin. The struggle continued as I suddenly fought for some control.

"Stop, Wayne. Please...don't."

The slap was fierce, slamming my head into the door. Shades of gray spun before my eyes, swirling me upside down and around in the cab of that vehicle. The disorientation was intense, blinding my senses. As the clouds faded from my vision, I could feel Wayne's hands pulling at my panties, his fingers leaving bruises against my thighs. I had no fight inside me, the wealth of it having been slapped away. Not since Candy had I felt so utterly humiliated. Not since Reverend Prescott had I felt so violated. Not since Lavinia had I felt so much pain. Not since Manroot left had I felt so alone.

Wayne whispered in my ear as he forced himself between my legs, his body intruding into mine, his hands mauling my breasts. "That's right, baby. I know you love me. Don't fight it. Oh, yeah. I love you, girl. I love you..."

Hours later when he left me standing at the bottom of my porch, a single light in the hallway to greet me, I could find no tears to cry. When Daddy James opened the door and saw the bruises against my face and the clothes torn around my body, there were still no tears. Not even as I stumbled up the stairwell to wash the offense down the drain could I force the hurt to shower from my eyes. Daddy James cried though. He cried loudly, his screams ringing like distant echoes in the back of a dream. His cries sliced through the midnight air, slapping against the breeze as he drove madly down the road and to the Tanner home.

"It's okay, Daddy," I whispered into the emptiness, the house having grown quiet around me. "It's okay. He loves me. It was only because he loves me..."

****

The next morning I rose and dressed like nothing had happened. The wound down the side of my face had already started to subside, the edges fading from black to blue to pink. Daddy James puttered over the stove, and outside, it was raining, a torrential wave of water falling from the sky. Everett sat at our kitchen table, his head in his hands. They both looked up anxiously as I made my way into the room.

"Good morning," I mumbled, avoiding the stares of concern that fell upon me. Daddy James dropped the pot of coffee back onto the stove. Everett rose from where he sat, reaching out an arm as though to steady me on my feet.

"Are you okay?" he asked, his voice saturated with worry.

"Yeah," I shrugged, reaching for a porcelain mug. "Why wouldn't I be?"

The two men passed a look between them. Daddy James dropped heavily into a kitchen chair. "Black, I know that boy done forced himself on you last night."

I gripped my coffee cup tightly. "Wayne loves me, Daddy. What happened was an accident. He didn't mean to hurt me."

The elder Tucker bit down hard against his tongue, his jaw tightening into a harsh line. Everett pressed his hand against my arm and I drew back quickly as if burned. Daddy James sucked in swiftly, slamming a palm against the table. He and I stared at each other, hurt clouding his eyes, emptiness filling mine.

I broke the silence. "I don't want to talk about this. Neither one of you understands. Wayne loves me."

"No," Everett replied. "No, he doesn't. He *raped* you. A man doesn't *rape* a woman he loves."

I felt my bottom lip start to quiver. "How do you know he raped me? How do you know I didn't want it?" My voice had risen three octaves higher as I shouted in his direction. Daddy James cringed and I suddenly wanted to draw back the knife I'd just plunged into his chest. I had only to look into his eyes to feel the pain I'd just placed into his heart.

"Leave me alone," I said, slamming out of the room. "Just stay out of my business."

Daddy James stormed, rushing behind me. His anger was turbulent, flooding the house with ire. "I didn't have to be there to know what he done, Black. You can cover for him all you want, and don't think for one minute that I'm gone believe that lie he told his Daddy 'bout you hitting your face on the dashboard when he stopped short to keep from running over some deer in the road. I know that was a bald faced lie!

"Now, you will not see this boy again. Do you hear me? I won't have it. If you're gonna live under my roof, then you will do as I say. Now, you want it over, it's over. I won't talk about it no more, but you will do as I say do and I say you will not see this boy ever again."

I sucked in air before letting my next words drop heavy to the floor. "Then I won't live under your roof. I am not going to stop seeing Wayne."

Daddy James eyed me from head to toe. Defiance had finally slapped him across the face and I watched as its bitter welt swelled within his cheeks.

"Then get out," he stated firmly, his pronouncement final. Daddy James slammed down the hall and up the stairs. His footsteps lumbered heavily against the hardwood floors. In the distance, I heard his bedroom door slam closed behind him.

At that exact moment, the front door opened, and I looked up to see Wayne standing in the archway, having heard the whole conversation from the front porch. "Let's go," he said extending his hand toward me. "We can come back for your stuff later."

Everett moved as though to step between us, then stopped, retreating back into the kitchen. A sudden sadness replaced the anger that had so consumed me just minutes before, the intense emotion edged in fear. This was not how it was supposed to be. This was not how I'd ever imagined leaving the shelter of my home. As Wayne guided me from the house to his truck, proclaiming that he would make things well, a wide smile plastered across his face, I knew in that instant that I had not hurt his heart. I had not been my mother. The damage to my own core, though, was devastating. Panic swelled from within as I reached out to be held, wanting desperately for someone to make it all better. Knowing that no matter what happened from that moment on, it never would be.

****

Sunlight peeked a lazy eye through the sheer lace curtain. Downstairs I could hear Daddy James and Everett whispering in quiet conversation together. Although deep sleep had eluded me, I did not feel tired. I did not feel much of anything, my emotions numb. After stretching the length of my body, I pulled the covers back up and over my head, sinking down into the warmth of the cotton sheets.

Inhaling Everett's scent off the bedclothes I filled my lungs with the aroma of the man who'd come to fill my heart as much as my grandfather did. Everett had helped right the many mistakes I'd made so long ago when I'd lost myself, the essence of my spirit wandering aimlessly in search of something I'd thought was gone from me. I filled my lungs once again, basking in the scent of my husband's love and strength.

I had not the energy to descend the stairs and join them. I did not possess the strength to endure the callers who would continue to come, filling our home with cascading arrangements of flowers and fruit. The house already reeked with the smell of cold chicken fried in hot Crisco in honor of my dead father and his memory as though the crisped shell of cooked meat could somehow ease the ache within the pit of our stomachs. Nausea rose in waves from my midsection as I thought about all the chicken that lay beneath foil covers in our kitchen.

A deep sigh escaped me, fleeing from me in rapid haste, afraid that it might get trapped. The duo of ghosts sat content at my feet waiting for me to continue the walk past the darkness they'd guarded for so very long. I clutched the covers tighter, swiping at the brimming tears with the back of my hand. I was not ready to walk the trail they'd laid before me but I knew I had no choice. I had to endure. There was nothing else left for me to do. I drifted once again back to days I'd longed to forget, the memories flooding my senses like bad smells from rotting meat.

The small apartment had been dingy at best. I'd tried desperately to make it feel like home but despite my best efforts it was still only a three-room flat in a dilapidated old building. A shaky back stairwell led to the only entranceway and the small domain boasted little but peeling walls and grimy windows. The refrigerator was only large enough to hold a carton of milk and a half dozen eggs and the cockroaches fought for control of the cupboards. A friend of Wayne's had found it for me and I'd moved in reluctantly, having nowhere else to go.

The first night had been the hardest. Lying atop an aged mattress, alone, had been terrifying. Wayne had promised to come be with me but had never shown. The night had been long and I cringed at the night noises that had disturbed any chance I may have had for some rest. A brief moment of slumber had been disturbed by the return of my nightmares and most of the night had found me cringing in tears against the wooden headboard.

The next day I'd waited hours for Wayne, who'd only laughed at my discomfort, promising that it would get better. I wanted desperately to believe the promises that swam off his tongue with relative ease. I wanted desperately to believe in something.

"What are we going to do today?"

Wayne shrugged, resting his body against the kitchen counter. "I got some business to take care of later, so I can't stay long. You need to be thinking 'bout getting a job though. I only paid the first month's rent and you gone need some money soon."

"A job?"

"Yeah, a job. Unless you got some money I don't know about, you gone have to support yourself somehow. I don't think your granddaddy's going to be giving you any money any time soon. Do you?"

I shrugged my shoulders, knowing he was right. I would have to look for something, but what did I know how to do? Three weeks later I found a job down in Elliston County, riding the bus forty-five minutes back and forth to waitress at the Truck Stop Cafe. The hours were long, the crowd unsavory, but nobody bothered me. There was an advantage to being James Tucker's granddaughter, an unmistakable "Keep Away" sign posted to my forehead.

Loneliness became routine and though I longed to call my grandfather, to hear the deep of his voice against my ear, I knew that I couldn't. I wasn't ready to admit my mistakes though, fearful that he wouldn't want to take me back. Instead, I worked a double shift from Friday to Wednesday, preferring work over getting any rest. Sleep was difficult at best, the nightmares overwhelming. My mother visited me regularly, having taken up residence within the depths of my anguish. I welcomed the rare occasion when one of my uncles would pay a visit in my dreams and allow me a brief reprieve from Lavinia's torment. Even my Aunt Eloise and the wealth of her tears were better than Lavinia's wrath and the darkness she fought to pull me into.

On Thursdays, the one day I had off, my time was spent inside waiting for Wayne to show up and during all that waiting I'd begun to read. On a regular basis I'd come to wear out the library card I'd acquired from the Creekton County Library. I enjoyed the companionship that came from strangers who asked nothing of me except to respect their need for quiet. The room was inviting, heavy oak bookcases lined floor to ceiling with books. The stories were numerous, tales of escape to places only imagined and I was reminded of the stories Daddy James had often amused me with.

At night, Langston Hughes whispered me to sleep, his poetry like soothing lullabies. Ntozake Shange woke me in the mornings, her vibrant rhetoric a welcoming alarm clock starting the day.

Shakespeare became my lover, teasing my womanhood with the lilt of his words. Edgar Allan Poe antagonized me, forcing me to question the darkness I believed myself to fear. Amiri Baraka debated with me and a host of characters and visionaries became my constant companions, visiting with me during those waking hours when I sat alone. Sometimes they even stayed to walk with me in my dreams, casts of characters guiding me where I did not know I could travel.

Wayne rarely came as he readied himself for school. His enthusiasm for me had dimmed after the only other time he'd tried to touch me and his manhood had withered in failure when I lay complacently beneath him. My fault, he had concluded. I'd somehow stripped him of his maleness, the pressures of my problems far too much for him to bear.

Although it should not have, the Sunday I'd planned a nice dinner, and he arrived five hours late, surprised me. Wayne entered nonchalantly, lifting his legs up onto the table top, dirt from his boots falling to the ivory cloth. I cringed in anger, the spoiled food laying cold on top of the counter. "Where have you been?"

He shrugged. "Business to take care of."

"What business?"

The silence was brief, a mere swallow of spit and an inhale of air.

"Well, you might as well know now. You gone hear it soon enough."

"Hear what?"

"Went to see Tanya Williams. Me and her had something to talk about."

I could feel the well of anger forming a heavy cloud in my head as I bit against my bottom lip.

"What?" I asked, my eyes following the movement of Wayne's fingers scratching at the length of his thigh.

"Tanya having a baby. She say it's mine."

Shock trickled. I'd not at all expected the words he had just uttered with little hesitation and even less remorse.

"A baby? But how..."

"How? Damn, woman, how stupid can you be! How?!" His laugh was cruel, his stare just shy of being hostile.

"When did you...? I sucked in a fountain of air, gasping deeply. "Well, it's not yours, is it?"

Wayne shrugged, his shoulders reaching skyward as he took a sip from the bottle of soda he'd just opened. The expression in his eyes seemed to dare me to say something, and then he sneered, a condescending grunt falling with an exhale of breath.

I snapped. The pounding across my brow was deafening, drowning out the "yeah" that passed over his lips, and the cobalt blue drinking glass that flew from my hand, shattering against the wall behind his head. My tears blinded me and the dishes flying in his direction as he tore out the door, slamming the screen behind him. The hurt in my heart was excruciating as rage tore through my body. How could I have let him betray me so casually? How could I have allowed him to think there could be any forgiveness for his every deception? How could I have been such a fool to have let him run me from my home and my grandfather's arms? What had happened to me and why was there no one to make it well again?

They all came eventually. All of them except Daddy James. I'd left them hanging on the other side of the locked door, as I pretended to not be inside. Earl had cursed me for not calling, then had cried for me before heading back down the stairs. Everett had only stood silently, outlining my frame through the wooden entrance as if he could see through it and me. There was only one knock I permitted entrance. Only one person I allowed inside.

Mrs. Tanner shook her head, her emotions fluctuating between pity and distress. She'd hugged me close, holding on as though afraid to let go. I hugged her back because I was.

"I went to see your grandfather."

"How is he?"

She nodded her head. "He'd be better if you were to go home to him."

I rose to go look out the window. "I can't."

She continued to nod. "Janay, first of all you need to understand why I'm here. If you were my child and this had happened between you and I, I would want there to be someone who could come to you and make sure that you were well. I know that your grandfather would want someone to do this for you, to make sure that you are alright."

I wiped a tear from my eye as Mrs. Tanner continued.

"I have always doted on my sons, but I have also been the first to admit when they've done something wrong. I can in all honesty tell you that Wayne is no good. God forgive me, because he's my child, and I raised him, but the boy is just no good. I should have warned you about him in the very beginning but I didn't expect this thing between you to last and I surely didn't think you'd suffer as you have."

My chin dropped to my chest.

"Now, I need to say something to you and what you do after is your choice. But you need to know that Wayne has gone. He's decided to forego college and go play basketball in Japan someplace. His father and I aren't happy about this but at this point, he is going to do what he wants, despite what we advise. He has packed his things and has left this other young lady, Tanya something or other, in the lurch. She was expecting wedding bells and a life-long commitment to a pro-ball player. Instead she's gotten a one way ticket to being a single mother, so you at least consider yourself lucky in that respect."

Mrs. Tanner took a deep breath shifting her weight from the heel of one shoe to the heel of the other. She resumed the conversation.

"I watched what was going on with you and my boys and I didn't say anything. I know now that I should have. You might not realize it, but Everett loves you. Wayne never did. And, I believe that if you are honest with yourself, you love Everett as well, or at least I think you could. Everett has a great heart and right now every square inch of it is wrapped up in you. There is absolutely nothing my son wouldn't do for you and he's hurting because he can't help you. You won't let him. But," she paused, "I also know that before you can even think about loving my son, you need to start loving yourself. And that's something we can't do for you. There isn't one of us who can make that happen if you aren't ready to make it happen for yourself."

The tears were drying against my cheek as I let Mrs. Tanner finish.

"Darling, you need to realize your own self-worth before you can see anyone else's. You are an incredible young woman. You have enormous potential. Your value is limitless, but you don't see it or believe it yet. And if you can't, then you can't expect anyone else to."

Mrs. Tanner reached out her hand and stroked my shoulder gently. I turned away from her, the tears beginning to fall in heavy waves for a second time. She nodded her head slowly.

"Your grandfather asked me to give you this." Reaching into her purse, she pulled out a large manila envelope. I took the mailer from her, pulling it close to my chest. Her gaze captured mine and held it, a mother's concern staring intently at me. "If you need anything, Janay, please know that you can call me. Even if you just need someone to talk to. I'm right here for you. Don't ever forget that, okay?"

I nodded as Mrs. Tanner wrapped her arms around me one last time before leaving. Staring behind her I waved as she inched her way down the precarious set of stairs, watching until she disappeared out of sight.

Back behind my locked door, I opened the envelope and emptied its contents against my mattress. Out fell a folded slip of paper, a bus ticket, a credit card inscribed with my name, two hundred dollars in cash, and a small white bible. Daddy James' neat printing lay inked on the page of notepad. "Black, you think the answers are here," he'd written. "So go, and may God go with you. Love, Daddy James."

Two days later I left for Angola.

****

The second Thursday of each month was visiting day at the Louisiana State Penitentiary. The bus from Creekton had left me in Angola four days prior so I had plenty of opportunity to rehearse what I was going to say to Manroot. I had a lot I wanted to say to my daddy.

At precisely nine o'clock that morning, I stood in line with a number of other women, children, and a few men waiting for the visitor check-in desk to open. At precisely five after nine two correctional officers in matching khaki uniforms walked in with clipboards in hand. A tall, thin red-haired man shouted for silence then directed us into a single line. I counted thirty-five people in front of me.

The wait was exhausting. Off in one corner a young Hispanic girl with skin like honey and waist-length hair the color of licorice vomited into a nasty metal garbage can. Around me children were crying and screaming as mothers pulled hair, slapped bare legs, or disregarded them totally.

As I approached the head of the line, I found myself getting even more nervous than when I'd first arrived. My stomach tossed and turned begging to join the Hispanic girl in the corner. I fought back the nausea.

The heavyset black man seated at the table glanced up at me quickly, then asked for my name.

"Janay Tucker."

"Social security number?"

The numbers rolled quickly off my tongue as I twisted a damp tissue between my palms.

"Inmate name?"

"Manroot Tucker."

The man looked up at me again, then jotted more information onto his thin-ruled notepad. Pulling a plastic bag from a cardboard box, he had me drop all my personal possessions inside, secured it before my eyes, and made me sign my name across the seal.

"Bus number one, stand over there," he commanded, pointing toward the door.

It was an old yellow school bus that transported us from the registration center through the barbed, wire-topped, prison gates. Guards stood in every corner, shotguns in front of their chests. An elderly white woman sat beside me, coughing phlegm into a lace-edged handkerchief, rambling on about her son Jeffrey.

"My Jeffrey ain't never did nothin' wrong. My Jeffrey don't belong here. My Jeffrey's a good boy. My Jeffrey..."

I nodded politely wanting to tell her that my daddy had never done anything wrong either. My daddy didn't belong here. My daddy had been a good daddy. Getting off the bus was the hardest step for me to take but I did it, following the crowd toward the prison doors. It was easy to figure out who'd been here before and who had not. Old timers knew the ropes and went through the motions effortlessly, whilst the few of us there for the first time, had not a clue.

I stepped through the caged door into the hands of a female guard.

"Arms out to your side," she commanded running her fingers under my arms and down my sides. Tears sprang to my eyes as she searched me, then waved me off to another line. Led down a narrow gray hall and into a holding room we were directed to sit and once again wait. The old woman still bemoaned her Jeffrey, until someone, I'm not sure who, told her to shut up.

It felt like an hour had passed before the female guard came to the door and began to call out names. I sat up anxiously, knowing that I was not far from seeing my father. Anxiety played at my limbs, pacing me across the floor, from one chair to another. And then my moment of reckoning arrived as the guard returned for the fifth time and called my name.

"Janay Tucker."

I rose, uneasy on my feet, and headed for the door.

"This way," the woman commanded, heading back down the hall from where we'd just come. A large man with an athletic build met us at the door. The woman nodded her head and turned away.

"Are you Janay Tucker?" he asked, searching the paper in front of him.

"Yes, sir."

"Manroot Tucker has declined your visitation. You will be returning on the next bus out."

I stared at him, dumbfounded. "What do you mean 'declined'. I came to see my father."

The man looked up, nodding his head. "I'm sorry. Your father doesn't want to see you."

His words stung, falling in a loud echo against my ears.

"No," I said, shouting louder than I meant to. "There must be some mistake."

The man stiffened, tightening his hold on his slip of paper. "There is no mistake. Manroot Tucker has declined your visitation. You will have to leave."

Sobs racked my body as they escorted me out of the prison and onto a waiting bus. I rode back alone, the driver stealing glances every so often into his rear view mirror. Only once did he attempt to utter words of consolation and in return, I fired a barrage of curses in his direction. I cried myself all the way back into town and through the door of my motel room. Hours later, it was Mrs. Tanner who answered the telephone. It was Everett who hung it up.

As I lay alone lamenting over Manroot's rejection, I could not help thinking that through all the years when I'd felt most alone, Daddy James had always been there by my side ready to pick up the pieces. Had I not been so foolish, he would be here now and I would not feel as horribly as I did. For the first time, when everything seemed hopeless and I felt most lost, it was neither Manroot nor Lavinia that my heart cried for, but Daddy James. Daddy James had always been my safety net and I'd taken his sturdy presence for granted much like I took the breath of life for granted. I'd been hateful and ugly toward him and he'd only been unwavering in his love and devotion, support and discipline offered in return.

What kind of child was I to be raised by so wonderful a man and to throw all that he'd ever done for me back in his face like it had meant nothing to me? Could there be any forgiveness for so great a crime? And what of my father who'd professed to love me always? Why would he turn from me when I only wanted to know him as I'd known him when I'd been six years old and he'd been large and loving in my glassy eyes? Could I not have created so great a mess to have dropped my behind into? And would I be able to pick myself up and out of my confusion and find my way back to the path that Daddy James had so lovingly laid out for me?

That night as I drifted off to sleep, I clutched at the small bible, the leather case inscribed with my name and birth date. I struggled to form the words to express the hurt that hugged my heart. Pray, my grandfather had said often to me.   Prayer, he professed, could work miracles. I was desperate for a miracle.

Everett arrived the next afternoon to take me home. Driving past the large brick structure behind the locked gates, I lifted my hand to give a slight wave and whispered good-bye to my father. It had to be enough that Manroot had at least known that I'd been there.

"What now, Black?" Everett asked, as we sat sipping thick, chocolate milkshakes and dining on grilled cheese sandwiches at a diner in Huntsville, Alabama.

"Well, I know what I've been looking for has always been right in front of me. I just couldn't see it."

He nodded as I continued.

"Daddy James has always wanted the very best for me. He's given me everything that I could have possibly wanted and he has never once asked for anything in return. I've let him down and I'm going to do whatever I have to do to make it up to him."

Everett smiled. I so loved his smile. Its warmth was reminiscent of my grandfather's. It was honest and genuine and when he caressed you with it, you could believe that it was meant to touch your heart.

"I've decided to go to school. In fact, I'm already enrolled at Creekton Technical College for next semester."

Everett looked surprised. "Where did that come from?" he asked.

"Well, Daddy James has a lot of property that needs looking after. He doesn't have any other children to pass it along to, but he does have me. I'm not going to be responsible for losing everything my grandfather and his grandfather worked so hard for. But I'll have to prove myself worthy, and I can't do that if I don't do what Daddy James wants, and he wants me to go to school."

"I think he was hoping you'd leave town and go see some of the world."

"I know but I've been away from Daddy James long enough. We're all each other have. I need him, and I want to be right by his side if he ever needs me."

Everett lowered his head slightly, twirling the red and white striped straw in his glass. "Black, I hope you know that you have me, too." He looked up hesitantly. "I mean...I really care about you. I..."

I reached out to stroke the top of his hand. "I know. I feel the same way about you, Everett. It's like I said, everything I've ever been looking for has been right here in front of me. But you know, I still have a lot of growing up to do. I've got to learn to love myself before I can love anybody else. Your mother helped me to understand that."

The man's smile swirled laps around me as he reached to let his fingertips linger like silk against my cheek.

I avoided sleep as Everett and I drove the long length of highway back toward Creekton, the conversation between us waning just before we'd merged onto Interstate 95. Everett drove in silence, his thoughts focused on the roadway ahead of us and the traffic that slowed our trek.

I had no desire to focus on anything so I slumped down low in the passenger seat, staring out the window at nothing, thinking only of the words on the Anita Baker cassette that played repeatedly out of the car's speakers. The easy rhythm of the soft jazz and the quiet of the car ride should have been enough to lull me into a deep sleep, but there was something inside me that refused to let Lavinia come slithering into my dreams to taunt me. I would not allow my mother to add insult to the injury that had already bruised my heart. I imagined her deriving some perverse pleasure at my father's flagrant rejection. My mother loving the fact that Manroot no longer loved me best.

As we maneuvered our way home, I thought about my mother. I wanted to believe that she would have liked me had she given me half a chance. I had to wonder why Lavinia had never wanted to give me a chance. She might have even loved me if she could have let me into her heart. I couldn't help but wonder if she even had a heart. I wanted to believe that my mother loved my father once because Daddy James had told me so. And Daddy James never lied.

I barely noticed the tears that slipped past the thick of my lashes. It was only when Everett wiped the dampness against the back of his fingers that I had any awareness I was crying.

Everett parked his car in front of the house and waited as I climbed the stairs. Eyeing the familiar structure, I noted the peeling paint and was surprised to discover how much I missed the earthy tones that stretched behind me. When I'd made it to the door, I waved him off, knowing that I had to do this on my own.

The old man's movements were slow as he made his way to the front door. Pulling the heavy wooden structure open, he leaned upon the frame for support. I stood nervously not sure what to say.

"Hey, Daddy."

He stared, reacquainting himself with my features, then pushed the screen door open for me to enter. I entered the foyer hesitantly, still not sure if my presence would be welcome. Then, without thinking another thought, I hugged my grandfather, my arms melting around his aged body, the tears washing over his chest. When I felt him quiver, his tears dropping with mine, I knew that I was home and back into my grandfather's heart to stay.

"Manroot wouldn't see me."

He nodded. "I know. You needed to find out yourself."

"But why? Why doesn't he love me?"

Daddy James eased into a seat in the foyer. "Black, Manroot has never stopped loving you. You wanted to believe that because he'd gone and you couldn't reach out to touch him with your hands, that he couldn't touch you with his heart. But this was the only way he thought he could do right by you. It was the only way *I* thought he could do right by you. We didn't know from one day to the next what might happen with your daddy. There wasn't one of us that wanted to risk seeing you hurt any more than you'd already been.

"Prison changed Manroot. Your mama dying destroyed him. He loved Lavinia. Loved her more than his own life. And when the love wasn't sweet and pretty anymore, he didn't know what to do with it. He didn't know how to keep it safe inside him and so he let it destroy him. If you had seen Manroot the way I've seen him since they put him in that place, then

Wayne would have only been the beginning. Every man like him and worse would have been okay for you. Your Daddy wanted better than okay for you."

"I used to hate him so much. I hated that he couldn't be here. I hated that he took himself away from me after my mama was gone. I hated him so much that I forgot how to love him. I thought it was all my fault and that he blamed me for everything that happened."

Daddy James nodded his head. "You didn't hate him as much as he hated himself. And he loved you as much as you loved him."

"I done you wrong, Daddy. I'm sorry. Please, can I come back home?"

Daddy James chuckled. "Black, you ain't need to be asking to come back. This is your home. You was born here and you was raised here. The only thing I ever expects from you is that you will respect yourself, me, and the rules I've set for us. Them rules is the same ones I put on your Daddy, on my other children, and on myself. If this is going to be a home worth being in then we all got to follow some rules, like them or not. You understand?"

I nodded. "Yes, sir."

Daddy James reached out to pat my back. "Now, I was just about to go fishing. There's fish in that pond that need catching."

I shook my head, the rise of a giggle easing past my lips. "Daddy, we ain't never caught no fish in that pond."

Daddy James pulled himself to his feet. "Guess that means you and I just ain't got it right yet. Guess we needs to be doing it more often."

****

Homecoming opened more doors than I ever thought I'd manage to fit through. For a while I tiptoed around my grandfather, wary of throwing our reunion off balance. With every smile he draped around my shoulders, guilt swelled like a cold rush of winter air within me. In no time though, my footsteps became regular and I was once again dancing up the dust in the fields.

School was proving to be a welcome challenge and I no longer sat miserable in classes. No one called me names. There were no taunts to greet me each morning or insults following me home. I was no longer fearful that my opinions would be ridiculed and my ideas disregarded. There was value in my words and thoughts, and class after class gave credence to my abilities. I relished the learning, appreciating the new found knowledge and every so often as I sat pouring over the text of my books, I'd catch my grandfather watching me, pride pouring from his gaze like a beam of light shining upon me.

I grew taller in spirit every day, no longer feeling the need to find my self-worth in Manroot's eyes. I'd embraced the fire and had not been burned. I wanted to believe that there were no more scars to battle, no more secrets to fear and hide from. But the nightmares continued. Lavinia continued to visit, my mother's blood bathing me in my dreams.

The clock on the kitchen wall read half past two. I sat quietly in the kitchen, the kettle on the stove beginning to hum softly. Lifting the container carefully, I poured boiling water into a large mug, dipping a Lipton tea bag in and out of the bubbling water. Daddy James shuffled in behind me, his slow gait in time with the darkness.

"I'm sorry, Daddy. I didn't mean to wake you."

"You ain't wake me. I was up reading when I heard you come down. You have another bad dream?"

I nodded as I filled a second mug with water, preparing a cup of tea for my grandfather.

Taking the seat beside me, Daddy James rested his hand on mine. "Is it the same dream, Black?"

I nodded my head, sliding onto the cushioned chair beneath me.

Daddy James tapped my hand gently. "Why you think you keep dreaming 'bout your mama?"

I shrugged, not sure I wanted to know the answer. "Don't know, Daddy. I just do."

The room grew silent as we both sipped hesitantly at the hot brew.

"What do you remember about your mama, Black?"

I twisted my face in thought, then shrugged my shoulders again. "Not much, Daddy. What I do remember I try real hard to forget."

Daddy James nodded his head. "Maybe you need to remember so them dreams can go away? Maybe you need to think about the time you was with your mama and all that happened to you."

Anxiety swept up and over me causing my hand to shake. Hot tea spilled out over my fingers and I jumped to cool my flesh with cold water from the kitchen sink.

My voice quivered as I spoke, a chill blowing through me. "Let's not talk about this now, Daddy. You look tired and I need to get to sleep. We both have a long day tomorrow."

My grandfather eyed me cautiously, still sipping at his own cup of drink. His eyes followed my exit out of the room. The next morning the familiar sound of Everett's car swept through the window and I jumped anxiously to peer outside. I watched as he exited the vehicle, gliding to Daddy James' side. The two men greeted each other warmly. Everett's visits had been infrequent since he'd gone away to seminary and though we wrote each other faithfully and spoke frequently on the telephone, I missed his companionship. I had waited anxiously for his return and was hoping that he would even consider coming back to work on the farm while he was home. Looking up toward the window, Everett waved his hand excitedly.

"Hey, Black!"

Daddy James gestured for him to go inside and I raced down the stairs to meet him.

"Hey, Everett!" I exclaimed excitedly as he swung me in his arms, lifting me off the ground. "Welcome home."

Everett held me at arm's length, studying me from head to toe. "You look great."

"Thanks, you too."

He pulled me close again, hugging me tightly, and I felt a familiar warmth rising from the pit of my stomach, tingling through my body.

"So, what have you been up to?"

I laughed lightly. "I don't know where to begin. You first."

Everett nodded as Daddy James came into the house. "You two cluttering up my house. Why don't you take it down by the pond whilst I fix us all some lunch?"

"Daddy, I can fix lunch. Why don't you sit down with Everett for a while?"

"I can sit down with Everett later. Right now you two needs to be getting out of my way."

"But Daddy James—"

The old man cut an eye in my direction, then spoke directly to Everett. "Boy, she's still hard-headed when she wants to be. I know you know how to listen. Take this girl down by the pond someplace so you two can talk. I ain't interested in hearing your noise. I've got lunch to fix."

Everett smiled. "Yes, sir, Mr. James." Grabbing my elbow, Everett pushed me out the door as Daddy James hummed behind us. Racing across the fields, Everett and I fell to the ground beside the water's edge. The sun glistened across the surface as newly sprouted blossoms peeked from the ground.

"So, start from the beginning and catch me up," Everett said, pulling at the blades of grass beneath us.

Laughter rang in our voices as we shared our news. I told him about school and the work I was doing on the farm. Daddy James had been giving me more responsibility with managing the land and I was doing a decent job of it.

"So, are you ready for graduation?"

I shrugged, laying back against the grass. "I almost wish it wasn't over. I've really had a great time. It hasn't been easy but I've enjoyed it."

Everett smiled down on me and I could feel the tingling inside growing warmer and warmer. We stared into each other's eyes, quiet wrapping an arm around us. Birds chirped in the distance and sounds bounced off the water before us, but all either of us heard was the deep beating of our hearts. I reached out my hand and pressed it to his chest. The pounding against my palm was heavy, beating in sync with the patter of my own heart.

"Black, may I kiss you?" he asked nervously, easing his body closer to mine.

I barely nodded my permission before reaching up to press my lips against his, the gentleness of his touch overwhelming. His lips skated easily across mine as he cupped his hand gently along the side of my face.

"I've missed you," he whispered, pulling away reluctantly.

I smiled, wrapping my arms around his neck. "Not nearly as much as I missed you," I whispered back.

We kissed again, loosing ourselves in the embrace, stopping only when we became aware of the length of our bodies pressed too closely together, rocking in slow motion against each other. Everett pulled himself away, rising up off the ground. Reaching out a hand, he pulled me to my feet.

"I'm sorry. I didn't mean to—" His voice dropped midsentence as he looked down nervously, suddenly embarrassed by the rise of manhood pressing at the front of his pants.

"Don't be sorry," I said, reaching out to take his hand in mine. "I'm glad you did. I wanted you to."

Everett nodded, then leaned to kiss my forehead. "Let's go get some lunch."

With our fingers locked tightly together, we headed back toward the house and Daddy James who sat waiting for us on the front porch.

"You two look hungry," he called out as we approached the steps. "Food's ready if you is." He smiled a grin of pure satisfaction.

"Yes, sir," Everett answered, squeezing my hand gently. "We're both ready to eat."

After saying grace, we ate heartily. The food was good. Short ribs, potato salad, hot buttered rolls, and string beans graced our plates. As we finished, Everett dropped his napkin neatly onto the table, then turned his chair to face Daddy James.

Daddy leaned back ever so slightly in his chair sensing the conversation was taking a serious turn. I looked at Everett anxiously wondering what it was he was about to say as his eyes darted back and forth between me and my grandfather.

"Mr. James, next week Sunday, I'll be giving my first sermon at Mt. Zion Baptist Church over in Carrboro. I would be honored if you and Black would be there with me and if you'd both have dinner with me and my parents afterwards."

Daddy James clasped his large hands in front of him, nodding his head slowly. "Boy, you know I wouldn't miss being there for you for nothing in this world. I'm proud of you, son. Very proud. Me and Black will surely be there. Won't we, Black?"

I nodded my head, meeting Everett's eyes and we both smiled shyly.

Draped in our Sunday best, the Tucker and Tanner families sat side by side in the first pew. With Daddy James on my left and Mrs. Tanner on my right, we watched with pride as Everett marched down the aisle alongside Reverend Earl Perry. Mrs. Johnnie Mae Perry, the pastor's wife, sat on the other side of Mr. Tanner. The Mt. Zion Baptist Mass Choir led the procession, ringing in the service with a glorious noise.

As they introduced Reverend Everett Tanner to the congregation, I shook excitedly, tears rising to my eyes. Mrs. Tanner clasped my hand beneath hers, smiling brightly at me as her son came to stand at the altar.

Everett preached and the words resounded around the sanctuary. His sermon was titled, *It's Not Over Until God Says It's Over*, and at some points I felt as if he was speaking directly to me. He stood brilliant in his black robe, a printed stole in pale shades of tangerine, peach, and lemon draped around his neck. Clearly he had found his calling, and it was fitting for this man whose heart was kind and whose love was genuine.

There was a new found lightness in my heart as the service ended and the congregation marched up and out of the church. Outside we waited for Everett, taking in the warmth of the sunny day, a clear blue sky draped over our heads. Mrs. Tanner chattered excitedly, anxious to embrace her son. Mr. Tanner's chest swelled with pride as people rushed to congratulate them on Everett's success.

The day was dizzying, spinning rapidly past us. As the sun settled behind the west fields, shading the mass of land before us, Daddy James, Everett, and I sat quietly on the front porch. Everett had dropped his parents off home after dinner and had returned to spend the evening, sipping on lemonade and eating pound cake that I had made the night before. The mood was reflective as none of us spoke, simply enjoying the quiet of each other's presence. Everett clearing his voice with nervous anticipation startled me from the silence.

"Umm umm. Excuse me, Mr. James, but do you think you and I could talk in private for a moment?" I turned to stare in Everett's direction, noting how he struggled to avoid my eyes.

Daddy James leaned forward in his chair, then rose from where he sat. "Why don't we take us a walk," he responded, stepping down off the porch. Everett nodded his head, then followed behind him.

"We'll be back," Daddy James called over his shoulder. The two men walked away from the house locked in conversation. I watched them with curiosity, wondering what it was they were discussing so intensely. The clock in the hall ticked slowly, dragging time behind it. By the time they'd returned I'd cleared away the dishes, had straightened up the kitchen, and was finishing the last page of a newly purchased *Southern Living* magazine over a cup of lukewarm tea.

Daddy James leaned down to kiss my cheek, squeezed my hand, then headed up the stairs toward his bed.

"Daddy? Are you okay?"

He nodded, wiping at his eyes. "Yeah," he said, his voice quivering ever so slightly. "I'm fine. Just going to my bed. You lock up when Everett leaves okay?"

"Yes, sir," I said, my gaze following behind him. When his bedroom door closed, and his footsteps no longer echoed across the floor, I turned to Everett. "What's wrong? What's going on?"

Everett smiled sheepishly. "There's nothing wrong. Come sit with me for a minute," he said, extending his hand and pulling me toward the front porch.

Outside we sat side by side on the porch swing. A full moon sat regally in the dark sky, bright stars bidding him his proper due.

"Everett, what's going on?" I started, turning to face him.

Everett pressed a finger to my lips to silence me, then rose to go stand by the railing. "Black, I've got to make some very important decisions in the next few days."

I looked at him questioningly as he continued.

"I felt really good this morning. After I got through with my sermon, I knew that I'd made the right decision about the ministry. I'm a preacher and I'm going to be a good one." Everett came to sit back down beside me. "How did you feel about me this morning? How do you feel about me being a minister?"

"Everett, you know I'm proud of you. You were wonderful. I know you'll be a great minister."

Everett nodded slowly. "I know that you've not been big on the church and religion, but did you feel better about being there today?"

I shrugged. "I wasn't uncomfortable if that's what you're asking. I mean, I felt more at peace than I've felt in a long time."

Everett sighed heavily, twisting his hands anxiously. His next question rang out nervously. "Do you think you could be comfortable being a minister's wife with all the responsibilities that would entail?"

I looked up, shocked. He reached out to take my hands in his. "Black, I love you. I've always loved you. I don't know what my life would be like if you weren't in it. I don't want to have to think about what it would be like if I don't have to. I want you to be my wife."

Everett dropped down on one knee, pulling a modest diamond engagement ring with a thin gold band from his shirt pocket. Slipping it onto my finger, he kissed my hand gingerly, then stared up into my eyes. "Will you marry me, Black? Will you be my wife?" He squeezed my hand tightly, then continued. "You have to know that if you say yes you won't just be marrying me, but you will also be marrying my collar. People are going to expect certain things from you. It's not easy being a minister's wife and I can't promise that it won't be difficult."

"What do you expect from me?" I questioned, my palms starting to perspire profusely.

"I don't doubt that you won't be a wonderful wife. I have no fears of you not making me proud to call you Mrs. Everett Tanner. I would hope that you can someday believe as I believe. I only want you to give your faith a chance. I would only expect that you will honestly try."

I leaned to wrap my arms around his shoulders. "Yes," I whispered. "I'd be honored to be your wife, Reverend Tanner. I love you, Everett. I love you so much."

WITH LOVE IN BOTH HANDS...

****

It was not supposed to be raining, I thought, looking past the sheer white curtains to the outside. Graduation day was surely not supposed to be a day for rain. Daddy James stood out on the porch, a cup of coffee in his hand. Joining him, I instantly knew that this was a morning after. A morning after rainfall had saturated the dark earth, filling it with sweet elixir for the sun to sip off during a hot day. There was stillness in the air as moisture dropped from the leaves of trees against the dark green grass and insects swam like tiny fish in miniature pools of fluid. Newly bloomed roses wafted their sweet aromas beneath our noses and the rising warmth was wrapping a comfortable blanket over the land.

Daddy James wrapped his arms around me, hugging me close. "What are you thinking 'bout, Black?"

"Trying not to think, Daddy. Just want to take it all in and hold it for as long as I can."

He nodded. "I'm mighty proud of you, Black. You done good, baby girl."

I hugged him tightly. "So did you, Daddy. So did you."

I glanced at my watch, then blew a quick kiss against Daddy James' cheek. "I need to make a call. I've got to close the deal on those two hundred acres down by Lake Orange before we leave here today."

"That can't wait until tomorrow?"

"The price is right now, Daddy."

He nodded his head. "Better you than me," he murmured, taking a sip from his cup. In the distance, he saw Everett approaching and he lifted his hand in greeting.

"That boy's here mighty early."

I looked toward where he was pointing. The morning sun was rising in the background, just beginning to peek from behind the fading clouds. A faint blush rose to my cheeks as I watched Everett's car slowly approaching.

"And, I'm not even dressed yet. I swear!" I exclaimed, hurrying back inside.

Daddy James laughed behind me.

It was a day of celebrations, one greater than the other. After an early commencement ceremony I passed my college diploma to Daddy James who beamed with pride. Hours later, Everett and I stood with our parents by our side, and took our marriage vows, standing in the very spot where Manroot had sworn to love Lavinia till death. Daddy James gladly gave me away, welcoming Everett as his son at the same time. When the Tanners embraced us, I gained a mother and a second father and it all felt as right as that morning rain. We were family, anchored by love. I'd come full circle and it felt good.

Later that night Everett sat down beside me, slipping off his shoes. Dark socks covered his wide feet, the thin nylon stretching up his lean legs. I found myself studying the outline of his toes, afraid to look up past his knees.

As he leaned down to kiss me, his lips barely brushing against mine, I could feel the beat of my heart beginning to race. My hand rose from my side to gently cup the side of his face, lingering against the warmth of his cheek. Though sweet the touch of him was, I pulled back reluctantly, rising from where I sat. On the other side of the room, I focused my attention on the tall oak tree outside the window.

"What's wrong?" Everett asked, coming to stand beside me.

"Nothing. I've never been happier." I smiled a slow smile. "I guess I'm just afraid that it won't last."

He nodded slowly. "Do you really believe that?"

I shrugged. "I keep waiting for something to go wrong, for some other catastrophe to drop down on me. Does that make any sense?"

Pulling me to his chest, Everett wrapped his arms around me. The embrace was protective, an attempt to shield me from my own apprehensions. "Yes, but I wouldn't worry if I were you."

I laughed. "You're optimistic."

"Yes, I am. I have more faith than you do. I have prayed over this long and hard. I have prayed for you and me every day since I knew that I was in love with you. I know that everything will be well with the two of us."

I shook my head. "I've just begun to start to believe in prayer. Prayer had never gotten me anywhere before. How can you have so much faith?"

"How can you not?"

I mulled over his question and just as I thought to respond, his kiss silenced me. "I love you, Janay Tanner. I will always love you."

I beamed, sunshine swelling within me. "I love you too, Everett Tanner. Very much."

He undressed me slowly, pausing every other moment to mutter his appreciation against my skin. I shivered beneath him, overcome by the intense emotions passing between us. Passion danced in our eyes as he stared into mine, pulling the essence of myself inside of him. Music chimed up between us and over our bodies, a subtle symphony blowing around the room. His fingers were tender, molding love out of my melted flesh. I could smell roses and lavender and jasmine as we swayed in perfect synchronization. It was love that seeped like warm honey from the fountain of my being, and from his. It was love that joined us and made us whole.

****

I stood in the kitchen window watching Everett, as he stood out by the pond, watching the sunrise. It had become a ritual between us, a rite of passage that announced the start of each new day. I often wondered about the conversation he was having with the God he worshipped so unabashedly, prayer flowing from his heart by way of his mouth. His hands were lifted toward the clearing sky, palms pressed high in praise. There was a part of me that envied my husband's ability to open himself so freely to things I had yet to understand. His faith was like that of Daddy James. It was so much a part of their essence that they lived it wholeheartedly, walked hand in hand with it daily, never allowing anything or anyone to stand in the way of it.

I heard my grandfather entering the room behind me, pulling a kitchen chair across the floor as he sat himself comfortably at the table, a cup of hot coffee in hand.

"Why did he fail me?" I heard myself ask, the words falling before I had chance to catch them.

"Who?" Daddy James asked.

"God. Why did he fail me? What did I do wrong?"

There was silence and it filled the room with heated anticipation as I spun around to face my grandfather. He looked tired, even after a full night's sleep. Age was dancing in his face, almost taunting his usual exuberance. He lifted his elbows to the table and pressed his chin into his hands.

"God has never failed you, Black. Never."

"Why can't I feel him, Daddy? Why can't I see him, and feel him, and talk with him the way you and Everett do? What's wrong with me?"

"Your faith will come in its own time, Black. You can't force it."

"I don't want to force it. I just want it to be there. Like yours and Everett's is. I just want—" I paused, suddenly unsure of what it was I did want.

Daddy James nodded. "Stop trying to make the pieces fit. They don't. Faith will fall on you when you open your heart and let it. You want someone to hand it to you packaged all nice and neat. You want to define it and understand it, instead of just letting it be what it is."

Neither of us said anything else and when Everett finally joined us, kissing my cheek as he entered the room, we were still spinning silence between us.

"Good morning," Everett cheered, taking the seat next to Daddy James.

"How are you this morning?" the older man asked, rising to refill his cup for a second time, and filling one for Everett as he did.

"I'm well, sir. I feel good this morning."

Daddy James sat back down, passing one mug toward Everett, as he pressed the palms of his hands against the other.

"What time are you leaving?" Everett asked.

"Where are you going, Daddy?" I asked, surprised that he had plans I knew nothing of.

Daddy James pursed his lips, pushing them out in thought before turning toward me.

"Angola. Going to see Manroot."

"Why didn't you tell me?"

The man shrugged. "Nothing to tell."

I rolled my eyes, leaning against Everett's shoulder as he wrapped his arm around my waist.

"Why are you going? Is there something wrong with Manroot."

My grandfather looked up at me, growing annoyance filling his eyes. "I just wanted to go see my son while I had some time. Everett can help keep an eye on things here. I just figured it was time."

"Does he know you're coming?"

"Black, what's wrong with you? This ain't the first time I've gone to see Manroot without telling you first. Why all the questions?"

I didn't know why, so I didn't answer. Everett squeezed my hand beneath his.

"Tell him I said hey. Tell him I miss him," I said finally, heading out the door. "Tell my daddy I love him."

Letter writing is a dying art. Typewriters had long since replaced the pen and ink, and computers had replaced typewriters. I couldn't remember the last time I'd written a letter to Manroot. There had been no reason to write, knowing he had no intentions of answering. Yet, I longed to know what was in my father's heart, to understand what thoughts traipsed through the man's mind.

With pen and paper in hand, I sat beside the still waters, forming words in my mind that dissipated with the light breeze that blew across the fields, the ink never falling against the stark, white paper. There was no point in writing Manroot. I knew that, but I also needed to spill my soul to anyone willing to listen. In the distance, I could see Everett doing battle with the tractor, the antiquated equipment giving him a run for his money. I had to smile, laughter brewing at the edge of my heart, as I understood his struggle, having myself gone up against the aged equipment more times than I cared to count. We needed a new one and I made a mental note to contact the John Deere dealer to see what might be on sale.

A sheet of paper blew away from me, the bright white sheet billowing across the lawn. I watched it as it rolled edge over edge. I suddenly saw myself rolling along beside it. My gaze returned to Everett, who had emerged victorious, the bulk of metal beneath him lurching across the backfields on his command.

Above me, clouds started to roll across the sky, filling the blue backdrop with abundant tufts of moisture-filled gossamer. The air was heavy and I could smell the impending rain preparing to drop down upon us. I lay back against the cool grass and stared up at the clouds. A memory of my grandfather's deep voice singing to me floated across my mind and I felt myself smile, feeling like the small child he'd cradled in his arms and had sung to. It was the first song he'd ever taught me and I'd sung it over and over for days on end until Lavinia had slapped it out of me, the lyrics having worn on her fragile nerves. *Jesus loves me, this I know. For the bible, tells me so. Little ones to him belong. They are weak and he is strong. Yes, Jesus loves me; yes Jesus loves me; yes, Jesus loves me, for the bible tells me so.*

Sitting back up, I pulled the paper close, the pen passing easily over the smooth surface. The first words I wrote were *Dear God.*

Jesus Loves Me resonated around the room, an orchestra of flutes and harps playing softly in the background. Sunlight streamed through an open window, shining on family who smiled lovingly in my direction. Uncle Titus reached out his hand to welcome me and I ran, excited to see him. I ran, suddenly feeling as if I was running in the wrong direction on a moving escalator, Titus moving farther away from me, no matter how fast my pace. The sunlight dimmed quickly, as if a shade had been pulled to block out the light, and then she laughed. Blood spewed from her eyes, and the scar on her cheek, pouring like water from her cackling mouth. I tried to sing, no longer hearing the flutes and the harps. When the first slap hit me, sending me to the floor, I fell into a thick puddle of crimson fluid. Lavinia stood guard above me, bellowing in my ear, trumpeting that nobody loved me, and I felt myself drowning, my mother's blood cutting off my air.

I awoke with a start, Everett shaking me from my sleep. Sweating profusely, dampness soaked my nightclothes, the bed sheets drenched in urine beneath me. When I met my husband's eyes, I could only cry and he held me, letting me sob into his shoulder until I couldn't cry another tear.

"I'm so sorry," I whispered, pulling the sheets from around the mattress. "I don't know why I keep wetting the bed like this."

Everett shook his head. "Stop. It's not your fault. Was it the same dream?"

I nodded. "My mother was haunting me again."

As I headed to the laundry with the soiled linens, Everett draped clean sheets against the mattress, making up the bed. I don't know how long I stood leaning against the washing machine before Everett came up and hugged me from behind, pulling me against him as he pulled my terry bathrobe tighter around my naked body. He kissed my neck, letting his lips linger against my skin.

"I turned on the shower for you. The water should be hot by now. I'll finish this," he said, pointing me toward the bathroom.

The flow of warm water felt good against my skin and I reveled in it until the first chill passed over my flesh. I had no desire to return to sleep and so I lingered in the bathroom until all the hot water was gone, and I knew I couldn't stay a minute longer. I dreaded sleep, fearful that the dreams would continue to come. Afraid that my mother would continue to visit me.

Inside our bedroom, Everett lay waiting for me, his bible propped against his thighs as he sat reading in the freshly made bed. He pulled me to him as I slipped naked beneath the covers, pressing my body against his.

"Make love to me," I said, closing the leather-bound book in his hands and setting it against the nightstand. "Please," I whispered, pressing my lips to his. When he kissed me back, his hands stroking the hurt out of my body, I knew that I would be fine. I knew that Everett would chase the bogey-woman away, just like Daddy James.

****

Daddy James was laughing into the telephone receiver as I made my way into the house from what had proven to be a long day of chores. I'd only half completed my list of to-do's and I wanted nothing more than to curl up in the window seat of our home with a good book and hot cup of tea. My grandfather waved excitedly in my direction, his cupped palm gesturing for me to come to his side.

"Hold on, she just come through the door...You too, son. It was good talking to you...I promise I'll stop by to see your mama real soon...Okay...okay...you take care. Hold on." Daddy James passed the telephone toward me.

"Who is it?" I asked, whispering the question as I cupped my palm over the receiver.

"Just say hello," Daddy James responded, turning an about face and heading into the kitchen. I sighed heavily.

"Hello?"

"So, how's married life treating you?" Earl said, laughing on the other end.

"Earl!" The excitement of hearing my friend's voice spilled out into the room. "How are you? Where are you? What's going on?" The questions spilled out of my mouth faster than anyone could have bothered to answer them.

Earl laughed again. "I'm fine. I'm still in New York. Girl, I love this city life! You don't know what you're missing."

I grinned widely. "I know you miss this small town living. Don't try to pretend you don't."

"I miss my mama, you, and your granddaddy. That's about all I miss about Creekton. So how's that man of yours?"

"Everett's great. I wish he was here so you could say hello."

"That's okay. Just give him a big hug and kiss from me. So what have you two been up to?"

"Working hard is all. Nothing special."

"They throw you out of that church yet? I know you been causing trouble up in there, getting your poor husband caught up in some mess between you and them Hail Mary church mothers!"

I laughed. "I've been a model minister's wife. I'm head of the Ladies Auxiliary and I even started a tutoring program for our young people."

I could almost envision my friend as he tossed the back of his hand to his forehead, throwing back his head in mock dismay. "Heaven help us all," he chimed over the phone lines. "Girl, I know you done fell down and bumped your head now."

"You're still a fool!" I laughed. "What have you been up to?"

"Same old stuff. I've been doing a lot of painting and beating a lot of pavement trying to get the galleries to show them."

"Is it not going well?"

"Let's just say it's going."

"Well, I know you'll do just fine. What are you painting?"

"Naked butts."

I almost choked as the mirth spilled out of my body. The two of us were roaring over the telephone lines. "I think you're the one who's bumped his head."

"I'll tell you a secret but you have to promise to keep it to yourself."

"You know I wouldn't betray your confidence. What is it?"

"I have a boyfriend. His name's Rick and he's a blue-eyed blonde."

I shook my head. "And how long has this one been around?"

"A long time. I think I'm in love."

I smiled. "Are you really happy, Earl?"

"I can be me in this big old city, Black. And don't nobody care that I'm not what they think I should be."

"I'm happy for you, Earl. You deserve it. I hope I can meet your friend one day."

"Me too."

Tears misted my view and I could hear Earl sniffling back his own sobs over the other end. "So, you keep in touch, you hear?" he said, his voice dropping to a whisper.

"You know I will. I love you, Earl."

My friend let his tears slide down his bronzed cheeks. "Thanks for being my family, Black. Without you and your granddaddy, I don't know where I'd be right now. I love you both for that."

A brief moment of quiet passed between us.

"I still have better legs than you do," I said, easing the serious moment. We both laughed. "Bye, Earl."

"Catch you later, alligator."

Months later, there was endless activity swirling around me. There was produce to sell, land to buy, acreage to manage, and a home to run. I spun from one day to the next, exhilarated by it all as Daddy James sat back and watched.

On that morning of reckoning, I arose wearier than when I had lain myself down to rest. Fatigue was lingering longer than normal as I struggled to pull myself together. Though my body begged for me to slow my pace, there was far too much to be done to even consider stopping to take a rest.

As Everett headed toward the fields and Daddy James to his gardens, I was wondering if I'd find the energy to pull it all together. Then, from where I stood on the front porch, nursing a hot cup of coffee, I saw the courier pull slowly into the drive, checking to insure he had the right address. The look on the man's pockmarked face was foretelling as he passed me the telegram, then tipped his hat good-bye. Pulling the message from the envelope I read it quickly, unforeseen closure coming with the words upon the paper.

****

Bright bouquets of spring flowers filled the large church. The sanctuary was a botanical plethora of tulips, irises, and lilies in every conceivable color. As Daddy James and I prepared to bid Manroot good-bye, I had to struggle to pull myself together to do what was expected. I had not one ounce of strength left to carry on.

Standing in the rear of the vestibule, I noted the curious faces and sympathetic eyes that strained in my direction. There was a flurry of motion beside me as the funeral home director prepped the family on what we should do and where we should go. I so wanted to remind him that we had been here before, more times than anyone cared to count. We knew the routines better than he did. Perhaps, I thought as I bit down against my tongue, if he'd had some advice on how to deal with the wealth of hurt that consumed us, his services would have been of greater use. But I said nothing out loud, biting back my thoughts. I only reached for Daddy James' hand as they pushed us toward the front of the church, and the open coffin at the pulpit. I hugged my grandfather close as we moved in the direction of the casket that held my father's lifeless body.

I paused two steps behind my grandfather as he stopped to whisper a private prayer over his son. The room seemed to suddenly spin in slow motion and for a brief moment I feared my legs would give out and send me straight to the carpeted floor. As I stepped forward into the space Daddy James had just occupied, the first rise of saline burned hot beneath my eyelids.

What remained of Manroot Tucker was a mere shadow of the man who'd walked out of our lives so many years ago. The man that lay before us was not the Manroot I'd loved and had once called Daddy. There was nothing left of the larger-than-life character who'd been my private giant. No laughter rang from his lips, no gleam shone from his eyes. The man before me had died years ago, having long since lost his way. I inhaled swiftly, the air punctuated with the sweet aroma of white roses and the stench of death. My grandfather wrapped his thick arms around me. As I lifted my gaze to his, I saw that his own tears had fallen to his cheeks. I brushed at

Daddy James' face with the tips of my fingers as we took our seats in the front pew.

The massive pipe organ hummed majestically in the distance, the organist's gaze focused intently on the pages of sheet music propped before him. Someone in the choir was singing softly, one of Daddy James' favorite hymns starting the service. As one of the deacons stepped to the podium to deliver a prayer, the hand of a haunting spirit slapped me full force, knocking the wind from my lungs.

The last time I'd seen my father, when I'd really gazed into his face, anger had creased the smooth marble of his dark skin. As he'd held my face, cupped gently in the palms of his hands, the love he'd held in his eyes had been coated with rage and disbelief. The tears fell quickly, the dark angels reaching out their cold hands to pull the flood of water from me. Every muscle quivered in convulsion as I struggled to maintain some composure. The sudden flux of memory flooded my being with a ferocity I'd not expected, and as I looked up into Daddy James' face, he spoke for me, his words voicing the thoughts I was struggling to fathom.

"It's gone be okay, Black. I know you remember, and it's gone be okay."

I nodded my head, holding tight to his optimism and even tighter to his grip, and then I wept just as I had wept over thirty years ago when my father's rage had rained down on us all, and my mother's blood had been spattered against me.

Everett delivered the eulogy and I saw the concern that spilled from his eyes as his gaze locked with mine. Two members of the Ladies Missionary Society stood over me, flapping fans that spelled out an advertisement for the local funeral home. I fought to focus on the tops of Sister Hattie's white nursing shoes, wanting to look anywhere except toward my father's body. I breathed a sigh of relief when they finally shut the casket, signaling that closure was not far behind.

It wasn't long before we three sat quietly by the graveside as they lowered Manroot's body into the deep, dark hole. Two men in matching gray uniforms struggled to keep the casket straight, as a third loosened the straps that held the container slightly aloft. When my father's body was firmly installed in the ground below, shovels of dirt packed tightly around him, I finally exhaled, releasing the breath I'd taken earlier and had held onto as if another wasn't promised to me. Beneath the green tent, I twisted uncomfortably in the folding chair placed at the edge of the gravesite for the family. Daddy James sat on one side of me, his felt hat clutched between his palms, and Everett sat on my other side, his arm draped over my shoulders.

I felt myself rocking slowly as I struggled to answer the questions that no one had dared to ask when I was a child. Daddy James listened intently, hearing the tale he'd heard only one other time those many years ago.

"Daddy had been so mad that night. That was the first time I'd ever seen him hit her, and he kept hitting her, and hitting her." I clutched at a soiled tissue, tearing the damp paper into small shreds. "But mommy didn't cry. She would just stand back up and laugh some more. I wanted her to stop laughing, so that he would stop hurting her but she wouldn't. It was as if something ugly had taken possession of her and she couldn't stop. And that laugh was pure evil. It was so cold and empty. I didn't mean to hurt her. I really didn't. I just wanted her to stop laughing, and just go away. Then she said she was going to take me away. She said I was never going to see Manroot again. I was so scared that I wouldn't be able to see my daddy anymore."

Tears rose to the edge of Everett's eyes as I continued. My husband tightened the hold he had on my hand.

"I remember going to the kitchen to get the knife. It was the knife she'd always scare me with. I thought if daddy had it he'd be able to scare her away instead. I kept trying to give it to him and I was screaming at him, but he wouldn't pay me any attention. They just kept yelling at each other, and he kept hitting her, and then..." I paused, gasping slightly, as the blurred memory came into focus. "Manroot hit her, and she fell backwards, right into the blade. Then I pulled it out and I kept stabbing her with it. I kept stabbing her."

I paused, my breath catching deep in my chest as the memory washed over my spirit. I lifted my eyes to meet my grandfather's intense stare. "I kept stabbing my mother," I said, unable to fathom how horrific the truth really was as I continued my story.

"I remember she called Daddy's name, and she was still laughing and then just like that she stopped. She stopped, and there was so much blood. It was everywhere. Daddy started screaming at me. I tried to tell him I didn't mean it."

I began to sob softly. "I tried to tell him, but he just grabbed me, and he kept shaking me, and he was crying too."

The tears were spilling out of my eyes, washing over my cheeks and down my husband's shoulder. I heaved a deep breath. "Manroot told me to forget about it. He said I could never tell anyone. Never. He said if I told they'd take me away and then he wouldn't be able to love me anymore. He said I'd never get to see Daddy James again." I looked back toward my grandfather, who sat staring at the freshly planted soil over Manroot's body. I caught my breath and continued. "Manroot said that he would explain it, and everything would be all right. But it wasn't. Nothing has ever been right. My mama was dead and they took my daddy away, and it was all my fault. It was all my fault."

"No," Daddy James said firmly as he cleared his throat. "If anyone is to blame it was Manroot. He had no cause to beat that woman like he done. Even if it hadn't happened then, we all knew there was going to come a day when he probably would have killed her. Your mama didn't want him anymore. He was hurt and he was jealous and he let it get the best of him."

Daddy James took a deep breath before continuing. "Black, what happened was an accident. Make no mistake about that. You were a child and you surely didn't mean for it to happen the way it did. Your daddy never wanted you to suffer because of it. Lavinia made you suffer enough. Your daddy suspected she was abusing you and he only wanted to try to make things right for you. I agreed with him. We thought if you could forget, then you could be happy. Your daddy and I made a big mistake. I'm so sorry, Black. I'm so sorry."

Everett pulled me into his arms and I felt Daddy James' large palm stroking my back. My sobs echoed in the stillness of the morning air and off in the distance I felt them leaving me, their ghostly presence disappearing in the wind. Beneath the rising summer heat we sat and cried until we were all cried out. With the tide of tears behind us, we bid Manroot one last good-bye and headed for home.

As the last mourner pulled out of the driveway, burning rubber kicked up dust down the road. Daddy James and I sat side by side, rocking slowly in the pine rocker. The day's heat was still heavy, not wanting to let go of the afternoon. Perspiration beaded lightly against both of our brows, lightweight, cotton clothing sticking against damp skin. The smell of fried chicken drifted from the kitchen. I sucked on a spoonful of strawberry Jell-O.

Everett came from inside the home to join us. "Are you feeling any better?" he asked, concern sifting from the fingers that kneaded the flesh along my shoulders.

I shrugged, not knowing if such a thing could be possible. He leaned to kiss my forehead, pulling me against him as I dropped my head onto his chest. The three of us sat in silence, listening to the sounds of nature that sprinted between the blades of grass, along the span of trees that sat to the north of the property, across the swell of pond water and out beyond the fields. We listened, each of us searching for the sounds that would whisper the answers that all would be well.

Rising from my seat, I reached for my journal and the blue ink pen that sat beside it. With no need to say anything, I headed for the pond and the sanctuary of water that always seemed to wash my anxiety away. Daddy James and Everett tossed each other a look, then my grandfather smiled as Everett nodded his head slowly.

Since that first letter, God and I had begun to converse regularly. I'd written pages upon pages of emotion to him, his answers coming back with the breeze. I'd begun to look forward to my time with him, finding peace like I'd never known before. I shared what felt comfortable to share, knowing that I had no need to push myself if I did not choose to. Today, though, I had much to let go of and even more to lay claim to. Even if I couldn't, I had hope that God would understand and that his understanding would eventually lead me to forgiveness.

Sunlight flooded the room. I reveled in the warmth that spilled out over me. I could smell the flowers, freesia, and roses wafting aroma through the air. When Manroot laughed, I turned to see my father smiling down upon me, holding out his hand for mine. The sunshine danced in his eyes, across his smile, flooding his dark complexion with an abundance of light. I laughed with him and when I put my hand in his, I could feel his thick fingers wrap around mine. I laughed again as I walked along beside my daddy. Uncle Titus and Uncle Chauncey waved, standing out in the fields as we passed them by. Even Aunt Eloise's surly face was lifted in spirit, joy shining from her gaze, her infant son cradled in her arms. She kissed us both, my daddy and me, and waved as we continued on our stroll.

I saw her standing by the water, humming softly as we approached. I was no longer six years old, my body full grown as my father kissed the back of my hand and winked his eye. He called me Beauty and smiled, then left me standing alone, the sun still shimmering down upon us. My mother waved, blowing kisses in my direction, and she laughed with my father as they walked away without me. Beauty lost, was beauty found, and it revealed itself in the ripple of water left by their footsteps as they disappeared, hand in hand.

The room was dark when I opened my eyes. Everett lay sleeping beside me, snoring ever so slightly into the pillow beneath his head. Easing my body out of bed, I headed downstairs to the kitchen to fill the teakettle. The back door was open, a warm breeze filtering in through the screen and when I looked out, Daddy James sat on the porch, swaying slowly in his seat.

He smiled as I sat down beside him, curling my body against his.

"Bad dream, Black?"

"No, sir. It was a good dream," I said, smiling back as I held his hand.

We sat and watched the flickers of a full moon dance against the water in the distance. The air was warm and shadows danced cheek to cheek in the midnight breeze. Knowing there would be no better time to share my last secret with the old man who knew me better than anyone else did, I cleared my throat, raising a carefully manicured hand to my lips.

"Daddy?"

"Uh huh?"

"I have something I want to tell you."

Daddy James nodded, shifting his body back against the waterproof cushions. "Your grandma use to say there had to be a passing of souls for life to be given. When she passed away you was born and her soul was passed on to you."

I inhaled deeply, holding the warm breath as though afraid to let it go.

Daddy James continued. "Manroot gone now and I reckon you'll be having that baby sometime soon. Mean we gone have us a hand full in that boy you carrying!"

The breath rushed past my lips. "How did you know?"

"That it's a boy?" Daddy James shrugged. "Don't. Just guessing. What you think it gone be, a baby girl?"

I shook my head. "No. How did you know I was pregnant?"

Daddy James laughed, dropping his arm against my shoulder. "Told you when you was just a little bitty thing that there wasn't nothing you could do that I wouldn't know about."

I twisted my face with disbelief. "Seriously, Daddy. How did you know?"

"I am serious." The man chuckled. "So, what you planning on doing?"

Rising, I leaned against the porch railing, staring out over the land. In the darkness, the rich earth stretched out before me, beckoning. The sweet smells warmed and caressed my face, tickling my nose and lips as I inhaled the pungent aroma.

I turned back to face my grandfather, the palms of my hands pressed warmly against the hint of new life. "Think I'll have me a beautiful baby boy in my grandmother's bed and raise him right here on Tucker land."

Daddy James nodded agreeably, coming to stand beside me. Entwining his fingers between mine, he hugged me close, brushing the bristles on his chin against my cheek. "I'm glad to hear that, although I guess we gone have to start calling it Tanner land."

I shook my head. "It will always be Tucker land, Daddy. I plan on making sure that when James Tucker Tanner is born that he knows that, too," I exclaimed.

I smiled as Daddy James stepped inside the door, moving to answer the teakettle's whistle. Over his shoulder, he called out to me softly.

"Yes, sir?"

"I love you, Black."

I smiled, a wide grin spreading though my soul. "I love you too, Daddy."

Daddy James nodded his head. "You and me have a lot to be thankful for, Black. Don't you ever forget it. You hear me?"

As the door swung closed behind him, I turned to stare back over the land. Stepping down off the porch, I crossed the damp grass, the dew pressing against my bare feet and the hem of my nightgown. Under the light of the moon, I headed for the pond, standing still beside the water. At the water's edge, I skipped a pebble for my mother, and my father, for all the hurt, and all the tears. The wet surface rippled and then, as the waters rested, with a level of comfort as though I'd been doing it every day of my life, I lifted my voice in prayer and gave thanks.

****

ACKNOWLEGEMENTS

I so love what I do! I have been so blessed and I understand that it has been a generous and loving God that has lifted me up and enabled me to do this. And I am so grateful.

As I navigated this journey it was not without a few bumps through the turns and when I most thought I might lose my way, family and friends reached out to put me back on the path. I would not be here if it were not for their unwavering love and support.

To my parents, Walter and Corrine Fletcher, you both have taught me that I can achieve all things as long as I hold tight to my faith, be humble in the face of adversity, and steadfast in my determination. You demanded excellance, nurtured greatness, instilled compassion, and inspired me to reach beyond the stars. Your lessons have been invaluable and all that I am is owed to everything that you have sacrificed.

To Matthew Gregory Mello, the light of my life, my personal "son-shine". I absolutely adore you my child! For you, I will move heaven and earth. Because of you, I am challenged to be the very best that I can be. I hope and pray that I am a shining example that you will always be proud to claim as your mother.

To Walter Woody Jr. for showing me that there are no limits when pursuing greatness and all pursuits are lost if there is no love. Thank you for your love.

And for their friendship and support, and for reasons that we alone may know, my sincerest gratitude to Tealecia Fletcher, Dr. William T. Fletcher, Susie Cole, Angela Thomas-Graves, Gregory Graves, Linda Fox, Westley Woody III, T'Keya Fox, Sarah Jenkins, Jacqueline Hinton Barrett, and Bridget Wilson. Your love thrives in all those each of you touches and I am grateful for it.

Lastly, to all those who helped make this book possible, thank you. Thank you, thank you, thank you!

ABOUT THE AUTHOR

Writing for as long as she can remember, Deborah Fletcher Mello can't imagine herself doing anything else. Her first romance novel, *Take Me To Heart*, earned her a 2004 Romance Slam Jam nomination for Best New Author. In 2005 she received Book of the Year and Favorite Heroine nominations for her novel, *The Right Side of Love*, and in 2009 won a Romantic Times Reviewer's Choice Award for her ninth novel, *Tame A Wild Stallion*. This year, Deborah's eleventh novel, *Promises To A Stallion*, has earned her a 2011 Romance Slam Jam nomination for Hero Of The Year.

For Deborah, writing is as necessary as breathing and she firmly believes that if she could not write she would cease to exist. Weaving a story that leaves her audience feeling full and complete, as if they've just enjoyed an incredible meal, is the ultimate thrill for her. Born and raised in Connecticut, Deborah now maintains base camp in North Carolina, but considers home to be wherever the moment moves her.

For additional information on Deborah, visit her at www.deborahmello.blogspot.com.

www.ingramcontent.com/pod-product-compliance
Lightning Source LLC
Chambersburg PA
CBHW071217250626
47163CB00001B/22

* 9 7 8 0 6 1 5 4 5 6 6 3 8 *